"SMACKS YOU RIGHT IN THE FACE with the cold-bloodedness of inner city gang warfare and the half-twisted mindset of the cops working to bust it . . . so vivid that your adrenal glands start pumping!" —*Oakland Tribune*

"VIVID . . . THOUGHT-PROVOKING, TROUBLING, AND SURPRISINGLY MOVING." —*Asbury Park Press*

"THE CHARACTERS ARE CONVINCING, THE SITUATION CREDIBLE, and the East L.A. milieu is rendered with the kind of jarring, jagged reality that makes you feel like you are there but wish that you were not . . . he knows all about cops, and he tells all." —*Los Angeles Daily News*

"DOES HE KNOW THE TERRITORY! . . . harsh, brutal and sobering." —*San Diego Union*

EARTH ANGELS

by
Gerald Petievich

A SIGNET BOOK

SIGNET
Published by the Penguin Group
Penguin Books USA Inc., 375 Hudson Street,
New York, New York 10014, U.S.A.
Penguin Books Ltd, 27 Wrights Lane,
London W8 5TZ, England
Penguin Books Australia Ltd, Ringwood,
Victoria, Australia
Penguin Books Canada Ltd, 2801 John Street,
Markham, Ontario, Canada L3R 1B4
Penguin Books (N.Z.) Ltd, 182-190 Wairau Road,
Auckland 10, New Zealand

Penguin Books Ltd, Registered Offices:
Harmondsworth, Middlesex, England

Published by Signet, an imprint of New American Library, a
division of Penguin Books USA Inc.
Previously published in an NAL Books edition.

First Signet Printing, March, 1991
10 9 8 7 6 5 4 3 2 1

The verses from the song "Earth Angels" are reprinted with the
permission of Dootsie William Publications.

 REGISTERED TRADEMARK—MARCA REGISTRADA

Printed in the United States of America

PUBLISHER'S NOTE
This is a work of fiction. Names, characters, places, and incidents
either are the product of the author's imagination or are used
fictitiously, and any resemblance to actual persons, living or dead,
events, or locales is entirely coincidental.

BOOKS ARE AVAILABLE AT QUANTITY DISCOUNTS WHEN USED TO PRO-
MOTE PRODUCTS OR SERVICES. FOR INFORMATION PLEASE WRITE TO
PREMIUM MARKETING DIVISION, PENGUIN BOOKS USA INC., 375 HUDSON
STREET, NEW YORK, NEW YORK 10014.

For Detective John Petievich:

Recipient of the Los Angeles Police Department Star of Valor for his actions in a 1981 shoot-out with gang members.

"When the Lord your God brings you into the land which you are entering to take possession of it, and clears away many nations before you, the Hittites, the Girgashites, the Amorites, the Canaanites, the Perizzites, the Hivites, and the Jebusites, seven nations greater and mightier than yourselves, and when the Lord your God gives them over to you, and you defeat them; then you must utterly destroy them; you shall make no covenant with them and show them no mercy. . . . But thus shall you deal with them; you shall break down their altars, and dash in pieces their pillars, and hew down their Asherim, and burn their graven images with fire."

—DEUTERONOMY 7:1–6

(Please turn the page for more reviews . . .)

LOS ANGELES POLICE DEPARTMENT

Levester C. Burrell
Chief of Police

TO: Chief of Police Levester C. Burrell
FROM: Captain Robert A. Harger, Central Bureau Detectives
SUBJECT: New specialized gang unit

1. This year's increase in gang murders—201 compared to 173 at this time last year—has made me rethink some of this bureau's organizational structure. With the increase in gang activity all over Los Angeles, it has become evident to me that the department would be well served by a new specialized unit targeted specifically against the perpetrators of the most heinous gang murders ... particularly those receiving the heaviest media coverage.

   The sheer volume of gang homicides has this bureau bogged down, and I'm afraid we're losing opportunities to destroy the infrastructure of the most violent gangs because our homicide detectives are simply overworked.

2. I would appreciate thirty minutes or so of your time to discuss the details of a plan I have outlined for a new specialized unit that would work separate from, but under the organizational aegis of, the C.R.A.S.H.

(Community Resources Against Street Hoodlums) detail now operating under my command. This unit would focus on the hard-core East Los Angeles street gangs that have been active in L.A. for more than fifty years. If this concentrated enforcement effort is successful against these, the most impenetrable of street gangs, we could later form units similar to fight the black gangs in the south end of town.

Because the gang issue has been all over the newspapers so much recently, I'm sure you'd have no problem selling this idea to the police commission. And with the election coming shortly, I predict the mayor would jump on the idea like a hobo on a hot dog.

Robert A. Harge

Robert A. Harger
Captain, Central Bureau Detectives

LOS ANGELES POLICE DEPARTMENT

Levester C. Burrell
Chief of Police

TO: Captain Robert A. Harger, Central
                Bureau Detectives
FROM: Chief of Police Levester C. Burrell
SUBJECT: New specialized gang unit

New gang unit authorized from first day of next
deployment period. Personnel: One detective
sergeant + three detectives.

Levester C. Burrell

Levester C. Burrell
Chief of Police

```
SPECIAL ORDER # 57543 (FROM CRASH SPECIAL UNIT)
DEPLOYMENT PERIOD #23
ATTN: CAPTAIN HOLLENBECK DIVISION
       CHIEF OF DETECTIVES
       ALL CRASH SUPERVISORS
       PAYROLL
SUBJECT: CRASH SPECIAL UNIT
AS OF THIS DATE THE FOLLOWING OFFICERS
WILL BE TRANSFERRED TO NEWLY FORMED CRASH
SPECIAL UNIT:
       1. STEPANOVICH, JOSE L., DET. SGT.,
          SER. # 613845 (SUPERVISOR)
       2. FORDYCE, TIMOTHY C., DET.,
          SER. # 423968
       3. ARREDONDO, RAUL A., DET.,
          SER. # 257491
       4. BLACK, CYRUS R., DET.,
          SER. # 992318
UNTIL FURTHER NOTICE, UNIT SUPERVISOR WILL
REPORT TO CAPTAIN HARGER, CENTRAL BUREAU
DETECTIVES, FOR CASE ASSIGNMENT AND
CONTROL.
```

ONE

Twenty-three-year-old Primitivo Estrada stood alone at the portaled entrance to the Our Lady Queen of Angels Church. Killing time, he rocked back and forth on the heels of his highly polished Stacey Adams shoes. Time was something he'd had plenty of ever since he'd been kicked out of high school in his sophomore year for having a gun in his locker. He had never held a job of any kind. Everyone called him Payaso.

Because of the August heat, the ruffled blue shirt and mothballed tuxedo jacket he'd rented for the wedding were soaked through. Above him, the sanctuary's multifoil windows reflected the surrounding jumble of apartment buildings, prewar bungalows, gas stations, taco stands, junkyards, and graffiti-adorned public housing projects that was East Los Angeles.

Payaso moved closer to the sanctuary door and opened it a few inches. Inside, it was standing room only. Father Mendoza, who the other *vatos* believed was a fag because he lisped, stood at the altar chanting religious bullshit. Kneeling in front of him were Smokey Salazar, vice president of the White Fence gang, and his cross-eyed bride Linda Medrano, whose gang nickname was Parrot. Careful not to make noise, Payaso eased the door closed again.

5

A loyal White Fence homeboy, Payaso had earned the rank of *veterano,* having served time in jail and reached his twenty-second birthday without being killed by an opposing gang.

Payaso had volunteered to stay outside and perform lookout duty. He figured he might as well because he knew he always cracked up in church. He'd kneel like everybody else and it would be all silent and everyone would like be praying. Then for no apparent reason he would just get the urge to laugh like hell. It was weird. It would start with a giggle and it wouldn't stop. He would like really crack fucking up during any church service. He used to think he was the only person in history with this inexplicable urge until he saw a movie at the Floral Drive-in Theater called *College Vacation.* In a scene he remembered vividly, all these college dudes laughed like motherfuckers during a church service and pissed off the minister. Payaso identified with this behavior and went back to see the movie four times.

Rocking back and forth, Payaso surveyed the line of customized lowriders parked at the curb in front of the church. The cars were all washed, polished, and decorated with paper flowers and streamers. At the conclusion of the church service the White Fence wedding party would be transported in fine style to the Knights of Columbus Hall on Soto Street for the reception.

Keeping his eyes on the street, Payaso lit a Marlboro. He took a long drag and gently blew a perfect smoke ring at the church door. He turned, aimed another ring at the woodframed house across the street, and for good measure, one more at the dingy El Cholo taco stand catercorner from the church.

For no particular reason, he thought of his mama, a fiery-eyed woman who showed her love by lying to the cops when they came to their tiny one-bedroom house on Ortega Street looking for him. At age thirteen, when he'd been a White Fence peewee, he'd learned his father really wasn't in the Army like Mama told

6

him, that Madre, with her long raven-black hair and her White Fence teardrop tattoo was full of shit. His father had most likely been one of the beer-bellied *cabrons* from the meat-packing plant on Los Angeles Street she invariably brought home on Saturday nights.

He recalled years of being carted next door with his brothers and sisters to Mrs. Valladolid's place to spend the night huddled together on her rancid living room rug. On Sundays Mama always served *menudo* and treated the kids extra nice. Payaso eventually figured this was to assuage her guilt for getting laid.

His first trip to the L.A County Juvenile Hall had been when he was twelve years old. He and some other peewees had been dropping bricks onto cars from the Soto Street freeway overpass. When the cops came, he and the others ran. He took a shortcut through a backyard, but his T-shirt got caught on the edge of a chain-link fence. A motor cop, whom he remembered as being ten feet tall, laughed when he found him, called him greaseball, and slapped him hard enough to make him see stars.

At Juvenile Hall, a bearded gringo counselor tried to reach Mama by telephone but, as luck would have it, it was Saturday night and she was off somewhere getting a piece of ass. So Payaso was placed in a padded isolation cell with a small window on the door and remained the night, intermittently jacking off to kill time. At about noon the next day Mama picked him up. Subsequently, he made six other trips to Juvie Hall and served both a thirty-day and a ninety-day sentence at the Fred C. Nelles Juvenile Detention Center in Whittier.

At eighteen, he was convicted of car theft and sentenced to a year in the Los Angeles county jail. He received a sentence reduction due to jail overcrowding and, with time off for good behavior, served three months and twenty-one days. While he was there, he used the guile he'd developed at Nelles and managed to negotiate a job in the jail kitchen.

Most of the mess duty was scrubbing institutional-sized pots and pans and cleaning out the kitchen's overflowing grease pit, but the position had distinct benefits. He was able to steal spoons and other utensils easily whittled into shanks for other White Fence homeboys serving time. He even provided weapons to prisoners in other cellblocks in exchange for Marlboros. He always checked out these buyers, though, to make sure he wasn't selling to a member or associate of a rival gang, who'd use one of Payaso's sharpened forks or spoons against him.

Another benefit of mess duty was that he was able to spit or urinate into the food served to the deputy sheriffs on the jail staff. Everyone knew the deputies would beat him to death if they ever found out, so this gained him respect from his comrades and moved him several notches higher in White Fence gang hierarchy.

Bored, Payaso wandered out of the shade to his Chevrolet. Parked fourth in line behind Smokey's, the car was a highly lacquered blue and had been lowered to within four inches of the street. Its seats were covered with pleated leather upholstery referred to in East L.A. custom-car circles as "tuck-and-roll." He reached through the window opening, unlocked the glove compartment, and took out a $1.98 spray can of Four Star paint and a cotton athletic sock. He looked about furtively to make sure no one was watching, then dropped down on his haunches to hide from passing cars. Holding the sock over the spray-can nozzle, he pressed the trigger firmly and allowed the spray can to hiss a healthy amount of gold paint into the sock. He set the paint can down on the sidewalk and, using both hands, cupped the sock like an oxygen mask over his nose and mouth, and took deep breaths.

Toluene-induced lightheadedness spread from his nasal passage to forehead, to his spine and the very center of his brain. Dope TV came on and his mind flipped through the channels. For brief, flashing moments he was relaxing comfortably in a dentist's chair with his mouth open wide, standing on the corner of Brooklyn and Soto streets watching the Cinco de Mayo parade, sitting anxiously in the principal's office at Castelar Elementary School waiting to get spanked with a thick wooden paddle, cavorting about while dressed as a monkey on Halloween, screaming while holding tight to the restraining bar in a roller coaster at the Magic Mountain amusement park.

He sprayed another shot of paint into the rag and sucked more paint fumes into his lungs. It was like sliding into soothing, tepid water as the high changed to the lighter-than-air, everything-is-OK sensation he'd first experienced as a nine-year-old when he'd inhaled model airplane glue. Clearly, as if the radios of a fleet of lowrider Chevys were playing simultaneously he could hear his favorite tune:

> *Earth Angel, earth angel, will you be mine?*
> *My darling dear, love you all the time.*
> *I'm just a fool. A fool in love with you.*

As the music played inside his head, Payaso dropped his whiff gear back into the car and came to his feet. *"All right,"* he said out loud as he grew well over eight feet tall and the deep pockmarks on his Bozo face smoothed out, his slack jaw tightened, and his crooked teeth straightened to perfection. *"All right,"* he growled as oversized, droopy ears slid back handsomely against the sides of his head, his cock elongated to ten powerful, erect inches, and his stooped shoulders puffed out to Rambo size. "*Hijo la,* man. *Mira,"* Payaso said to every *chingone* in East Los Angeles—and for that matter across the L.A. River to the mayor in City Hall downtown and every sombrero salesman on the touristy Olvera Street. He *was* fucking Rambo. *Mira. Eses! Look at my goddamn dick!*

Right then, right at the pinnacle of his spray-paint buzz, a red pickup truck pulled up in front of the church.

The driver and passenger in the cab were wearing white undershirts, as was the green-eyed, glaring *vato* sitting on his haunches in the bed of the truck with his back against the cab. Payaso recognized him immediately as an Eighteenth Street gang shooter known as Greenie. He was wearing a knit watch cap with a small roll at the bottom pulled down tightly over his ears and a pair of stiff-starched blue jeans with small rolls at the cuff and slit up the side—what all the East L.A. gangs called "counties." Greenie was holding something covered with a towel.

Payaso backed toward the door of the church.

"Where are you from?" Greenie yelled, raising a sawed-off shotgun from under the towel and aiming it directly at Payaso.

"White Fence!" Payaso yelled, scrambling to open the church door.

With the blast of the shotgun, Payaso felt himself being lifted from the planet Earth by sharp, burning hooks and catapulted into the red-carpeted aisle of the crowded sanctuary. A frightened roar came from the wedding crowd. Payaso's head smacked the musty church carpet. "Eighteenth Street!" a man shouted. There was the sound of running. More shotgun blasts. People screamed, shrieked. The cathedral erupted into hysteria.

Lying on the church carpet, Payaso tried to sit up, but couldn't. In fact, he couldn't catch his breath, not even one. His mouth, which suddenly felt like wet clay, opened wide for air. In front of him he could see tilted pews and an altar. His body was leaking warmth and he was taken by a wave of nausea.

Tires squealed as the pickup truck sped away. Voices and more footsteps on the carpet. Hands touching him. Shouts for an ambulance, blurry faces blocking his view of the altar. He felt himself being lifted. People were saying things in Spanish and English to comfort him. But he still couldn't breathe.

As the world turned into pastel grays, then bright,

inside-the-eyelid pink, Payaso thought he smelled Four Star paint . . . or, *Hijo La* man . . . was it the rank odor of Mrs. Valladolid's rug?

Suddenly he was immersed in a sea of warm black ink.

TWO

Minutes after the shooting, the dimly lit church became a maelstrom of police activity as uniformed officers and detectives herded wedding guests into the street and roped off areas with yellow evidence tape, shouting conflicting commands at the crowd in an attempt to establish order. As all this was occurring, a deep and desperate sobbing echoed throughout the sanctuary.

Detective Jose Stepanovich, a clean-cut young man wearing a tailored blue sports coat and gray slacks, looked down at the wounded man lying just inside the front door. He recognized the victim immediately. If he remembered correctly, the moniker was Payaso.

Stepanovich had grown up in East L.A. and had spent his entire nine years in the Department assigned to the area. There were few members of the more than thirty street gangs in the division he didn't know by sight. Stepanovich knew that Eastside gang members lived and died in their respective gang territory like peasants in a feudal state. He'd figured out long ago that knowing their cars, nicknames, girlfriends and hangouts was critical in solving a gang murder. Locked into their respective turf, the White Fence, Frogtown, Maravilla, Happy Valley, Clover, Third

Street and Alpine Street gangs were easy to find. Even if they fled to Mexico to hide out with relatives after committing a murder, in a few months they usually returned to their home turf.

This special talent for being able to interpret and predict the activities of the street gangs had earned him a call from Captain Villalobos of Hollenbeck Division to brief the East Los Angeles Rotary Club on the problem. When questioned about the prognosis of the gang situation in general, he was smart enough to evade any direct answer rather than betray his true feelings, that the only way to solve the problem was to lock up each and every gangbanger and throw away the key.

A balding, taciturn paramedic whom Stepanovich had seen at the scene of the six other East L.A. gang shootings during the last month extended a clear plastic tube from a plasma bottle and attached it to a hypodermic needle. He lifted Payaso's right arm and stabbed the needle into a bulging blue vein that snaked between tattoos of a three dimensional Latin crucifix and the word "VIDA LOCA" just above it.

Payaso's eyes rolled back in his head, and his jaw hung slack as white spittle leaked from the corner of his mouth. He didn't appear to feel a thing.

Stepanovich stepped back and, moving his hand into a pillar of blue light streaming from a stained glass window, checked his watch. He took out a pen, noted the time on a leather-covered notepad given him as a police academy graduation gift by Nancy. She'd filed for divorce when a marriage counselor suggested that marrying a cop might have been a mistake for a dependent personality who needed a spouse around nights and weekends. Stepanovich ambled to a cluster of policemen and tan-uniformed coroner's deputies kneeling in the aisle.

Raul Arredondo, a husky, hawk-faced young detective who often worked with Stepanovich, came to his feet and stepped back to allow Stepanovich a view of the tiny corpse on the floor: a girl whose age Stepanovich guessed at about nine years old, dressed in pink taffeta, white panty hose, and shiny patent leather shoes. There was a small, bloodless opening below her chin and an enormous, gaping exit wound on top of her head, exposing wet brain tissue. Her wide brown eyes and small mouth were open in death. A few feet away, a woman Stepanovich guessed to be the child's mother was being restrained by two other women as she rocked back and forth, sobbing hysterically.

A feeling beyond anger overwhelmed Stepanovich. Like many cops, he'd become inured to violent death: gory gang murders, suicides, blood-splashed traffic accidents, and drowning victims staring up at him from the bottom of swimming pools. The sight of a dead child, though, still pierced him to the core. "Damn," he heard himself saying.

"She caught a stray round," Arredondo said, trying to hide the emotion in his voice.

Detective Captain Bob Harger passed Stepanovich and stepped up onto a nearby pew. Only a few years older than Stepanovich, he was attired in a short-sleeved white shirt and pleated trousers secured by a black weave-pattern leather belt. On the belt were two four-inch barrel revolvers in zebra-skin holsters.

"Officers, take your commands from me!" Harger shouted in a foghorn voice that reminded Stepanovich of the officer-survival lecture Harger regularly gave to police academy recruits. He pointed his right hand as if it was a gun: "I want a rope line from here to the door." Then his left pointed the opposite way: "Give me all witnesses over here in this corner. Stepanovich, keep this area clear."

Stepanovich gave a "Yes sir" to the order and moved to obey. As he ordered wedding guests toward the rear of the church a TV news crew stepped inside the door. The camera focused on Harger.

"Seal the front door!" Harger shouted to a uniformed sergeant. "No prints and photos until the detectives finish." With a few more commands, Captain Harger turned an utterly chaotic crime scene into a "manageable police problem," to use the lexicon of the in-service training classes.

As far as Stepanovich was concerned, Harger was a born leader. He wasn't just a champion on the police handball court, but actually taught a class in the sport. Not only was he a decorated Vietnam War veteran, but a major in the Army Reserves. And it was well-known he had shot it out with bad guys more than once during his career. But perhaps most of all, Stepanovich admired Harger's humility: he preferred to chug beers with the men rather than schmooze with the brass. He was an ass-kicker, a policeman's policeman, in direct contrast to many of the up-and-coming young LAPD lieutenants. Stepanovich and other street detectives referred to these policemen as pogues: aggressive, ass-kissing yuppies who excelled at nothing more than scoring high on the written portion of promotional examinations.

In fact, one of the most oft-told LAPD war stories concerned Harger. As Stepanovich heard it, in a struggle with an armed robber for a weapon Harger had managed to turn the barrel of the gun toward his opponent. As the desperate man scrambled frantically, Harger had smiled broadly, then fired the weapon directly into the man's mouth. Perhaps because the legend fulfilled the subconscious wish of every cop who'd ever felt his bowels weaken during such a struggle, the story had become a Los Angeles police legend. In some versions of the tale the crook, whose teeth were blown down his throat, was a dope dealer. In others he was a child molester.

"Harger the Charger, a man with a whole bucket of balls," said Detective C.R. Black, a tall, rangy man looming behind Stepanovich.

Black looked much older than his thirty-five years. He had worked as a hod carrier in Bakersfield, California, before joining the department, and though he had a red and leathery neck as a result, his face held the toxic pallor common to cops who preferred working nights. His slicked-back black hair was thinning, the roots smothered by years of wearing a black uniform hat. He was wearing cowboy boots and a brown, Western-style polyester suit jacket that reeked of tobacco smoke. "Stones," Black said. "A basket of fucking stones."

"A real street cop," said the boyish, freckled Detective Tim Fordyce, standing to Stepanovich's right spinning a roll of evidence tape on his index finger. His detective badge was pinned to the lapel of a green corduroy sports coat, the only jacket Stepanovich had ever seen him wear. Fordyce was a meticulous, frugal young man who lived with his elderly parents, liked to talk computers, and professed to live for the weekends he spent in his Winnebago. Stepanovich liked Fordyce, but because he always seemed to avoid taking a definite position on anything, considered him to be less than stalwart.

Two hours later, the atmosphere in the church had changed. Frenzy was replaced by orderly and dull police procedure as men collected shotgun pellets, wadded them into small clear plastic bags, and measured and remeasured ballistic distances. Photos were retaken, and potential witnesses were interviewed.

Because he spoke Spanish, Stepanovich's job had been to interview these potential witnesses. As with virtually every gang murder, no one interviewed, even those who'd been within a few feet of the victims and perpetrators, admitted seeing anything.

Stepanovich found this response unsurprising. Unlike the black gang murders in South L.A. based on disputes over the sale of narcotics, retaliation murders committed by Hispanic gangs were based strictly on gang rivalry. It had been that way ever since the Mexican immigrants arriving after the turn of the century had settled in East L.A. and found themselves clinging to others from Zacatecas, Guadalajara, or Tecate. Gangs had formed and through the years loyalties had never weakened. Every building and every wall in East L.A. was tattooed with gang *placas:* coded challenges that glorified individual gangs and marked territorial boundaries: the graffiti of death.

One of the last potential witnesses left to interview was a thirtyish Mexican man with a Fu Manchu mustache who was slouching in a pew close to the door. As Stepanovich sat next to him, the man opened his eyes and sat up.

"May I have your name, sir?"

"Albert Garcia."

"Were you sitting here when the shooting occurred?"

Garcia nodded.

Stepanovich wrote his name on a fresh sheet of paper. "What did you see today, Mr. Garcia?"

"I didn't see nothing," Garcia said, rubbing his eyes as if he'd awakened from a long nap. "I didn't see shit."

"Anything you tell me will be kept in confidence," Stepanovich said, noticing Garcia's grime-caked fingernails.

"That don't mean dick in East L.A."

"Sitting here would give someone a wide-open shot of anyone coming in the door. There's no way a person could miss seeing what went down."

"I saw the same thing everybody else did," Garcia said. "The door flies open and this dude comes in shooting."

"What kind of a gun did the man have?"

Garcia looked about at the remaining wedding guests staring at him and shrugged. "I got my ass down. I didn't see nothing."

"Did the man say anything?"

Expressionless, Garcia shrugged.

"How many shots were fired?"

"Three or two, I think. The sound hurt my ears. That's all I know."

"What was the man wearing?"

"I don't remember."

"What did he look like?"

Garcia rubbed his nose. "Don't remember."

"You couldn't have missed getting a good look at the guy."

"He was a Mexican," Garcia said. "That's all I know." He exchanged a smirk with another man sitting across the aisle.

"Would you recognize him if you saw him again?" Stepanovich asked coldly.

"If I did, I wouldn't tell you."

Because Garcia was the twenty-seventh witness he'd interviewed, Stepanovich wrote the number twenty-seven in the upper right-hand corner of the report form and drew a circle around it. As he did, a mordant thought occurred to him: tomorrow or the next day there would be another shooting somewhere and the numbering of another list of fruitless interviews would start all over again.

"Can I go now?" Garcia asked.

"Where can you be reached during the day?"

Garcia recited the address of the gas station where he worked, and Stepanovich entered the information in the proper section on the report form. "You can go."

As Garcia stood up and sauntered down the aisle toward the door, Stepanovich made a final note by Garcia's name. It read:"Probably saw it all. Reinterview."

After the last of the witnesses had been interviewed, Stepanovich and the other three detectives gathered in the sacristy, the only place in the church where they could speak without being overheard. Captain Harger, standing in front of a tall armoire bursting with colorful vestments, waited patiently until the men had quieted down on their own rather than demanding order. As usual, Stepanovich was impressed.

Harger aimed an index finger at Stepanovich. "What do we have?"

Stepanovich took out his notebook and flipped to a page. "The shooter arrives in the bed of a red pickup truck. He fires once, blowing victim number one into the church. Shooter follows him inside, shouts 'Eighteenth Street,' fires twice more, and hits victim two. The shooter is described as a male Mexican wearing county pants and a white T-shirt. In his late twenties or early thirties, using a piece that is most likely a sawed-off twelve gauge."

"If anybody recognized the asshole, they aren't talking," Black said.

Harger turned to Arredondo. "Outside?"

Arredondo adjusted his trousers. He flipped open a pocketsized leather notebook with the letters "L.A.P.D." tooled across the front. "The old lady who runs the taco stand across the street saw the shooter jump into the bed of a red pickup truck for the getaway . . ." He turned a page. "A postal carrier two doors away says there was a getaway driver, possibly one other dude in the passenger seat. She says she won't testify."

Harger turned to Fordyce. "What do the people at records say?"

Fordyce ran his fingers through his thin brown hair. "The computer shows no red pickup truck tied to any known Eighteenth Street gang member. But once I get on the machine myself, I'll be able to check other criteria."

Harger nodded and Fordyce fell silent. "Physical evidence?"

Black held up a small, clear plastic bag containing shotgun wadding. "Nothing but some wadding and pellets. Nowhere to go with them really."

Harger made eye contact with each man: a brief glance that, as far as Stepanovich could tell, was devoid of condescension. "The Chief authorized this special unit and he expects results. This is our first case and I want every clue taken as far as it will go. If it means working all night, gentlemen, I hope you like coffee. If you need special equipment, just ask and ye shall receive."

"With all due respect, sir," Arredondo said, "some gang murders are just unsolvable."

Harger cleared his throat. "I picked you four for this assignment because you've all worked East L.A. and know the M.O. of the gangs. There's going to be a lot of overtime, and if it gets too much for any of you, just say the word and I'll have you replaced. No hard feelings. But as long as you're in this unit, I want you out there among 'em. I want the gangbangers in this part of town hit like they've never been hit before. As to whether a case is unsolvable? We'll talk about that after every peewee, every *veterano* in East L.A. has been turned upside down and kicked in the face. I want these punks hassled, their shit turned over. When they see you coming, I want them to know darkness has fallen."

There was a heavy, almost embarrassed silence for a moment after Harger had finished. Stepanovich could hear the others breathing in the tiny room.

"May I ask a question?" Black said.

Harger nodded.

"What can we do to solve a gang murder that a divisional homicide detective can't?"

Harger made a sardonic expression. "Realistically, we may not be able to make a case on every gang shooter. But what we're going to do is show these *pachucos* there's a price to pay every time they pull the trigger. We'll be answering directly to the chief of police and no one else. And the Chief tells me he isn't going to be worried about the details of how we do our job—just the results. The chain of command is *him* to *me* . . . to *you*. No adjutants or commanders or captains nosing in. That spells 'elite unit,' gentlemen, and I hope you read that loud and clear."

Stepanovich admired the turretlike manner in which

Harger revolved his head to make eye contact with each one of them.

"Stepanovich, you're known as the gang expert. Tell us what happened here today. I'm talking the big picture."

"This church is located in what Eighteenth Street considers their territory, sir. Last week Payaso, victim number one, and some of his White Fence pals, including the groom Smokey Salazar and a couple of other *veteranos*, Gordo and Lyncho, insulted Flaca, one of Eighteenth Street's women, by pinching her ass as she walked through Hollenbeck Park. Today's move is retaliation."

"An insult," Harger mused. "Eighteenth picks a shooter, drives him to church, and ends up killing a child?"

"That's the way I read it."

"Do you think Payaso knows who shot him?"

"Gang members always know the members of the other gangs," Black said before Stepanovich could answer.

Harger nodded and put his hand firmly on Stepanovich's shoulder. "I want you and Arredondo to do the hospital follow-up," he said, making a turret turn. "Black, grab a couple of blue-suiters and recanvass the neighborhood. Fordyce, make the computer hum. Get a list of every red pickup truck registered in East L.A. from the department of motor vehicles, and let's dig out the names of known Eighteenth Street shooters and their associates."

Black cleared his throat. "Elite unit or not, it may not be possible to stop the gangs from killing one another. They've been doing it in this part of town for a hundred years."

"All I'm asking is for you men to trust me and give me your best effort. I'll take the heat for any failure. But frankly, I've studied each of your backgrounds and I'm confident that with a solid team effort, we can hit the gangs like a steamroller. If I didn't believe that

I wouldn't have accepted this assignment from the Chief."

"Count me in," Stepanovich said to break the sudden silence in the room.

"Me too," Arredondo said.

Black rubbed his hands together. "I say, let's go to work."

THREE

On the way to the county hospital, Stepanovich turned onto Third Street and cruised past the places of his childhood: old brick buildings, a tortilla factory, a mom-and-pop market once owned by his best pal Howard Goldberg's father, and a twelve-unit stucco apartment house occupied by mostly Serbians and Russians and in recent years by undocumented workers from Peru and Colombia. The tiny two-bedroom house where his mother lived, where he'd spent his childhood, was on Vega Street, less than a block away.

Farther east, he cruised past Evergreen Cemetery, a grassy expanse of graying and blackened tombstones bounded by a chain-link fence. As a child the cemetery had been his favorite place for kite flying. Now, bordered as it was by a freeway, a service station, and some rotting wood-frame dwellings housing extended families of illegal Mexican aliens, the urban graveyard seemed to him the ugliest piece of land in Los Angeles.

He remembered hot summer nights when he and Howard Goldberg, guided by the bat-vision of childhood, would race about between the tombstones and launch commando-style raids on the neighborhood ice cream truck that passed by the cemetery every hot night at about nine. Out of the darkness he would race into the dimly lit street and hop up onto the rear bumper of the truck. Holding on with one hand to the light fixture affixed just above the truck's small rectangular door, he'd lift out cartons of Popsicles and strawberry sundaes and drop them gently to the street for Howard to pick up and carry back into the cemetery for a robber's feast. At the age of ten, it was the ultimate excitement, and they were lucky enough never to have been arrested. Unfortunately, in a night of horror he'd never been able to forget, Howard had tripped in the street and been run over by a speeding drunk driver, crippling him for life.

Even at that early age, Stepanovich had wanted to be a policeman when he grew up. His father, a railroad switchman, had died of a heart attack when Jose was five, and the dominant male figure in his life became his father's brother, the clean-featured, sharply dressed burglary detective Nick Stepanovich.

Uncle Nick had a permanent charge account at the exclusive Murray's Clothiers and enough girlfriends to start a harem. He always seemed to have liquor on his breath, but never seemed drunk. He brought gifts, mostly food, to the Stepanovich household every week. In fact, on Serbian Orthodox holidays the take included expensive turkeys, hams, wheels of cheese, candies, and enormous baskets of fruit. His frugal mother was always evasive when he asked about Uncle Nick's gifts. But once the inquisitive child found a printed greeting card inside the colored cellophane covering one of the elaborate Christmas fruit displays Uncle Nick had brought over the day before the Serbian saint's day. It read:

Dear Mr. and Mrs. Melvoin:
I hope you enjoy your stay at the L.A. Biltmore Hotel.

Larry Hess
General Manager

The kindly Nick took Stepanovich to boxing matches at Olympic Auditorium, always flashing his badge to get in, and to burglary division picnics. Once, having stopped by the house to drop off a large package of porterhouse steaks and a case of canned goods while on duty, Uncle Nick spotted a fugitive meandering down the street. Stepanovich would never forget Uncle Nick, like a magician, actually pulling a gun from under the jacket of his sharkskin suit, chasing the crook, and single-handedly tackling, wrestling, and handcuffing the man. With the neighbors watching in awe, Nick dragged the prisoner to his detective car and tossed him into the backseat like a sack of grain.

The capture was Jose's recurrent childhood dream.

At eighteen he had enlisted in the Army and spent two years in Vietnam. With a hunger for excitement, for the bizarre, only made keener by the ennui of military law-enforcement duties, he had submitted his application to the L.A. police department the day he was discharged.

Stepanovich pulled up to a stop sign and a leggy Mexican woman wearing a hip-hugging knit skirt stepped off the curb and crossed the street in front of the sedan.

"There's a bitch who wants it," Arredondo said, taking a small comb out of his lapel pocket. He raked it through his thick black hair and rapped it sharply on the windowsill.

"How can you tell?"

Arredondo shoved the comb back in his shirt pocket. "Strides."

"Strides?"

"Last week this broad moved into an apartment down the hall from me. I hawk on her immediately: big tits, great ass—a ten on a ten scale. That night I'm just sitting there in my apartment watching this English movie and there's a knock on the door. Guess who? None other. She asks if she can borrow a screwdriver. I play it cool, give her a screwdriver. A few minutes later, she brings it back. I ask her if she wants a Budweiser, put some Lola Beltran sounds on the old stereo. An hour later I'm doing her doggie-style on the living room floor and she's liking it, screaming 'Fuck me harder!' and all that shit. I'm talking begging for mercy, dude."

Stepanovich stopped at a traffic signal across from a check-cashing establishment emblazoned with signs in Spanish.

"I reached my rocks during 'Coucouroucoucou Paloma.' Afterward the bitch tells me she doesn't know what made her do it blah blah blah, and she'd like to see me again yakety yak—she has to be at work in the morning. She leaves. There I am still watching this English movie and I've done a ten on a ten scale." He picked up a logbook resting between them on the seat and began filling in blanks. "If she has AIDS, you're talking to a dead man. But the risk is all part of it. Russian-roulette sport fucking."

"Long strides. I still don't get it."

"All women who walk with long strides love to fuck. It's a sure sign."

"You're crazy."

At L.A. County General Hospital, Stepanovich and Arredondo followed a cement-and-tile corridor past dingy waiting areas packed with pregnant black and brown women. They turned a corner into an acrid-smelling hallway and maneuvered their way past a janitor mopping up a puddle, patients on gurneys and in wheelchairs, and shuffling orderlies and nurses.

Finally they came to a glass-enclosed nurses' station. A tall black nurse was sitting at a desk. She had corn-rowed hair, heavy green eye makeup, and white lipstick accentuating tobacco-stained teeth.

Stepanovich showed her his badge. "Primitivo Estrada. Can you tell me his condition?"

The nurse looked up, lit a long, slim cigarette with a

tiny throwaway lighter, and coughed some smoke. "The gunshot victim?"

"Right."

She set the cigarette in a small glass ashtray and used a long red fingernail to pick something from the end of her tongue. With the same finger she opened a three-ringed notebook that was sitting on the desk and thumbed through the pages. "Condition critical. He's in room 309. That's post-op intensive care."

"Is he able to talk?"

She shrugged. "He's been completely out of it."

"Is he going to live?"

"You should probably ask the doctor that."

"I'm asking you."

She picked up the cigarette and took a long drag. "Odds are the boy is headed for the big hacienda."

"Any objection if we talk to him?"

"Any requests for interview by law enforcement officers are supposed to go through the security office. That's in the next building over. You fill out a form. You bring the form back here, and when the nursing supervisor has time, she looks at it to see if it's OK. Make sure it has a date/time stamp on it. Sometimes they forget to put the stamp on it. Then you have to go back to the security office."

"Thanks," Stepanovich sighed, and he and Arredondo filed down the hall.

At Room 309, Stepanovich pushed open the swinging door. The room held four occupied beds and reeked of a sweet, indescribable odor reminding Stepanovich of the dead-body calls he'd handled when assigned to uniform patrol.

He and Arredondo approached a bed in front of a flyspecked window. Payaso was lying on his side. His chest and back were covered with thick white surgical dressing and tape, and clear tubes issued from his right arm, nose, and penis. His breathing was labored and spittle had dried at the corners of his mouth. His tattoos appeared lifeless and faded on his cocoa skin.

Stepanovich tugged the curtain from the wall to shield them from the view of the other patients. He leaned close to the wounded man. "Payaso," he whispered, "can you hear me?"

Payaso gurgled, gagged, took a few rapid breaths, then rested. "Mama," he said finally without moving.

"Do you have pain?" Stepanovich asked in a fatherly tone.

Payaso's lips moved. "Aaaaaah."

"Who shot you?"

Payaso's lips twitched a little.

"Tell me who shot you, Payaso."

Payaso's tongue struggled to moisten his lips.

"Can you talk?" Arredondo asked.

"Mama," Payaso said finally. "Mama."

Stepanovich leaned closer to the wounded man. "Mama wants to know who shot you," he whispered.

"Mama."

"Diga Mama," Arredondo said. "Was it someone from Eighteenth who shot you?"

Stepanovich picked up Payaso's left hand and massaged it gently. Payaso swallowed with difficulty. His jaw worked a few times as if he was trying to form a word.

"Your mama is here," Stepanovich said in the Spanish his Mexican mother had taught him. "Tell Mama who shot you, *mijo.*"

Payaso strained to open his eyes. He blinked rapidly. Then his eyes closed again.

Stepanovich tapped Payaso's arm. No response. Then he gripped his bare shoulder and shook firmly. "Wake up."

Payaso opened his eyes and looked at them. His head moved weakly. Both Stepanovich and Arredondo leaned closer.

"Mama is here, amigo," Arredondo whispered. "Tell her who shot you."

Payaso gurgled.

"Mama esia aqui," Stepanovich said.

Stepanovich leaned to within inches of the man's face. He smelled hospital breath.

Payaso's eyes darted. His lips pursed to form a word.

"Talk to me, Payaso."

"Fuck you, cop," he murmured. Then his eyes closed and he breathed deeply.

Stepanovich and Arredondo looked at each other.

Stepanovich threw open the curtain partition and sauntered to the window. He looked out at the heart of East L.A.: a huddle of sooty medical buildings, some ambulances parked in a lot. Down a sloping road leading past the hospital entrance was the juvenile jail facility, a modern two-story edifice that looked like a college classroom building surrounded by a high chain-link fence.

"He'll be a solid gangbanger right to the end," Arredondo said.

"He's not gonna die. Even the hard-core gangbangers talk before they die."

They left the room. Outside in the hallway, Arredondo stopped to use a pay telephone.

A young nurse, a slender Hispanic woman with dark, brooding eyes, approached Stepanovich. Her jet-black hair delicately framed her face and was pulled into a knot in back. Her complexion was a vibrant Aztec beige that Stepanovich guessed required no makeup of any kind. She had full hips, long legs, and her starched nurse uniform strained against full breasts. The plastic name tag she was wearing read: "GLORIA SOLIZ, R.N."

"I'm the nursing supervisor for this ward," she said in a less-than-friendly tone.

"We're with LAPD," he said, unable to take his eyes off the pencil-line scar high on her left cheek.

"That doesn't give you the right to bother someone who is fighting for his life."

"We're investigating a murder."

"This is a hospital. If you want to interview patients, I'd appreciate it if you would go through the proper procedures with the security office."

"We'll be sure and do that next time."

"You cops must go to some school to learn how to act like that."

"Pardon me?"

"Condescending to people. Policemen practice it like an art."

He shrugged. "Just trying to do a job."

"Don't do your job in my ward. This is where people come to get well. If Mr. Estrada was a policeman, would you want someone to disturb him?"

"No, but Mr. Estrada isn't a policeman. He's a gang member who may know who murdered a nine-year-old girl today."

"I'm not trying to be confrontational."

"Yes, you are."

She shook her head disdainfully and headed down the hallway. Stepanovich was transfixed by the movement of her hips.

"Who's the medium strider?" Arredondo said, setting the telephone receiver back on the hook.

"A lady I'd like to get to know," Stepanovich said without taking his eyes off her.

FOUR

Stepanovich drove out of the hospital parking lot and cruised along a road that followed the perimeter of the hospital complex. He turned right on State Street and drove across a bridge spanning the freeway. At the end of the bridge he slowed down and pulled to the curb in front of Manuel's taco stand, a shiny red hut with three stools at the service window and two picnic tables covered by a patio roof.

Without exchanging words, he and Arredondo climbed out of the sedan. Manuel, a heavy, thirtyish Mexican wearing a stained butcher's apron and a Dodgers baseball hat, prepared tacos, wrapped them in wax paper, and handed them to the detectives. Stepanovich made no attempt to pay because he knew Manuel would refuse him. Years ago he'd arrested a member of the Happy Valley gang who'd robbed, then pistol-whipped Manuel into unconsciousness. Since then Manuel had refused to accept Stepanovich's money. Though he knew Internal Affairs Division frowned on accepting such gratuities, nevertheless Stepanovich stopped by a couple of times a week. He figured Manuel could afford a few tacos, and besides, while he was there he was providing Manuel free protection from armed robbers.

31

Holding the tacos with their fingertips, Stepanovich and Arredondo stood on the sidewalk in front of the place and ate in the knees-apart, leaning-forward, dripping-taco position.

Manuel wiped his hands on his apron. "Who claimed at the church?"

"Eighteenth," Stepanovich said with his mouth full.

"Is it true they killed a little girl?"

Stepanovich nodded.

"I hope you waste the fuckers when you catch 'em. The streets ain't safe no more. The goddamn *pachucos* are everywhere. They just strut around and people are afraid to do anything. You should do it Mexican style. You don't see no *pachucos* strutting around below the border. Down there they shoot your ass on sight. If you get out of line, the police take you outside of town and let you have it but good."

"That's a good point."

Three young women wearing short skirts and hair ratted high stepped up to the other side of the counter, and Manuel turned to wait on them.

Stepanovich finished his taco and used a paper napkin to wipe his mouth and hands. On the crowded freeway below, long ribbons of blinking taillights led from L.A.: clones in Volvos and Hondas raced toward stucco suburbs named Villa Park, Greenbriar Park, and Frazier Park. He wondered where Gloria Soliz lived.

"It's all the luck of the draw," Arredondo said with his mouth full. "If the little girl's parents hadn't brought her to the wedding, she'd still be alive. If she'd have been sitting in the next seat, the bullet would have missed her."

"We're gonna put this case together," Stepanovich said, still staring at the freeway.

Arredondo wiped his hands with a handkerchief. "Even if we find out who the shooters are, we'll probably never be able to convict 'em."

"We'll see."

"I'd like to find the guy who did it and blow his goddamn brains all over the street."

An exhausted Stepanovich nodded. He took a deep breath, then checked his wristwatch. There were no hot leads and he suggested they call it quits for the day.

After dropping off Arredondo at the Hollenbeck Station parking lot, Stepanovich drove a mile or so past the small factories, machine and auto-repair shops along the heavily traveled San Fernando Road to the suburb of Glendale.

Glendale was a well-established suburban community of apartment houses, single-family homes, and a thriving commercial area with an air-conditioned shopping mall. Like most other Southern California city officials, the Glendale city fathers had allowed many new apartment houses to be built to accommodate the city's share of the recent influx of immigrants. While most of those who'd flocked to L.A. were Mexicans who gravitated to minimum wage jobs in factories, restaurants, and car washes, the people settling in Glendale were mostly Asians, Cubans, Armenians, and East Indians, a middle-class group of entrepreneurs who purchased small restaurants, bakeries, service stations, and the cheap motels along Colorado Boulevard.

The city's luxury homes were situated at the north end of town at the base of the foothills and looked down at Brand Boulevard, the main thoroughfare, recently widened to fit in more car lots and banks. Around the new apartment buildings both east and west of Brand, fast-food establishments, a gym called the Fitness Connection, and even a couple of singles bars thrived.

Stepanovich turned right off Brand and halfway down the block slowed in front of the Lakeview Arms apartment house, where he lived. Except for the "LAKEVIEW ARMS" sign adjacent to the glass security door at the entrance, the place looked exactly like all the other buildings lining the street. Like most nights, the parking places near the entrance were already taken. He refused to pay the thirty dollars extra to park in the underground garage and hadn't been issued a monthly Lakeview Arms parking permit. He cruised down the street and maneuvered into a parking space near the corner.

After locking his car, he trudged back up the street past two-story stucco apartment houses with names—The Pines, Roma Gardens, The Mediterranean—that could only have been picked from the Southern California Book of Meaningless Apartment Names. He opened the security door without using a key. The lock had been broken during a daytime burglary over a month ago, and the owner, a yacht builder who lived in a mansion in Laguna Beach, hadn't gotten around to having it repaired. Inside, Stepanovich was hit with a familiar chemical odor wafting from the super-chlorinated swimming pool situated between the apartment structures. Lakeview's Lake. He stopped at his mailbox and, dodging some plastic lounge chairs, he made his way along the perimeter of the pool to his apartment. He unlocked the door, flicked on the light, and stepped in.

The living room was bare except for a brown bean-bag chair and a card table he'd borrowed from Arredondo after Nancy had stripped the place of everything, including the console television and an over-priced sofa and recliner chair she'd purchased with a loan from the Department credit union just before walking out on him.

He sat down at the card table and sorted through the mail: a newsletter from the Police Protective League, one of Nancy's art magazines, an official-looking brown envelope bearing the printed inscription: "DATED PRIZE MATERIAL FOR JOSE STEPANOVICH"—junk, he surmised—and a letter with a Brentwood address he recognized as Nancy's boyfriend's. Bruce was an interior decorator and marathon jogger who worked with Nancy at the California Design Center. He noted with his usual irritation that she used her maiden name.

The letter was in her clear, almost calligraphic hand:

Hello,

I've been trying to reach you by phone for weeks, but as usual you haven't been home. So what else is new?

The reason I was calling is that I'm not receiving all my catalogs and magazines. Though I know from first-hand experience how careless you are about such things, I would appreciate it if you would forward all mail addressed to me. Though the post ofice has had my change-of-address form for months, you know how truly screwed up they are. I of course have no way of proving it, but my guess is that you are throwing away everything arriving with my name on it. Or at least everything that doesn't seem important to you. Please do not ignore this letter. I want, and have a right to, all my mail whether it is junk mail or not. Though I'm fully prepared to never see any of the second-class mail, I'm asking you to be at least halfway considerate about this.

I'm sure you're not interested in the least, but I've done a lot of thinking in the past months and I'm convinced that my moving out was best for both of us. We were living as strangers. Strangely enough, by being away I've come to have a better understanding of you as a person. As I see it, the problem is that you have no life away from your job. It was the same with your Uncle Nick. He preferred to drink all day at the VFW hall and retell tired police stories after he retired rather than play golf or take up any new activity. Though I'm sure you never realized it, when you and he were to-gether all he ever talked about was police work: gangs, violence, and death. The fact that he died less than a year after retiring should have shown you what happens when you live that way.

Well, enough of that. I know you aren't listening. Bruce and I just got back from a Club Med vacation in

Gerald Petievich

*Puerto Vallarta. Entirely <u>too much</u> food and sun so I'll
have to hit it <u>extra</u> hard in my aerobics class.*
　　Please don't be a prick about forwarding my mail.
Nancy

He tossed all the mail, including the art magazine,
into a plastic trash can under the kitchen sink, and
opened a window to let in some fresh air. Down the
street he could see the streetlights of Brand Boulevard. Though it wasn't Greenwich Village or even San
Francisco's Union Street, there was a movie theater
and a couple of decent restaurants within walking distance, and a laundry and a post office that came in
handy nowadays. Best of all, the apartment was af-
fordable and he was outside the city limits of Los
Angeles, a town he no longer considered habitable
because of gangs and crime.

Actually, the apartment and location had been Nancy's choice. She had gone to Glendale High School
and loved the town. When first married, the two of
them had attended cocktail parties and barbecues at
the homes of Nancy's married Glendale friends.
Stepanovich had little in common with the other guests
and felt alienated trying to make conversation. Like
all policemen, he felt there was no way an outsider
would understand his work. Even after long days at
work, he found himself preferring to stop by the Rumor Control Bar and drink scotch with the other detectives rather than stand around at some suburban
barbecue holding a plastic glass of lukewarm chablis
and listen to yuppies clack about the price of property.

After attending such functions, he and Nancy always seemed to edge into arguments that ended with
Nancy crying and accusing him of being hostile and
noncommunicative. Looking back, he probably had
been. They'd once been desperately in love, but he'd
eventually stopped looking at her as the long-legged
beauty he'd married and began seeing her as a carping
roommate.

Now, he thought, when Nancy married Bruce, a wimp
who wore button-down shirts and flashed an instant

36

shit-eating grin, she'd always have a party companion.

He opened the refrigerator, took out a half-empty carton of milk, and held it up to his nose: sour. He poured the curdled liquid down the drain. Promising himself to get to the store as soon as he had time, he took a glass from the dish drainer, flipped on the faucet, and filled the glass with water. He drank and set the glass on the sink. The taco at Manuel's had been the only thing he'd eaten all day and he was still hungry. He considered heating one of the TV dinners he had in the freezer, but decided against trying to sleep on a full stomach. In the morning, after signing in at Hollenbeck Station, he and Arredondo would stop at the Zacatecas Café on Evergreen Street for a combination plate with all the trimmings.

Stepanovich's bedroom was furnished with a bare mattress on the floor, one of Arredondo's card table chairs, and a portable radio. The clothing he'd kept in the dresser Nancy and Bruce had taken to Brentwood was now stacked on the floor of the closet next to his shoes. A tennis racket and some cardboard boxes he'd filled with police academy textbooks, and a few framed photographs of himself and Uncle Nick standing with his mother and father at the Los Angeles County Fairgrounds, were all he'd held on to.

Stepanovich removed his sports coat and slid his gun, bullet pouch, and handcuffs from his belt and set them on the chair. He stopped undressing and checked his watch. It was almost midnight. His mind made up, he quickly put his police equipment back on his belt and left the apartment.

It took him about ten minutes to get to the L.A. county hospital. He parked his car in the same spot he'd used earlier in the evening and entered the front door. Because of the hour, the pale green corridors were dimly lit.

He found Gloria Soliz at the nurses' station in the intensive-care ward, writing on a metal clipboard. He stood in front of her until she finally looked up and saw him.

"Mr. Estrada is still too sick to be interviewed," she said when she recognized him.

"I'm not here about him. I had to pick up something from hospital records, so I thought I'd stop by and apologize for the misunderstanding earlier."

She stared at Stepanovich for a moment, but she didn't smile. "That's nice of you. But no apology is necessary."

"I guess I came on a little strong."

She came to her feet. "No problem. Is there something I can help you with?"

"When is the shift change for this ward?"

"In a few minutes."

"Would you like to go out to breakfast?"

She looked about to see if anyone was nearby. They were alone. "It's late and I—"

"We could just grab a bite."

"Thanks, maybe some other time." The phone on her desk rang. She let it ring twice before picking up the receiver.

Stepanovich took a deep breath, let it out. Shuffling back down the hallway, he stopped at the elevator and looked back. Still holding the phone to her ear, she was standing in the hallway watching him. She darted back into the nurses' station.

Outside the employees' entrance to the hospital, Stepanovich sat in his car and watched as ambulances intermittently charged toward the emergency entrance. The image of the dead little girl lying on the church floor began to obsess him. But he recognized this as a normal response to the horrible events of the afternoon. Though it was no particular consolation, he knew the next violent death scene would, like a boxcar on a track, shove today's tragedy to the back of his mind. He just hoped like hell the next victim wasn't a child.

A few minutes later, off-duty nurses and doctors began streaming out the door. He straightened to get a better look. As the flow of departing hospital employees began to dwindle, Gloria Soliz emerged. She didn't notice him. He started the engine. She walked across the parking lot to a late-model Volkswagen. As she reached into her purse for her keys, he cruised across the parking lot and pulled up beside her.

"Sure you won't change your mind?"

She turned in surprise.

"Breakfast is the most important meal of the day."

She smiled broadly, shook her head. He climbed out of the car and opened the passenger door of his sedan. She stood there for a moment, then climbed in.

"How about Artie's coffee shop?" he said, steering down the descending driveway and onto the street.

"Where all the cops hang out."

"Some of them," he said, smiling, for the car was filled with the pleasant scent of her perfume.

"Cops love to do things in groups, don't they?" she said as he turned onto Mission Road, a thoroughfare lined with auto-salvage yards and railroad sidings.

"I'm sure nurses socialize now and then."

"It's different."

Artie's, an open twenty-four hours establishment, was located next to a freeway at the edge of downtown. The place was deserted except for a group of motorcycle cops seated at a table in the corner.

Stepanovich and Gloria sat in a window booth overlooking the parking lot. The waitress, a tiny Filipino woman with thick eyeglasses, poured coffee, took their orders, and moved away.

Stepanovich sipped coffee and felt it warm his insides. "I hope you don't think I'm coming on too strong."

"I've found that cops always come on strong."

"Why don't you forget the cop stuff? Pretend I'm a rich doctor."

For a moment he thought she was going to take offense. Then the corners of her mouth turned up slightly. She smiled and shook her head. They both laughed and Stepanovich thought she seemed to relax.

"Where'd you go to school?" he asked.

"UCLA."

"I meant high school."

"Roosevelt. How about you?"

"Garfield."

"So you grew up in the barrio too."

Eating breakfast, they talked of growing up in East Los Angeles, and found they'd attended some of the same dances and even knew a few of the same people.

"Why nursing school?" he asked.

"I wanted to help people. I still do. And there's plenty of people to help when you're a nurse."

"Why didn't you move away from East L.A. when you got out of nursing school?"

"It's home to me. My family is here."

"So are the gangs."

She gazed out at the parking lot. "Gangs are a fact of life," she said resignedly.

"A fact of life I'd like to erase."

"A lot of them are just kids who don't know any better," she said. "Some have parents who were gang members."

"My mother was Mexican, my father was Yugoslavian. Even though we weren't Catholic, they sent me to Catholic school to keep me away from the gangbangers. But it didn't help. The gang punks used to catch me on my way to school and beat the shit out of me anyway."

"So now you're getting back at them."

"I guess you could say that. Yeah, as a matter of fact, I am.

"You're not going to change anything."

"The gangbangers I've put in San Quentin are reading comic books right now instead of on the streets shooting innocent people."

"A policeman's dream. All the criminals locked up in cages."

"Do you have a better idea?"

"No, but on the other hand, I don't see the world as

the unattractive place you do," she said demurely.

Nothing was said for a while, and she avoided his eyes when he tried to make her share a smile that would ease the uncomfortable silence.

"Are you married?" he said.

She shook her head. "Never really had time, I guess. And you?"

"Just divorced. I haven't been out much recently."

"How long were you married?"

"Five years. The marriage counselor said we might have made it if I weren't a policeman. Nancy couldn't handle the long hours."

"Why didn't you quit the police department and get a job with shorter hours?"

"I waited in line to become a cop. I worked like hell to make it through the police academy. Why should I quit?"

"To save your marriage."

"I married the police department before I married my wife."

"Being a cop isn't just a job for you, is it? It's power and status—machismo. It's a way of life." Gloria touched her lips with a napkin. "I'm sorry. I didn't mean to get personal."

"How do you know so much about cops?"

"I grew up in East L.A., remember?"

"Would you like to go out sometime?" Stepanovich heard himself saying.

She looked into his eyes for a brief moment, then finished her coffee. "I don't know."

They were both quiet for a moment. Then she pointed out that she'd just worked a double shift and felt like she was going to fall asleep at the table. Stepanovich paid the bill. They walked out of the restaurant, and he drove her back to the hospital parking lot. As he pulled into a space next to her car, he said, "I'd like to see you again."

"I'm afraid I have a very busy schedule—and journal articles to catch up on. Besides, I'm not much of a social butterfly."

"Neither am I, but I'd still like to see you," he said. "May I have your home number?"

She took out a pen and a tiny pad, wrote down the number, then tore the note from the pad and handed it to him. "My days off are Tuesday and Wednesday. And thanks for breakfast."

He considered kissing her, but didn't want to seem too aggressive. Instead, he climbed out of the car and opened the door, hoping that she wouldn't think the gesture condescending. She climbed out of the car and kissed him full on the lips. "Good night," she said, pulling away from him. She climbed in her VW, started the engine, and drove out of the parking lot.

She was on his mind as he drove back to his apartment.

Later, naked and covered only with a sheet, he was still thinking about her. Unable to sleep because of the heat, he reached out to the portable radio, tuning past a religious station, an all-night talk show, some screaming rock music. Restless, he turned it off. Lying there with his eyes closed and his arms extended straight out, listening to the cars whizzing past the apartment house, he finally began to feel drowsy. He imagined Gloria standing in the hospital hallway. Farther down the corridor, sprawled on a bloodstained church carpet, was the corpse of the little girl . . . and behind her Payaso was lying in his hospital bed attached to life-giving plastic tubes. In this dream the scent of Gloria's perfume acted like a powerful narcotic that suppressed any power he had even to say, "Hello."

When Stepanovich awoke the next morning, Gloria was still on his mind.

FIVE

Arredondo was waiting at Hollenbeck Station. He said he was starving and suggested the Zacatecas. Though Stepanovich was still full from the breakfast at Artie's, he knew Arredondo was unbearable to work with when he was hungry. Besides, at the Zacatecas they could eat for free.

He parked in the red zone in front of the small family restaurant housed in an old two-story brownstone. Across the street was the Chickasaw Street Elementary School, where a month before two students had been killed in an unsolved drive-by shooting Stepanovich believed had been committed by the King Kobras gang. They entered through a tattered screen door and crossed the dingy linoleum to a table in the corner, where they could keep an eye on the door and the bay window in case the King Kobras decided to drive by and shoot up the place. A full-skirted, smiling young Mexican woman with a streak of peroxide-blond running through her black hair came to the table, and they both ordered combination platters. The waitress served them quickly and they gorged on enormous quantities of *chorizo* and eggs, *flautas*, and piles of flour tortillas smeared with butter.

When the waitress brought them a bill after they

finished eating, Arredondo headed into the kitchen to make small talk with the proprietor, Mary Valenzuela, knowing that she would recognize them and tell the waitress the meals were on the house. Mary hadn't charged Stepanovich since he'd interceded with the court to help her son Efriam get released from L.A. County Jail. Stepanovich had convinced the boy to testify against some Third Street gang shooters, and though Efriam had died from an overdose of heroin while celebrating getting out of jail, Mary was still grateful to Stepanovich for the favor.

While Arredondo was in the kitchen, Stepanovich took out his notebook and reviewed the notes he'd made on the church shooting.

A few minutes later, Arredondo returned to the table and sat down. "I'm glad I went back to say hello. Mary looks like she might need a little fucking."

Stepanovich found the page he was looking for. "What did she say?"

"Just small talk, haven't seen you guys in a long time yakety yak, but extra friendly. A bitch in heat. Women can't hide it."

Heavy-busted Mary Valenzuela emerged from the kitchen and whispered something to the waitress, who in turn came to the table and snatched up the bill. "Sorry," she said apologetically, hurrying to another table.

"The price is right, amigo. Where we headed?"

"El Sereno."

"Who's there?"

"Albert Garcia. One of the witnesses from yesterday. I read him as knowing the secret."

"How so?"

"He was right by the sanctuary door. There's no way he wouldn't have seen the shooter, and he was extra shaky during the interview," he said as they walked out the door.

It was Arrendondo's turn to drive, and he climbed behind the wheel and started the engine. Bloated from the combination platter, Stepanovich leaned back in the passenger seat and closed his eyes.

Arredondo pulled into traffic. "Did I tell you about the broad I spent the night with?"

Stepanovich shook his head without opening his eyes.

"A schoolteacher I met at Monahan's bar last night. A real space cadet, this bitch. I put the word to her at the bar. She'd had a few drinks and buys my action right then and there. She wants to go to her place. I follow her in my car. A nice pad. I fuck this broad across the living room and into the bedroom—every which way. I'm power-fucking and she's loving it. Finally we drop off to sleep. The next thing I know I wake up in the middle of the night to this buzzing sound. Bzzzzzzzzzzzzzzzzzz. I lie there listening. I pull back the covers. This bitch is lying there in the darkness giving herself a workout with her trusty vibrator. I said, 'What's this, baby?' This bitch isn't embarrassed in the least. She says, 'Turn on the lights, dude. I want you to see me do it.' "

The police car pulled to the curb in front of a graffiti-stained duplex on Eastern Avenue. Stepanovich climbed out and, with Arredondo following, trod down a gravel driveway past the house. The rear unit was a hovel the size of a small garage. Like most of the others in the neighborhood, its windows were lined with wrought-iron bars, and the interior was hidden behind makeshift drapes of sheets and newspaper. A front door reinforced with a metal plate around the jamb was protected by a tiny screened-in porch that reminded Stepanovich somehow of a pet store aviary. The screen door was unlatched. Boards creaked as he stepped onto the porch. He tapped a knuckle on a door.

There was the sound of movement inside, and the door was pulled open a few inches by a dwarfish Mexican woman whose hair was wrapped loosely in a towel. She was wearing a grimy blue robe and a pair of yellow dishwashing gloves that were sudsy.

Stepanovich held out his badge. "Does Albert Garcia live here?"

Holding her robe closed with her wet, gloved hands, the woman shook her turban. "Nobody here by that name," she said in barrio dialect.

"How long have you lived here?"

"Ten years. What's this about?"

"Have you ever heard of Albert Garcia?"

She shook her head. "I don't know no one named Garcia."

"We must have the wrong address. Sorry to bother you," Stepanovich said.

The woman shut the door.

Without saying a word to each other, the detectives strolled to the front house and knocked on the door. An obese Mexican man with shaving cream covering one side of his face opened the door. Stepanovich showed his badge. "We were just speaking with Albert Garcia next door. His car was broken into last night, and he said you might know who did it."

"I don't know nothing about Garcia's car. But if someone broke into it, it's his own fault because he leaves it parked on the street. I've told him to pull it in back."

"Sorry to bother you," Stepanovich said. They marched back to Garcia's door, and Stepanovich pounded loudly this time. When the woman opened the door, he and Arredondo pushed past her into a small living room furnished with a cheap red sofa and chair, a framed lithograph of Pope John XXII, and a kitchenette table.

"You can't just come in here!" the woman shouted.

Albert Garcia, wearing Levis and a T-shirt, was sitting on the sofa looking sheepish.

Stepanovich advanced to the sofa. "Sorry to bother you, but at the church yesterday I got the feeling you'd prefer to talk in private."

Garcia's eyes darted back and forth between the

detectives. "Like I told you, I didn't see *nawthing*."

"A little girl had her brains blown out yesterday. If we can't find the ones who did it, someone else could get killed," Stepanovich said.

"I'll be the one who gets killed if I rat for you."

"There was a hundred people in the church. So if you could see your way to tell us what you know, the shooter would never know exactly who handed him up. We could arrest him and your name would never so much as come up."

"Bullshit. There ain't no secrets in this barrio."

Stepanovich felt his muscles tighten as he glanced at Arredondo. The other detective took the frightened woman by the arm and led her into the other room.

"Where you taking her?" Garcia cried as the door slammed.

Stepanovich grabbed Garcia by the neck with both hands and yanked him fully to his feet. "I'm working on a murder, you piece of shit," he hissed. "Now, either tell me what you saw or you're under arrest as a material witness."

"Leave him alone!" the woman shrieked from the other room.

Stepanovich spun Garcia around, took handcuffs from his belt, and ratcheted a cuff onto Garcia's right wrist. He twisted sharply and Garcia cried out in pain.

The woman cried, "He didn't do nawthing! Leave him alone!"

"I got a look at him, but I don't know who he is," Garcia whispered.

"Age?"

"About thirty."

"That won't get it."

"He was a *veterano,* but I don't know his name. I swear." Arredondo ratcheted the other handcuff onto Garcia's left wrist. "He had green eyes."

"You're sure about that?"

"Positive. There ain't that many Mexicans with green

eyes. That's all I know. Please don't take me to jail. I gotta go to work today. I'll lose my job."

Stepanovich paused for a moment, then used a handcuff key to unlock the handcuffs. As Garcia rubbed his chafed wrists, Stepanovich crossed to the bedroom door and opened it. The woman rushed out to Garcia and threw her arms around him. Arredondo followed Stepanovich to the door.

"I don't like the gangs any more than you, but I gotta look out for my own ass," Garcia said.

"Where are you going to be for the rest of the day?" Stepanovich asked.

"I was just going to work."

The detectives headed out the door.

"I don't get to carry no fucking gun to protect myself like you cops!" Garcia yelled at them as they headed down the driveway.

"It's Pepe Gomez," Stepanovich said as he and Arredondo climbed back in the car.

"The name rings a bell."

"They call him Greenie. He's an Eighteenth Street *veterano* good for at least four drive-by murders. He lives in the apartments at Eighteenth and Toberman and likes to use a sawed-off piece."

"I remember him. He did a deuce for robbery at Chino awhile back."

Stepanovich and Arredondo drove downtown to Parker Center. In the records bureau on the third floor they obtained a mug shot of Gomez from his arrest file. With the help of a clerk, they rummaged through at least a hundred other files until they came up with four other mug shots of Mexican men with green eyes who looked somewhat like Gomez. Stepanovich removed a booking photograph of each man from the file and numbered and stapled the photos onto a manila file folder. It was almost three by the time they finished.

It took less than ten minutes to get from Parker Center to the service station where Albert Garcia was employed. He was changing a tire in the automotive bay and there was no one else in the station. Frowning when he saw them approach, he set down his tire iron, pulled a soiled blue rag out of his rear trouser pocket, and wiped his hands. Stepanovich handed him the manila folder bearing the mug shots. "Recognize anyone here?"

"I told you I didn't want to be no witness."

"We already have a case, but we just want to make sure we have the right guy," Arredondo lied.

Garcia accepted the folder reluctantly, studied it. Handing the folder back, he pleaded, "I gotta live here, man. I can't be no witness."

"The little girl who was killed could have been yours," Stepanovich said.

"The homeboys know who did it," Garcia said. "They'll take care of him."

"I'm just asking you to point your finger at one of these pictures if you see the man who did it. Just point your finger and we walk away and leave you alone. I'm not asking you to come into court," Stepanovich said. He'd used the line before.

"You wouldn't be here if you didn't need me as a witness. I got a business here. I got a family to feed."

"You're chickenshit, eh, *cabron?*" Arredondo said.

Garcia glared at Arredondo. "You calling me chickenshit?"

"I'm saying that your mother and father are chickenshit and they raised chickenshit—*ka ka pollo.*"

Stepping between the two men, Stepanovich gently took Garcia by the arm and ushered him into a corner.

"I ain't afraid of him because he's a cop," Garcia said, glaring at Arredondo. "Fuck that asshole."

"Look, I don't have a choice of who I work with," Stepanovich said. "That guy is up for promotion and he'll do anything to make a case."

"I ain't getting involved in no court bullshit. You can go ahead and lock my ass up, but I ain't going to court. Go ahead and put on the cuffs because I ain't crazy. This is East L.A., man. This is where rats get their fucking heads blown off."

Arredondo glared at Garcia, then strolled outside.

Stepanovich stepped closer. "All I want you to do is tell me whether I'm going in the right direction," he pleaded. "As far as putting the case together, I'll handle all that. I'll get the evidence another way. I can say that a confidential informant told me who did the shooting, and your name will never so much as be mentioned in court. The little girl didn't deserve to die like that. She's gone now and will never have her chance at life. And think of her mother. Her life will never be the same."

Garcia's mouth straightened into a tight line.

Stepanovich handed him the folder. "There's no one here except you and me. Just tell me if one of these people is the man who did the shooting at the church. You don't have to say which one."

Garcia watched Arredondo climb back in the police car.

"Please," Stepanovich said, looking Garcia in the eye.

Garcia glanced at the folder and handed it back to Stepanovich. "He's on there. That's all I'm saying."

"I'd consider it a personal favor if you would give me a hint."

Frightened, Garcia ran his hands through his hair. "No. Because I know you'll call me into court."

"There's no way you could be called into court for blinking, right?"

"Huh?"

"Like this. I point at the pictures one by one, and if you see the guy, you blink."

"I don't trust you people."

Stepanovich pointed to the photograph of Pepe Gomez. "I'm not asking you as a cop. I'm asking as a favor. Man to man."

Garcia stared at Stepanovich for a moment, then looked down at Gomez's photograph. He blinked.

"Thanks," Stepanovich whispered.

"If you call me to court, I don't know nothing!" Garcia yelled as Stepanovich headed back toward the police car.

Stepanovich opened the passenger door of the sedan and climbed in.

"What happened, homeboy?" Arredondo said, starting the engine.

"He did Greenie. Let's go back to the office so I can write a search warrant."

"You really have a way with these people," Arredondo said facetiously. "But I'm the one who pushed the man right into the trap. We had that dude going every which way. Vertigo, man."

"Couldn't have done it without you," Stepanovich said, pulling out the driveway and into heavy traffic.

A windowless room in the basement of Hollenbeck Station, the CRASH office was crowded with desks and a police computer hookup. The walls were covered with neatly drawn link-analysis charts that showed the leadership of the most active gangs, personnel deployment rosters, and gang-detail wanted posters. Neither Stepanovich nor the others in the unit had much use for the charts, but they gave the captain something to point to when ushering community leaders and other visitors through the station.

Stepanovich's desk was in the corner of the police bull pen, banked by two metal filing cabinets that provided him a measure of privacy. After he phoned Harger at the police academy and briefed him on the developments in the case, Stepanovich spent the day writing and rewriting the search warrant for Greenie's apartment. Because writing a search warrant was a one-man job, Arredondo and the other members of the task force lounged about the office killing time. Their conversation half filtered through Stepanovich's consciousness as he concentrated on the paperwork—copying parts of other search warrants he had written, replacing those facts with the facts of the case at hand, then sprucing up the text to make it sound original.

"I learned computers in the Navy," Fordyce said proudly from his seat at the computer terminal. "When I first came on the department I broke my ankle and they assigned me to the records bureau. Pretty soon I was giving lessons to the clerks."

Arredondo, his feet up on a desk, said, "If you know about computers, why waste your time being a policeman?"

Fordyce shrugged and gave a boyish grin. "Actually, I always wanted to be a teacher and work with kids, but I didn't have a college degree."

"So now you put kids in jail," Black said, turning from his desk. Leaning over a brimming trash can, he opened his mouth and spat a large purple wad of chewing gum neatly into the receptacle.

Fordyce winced self-consciously. "You always have something negative to say."

Black took another stick of chewing gum from a purple package on his desk, "Me, I always wanted to be a cop," he said, unwrapping the gum and forming it into a carpetlike roll. "I liked it in the Army as an MP—all of it: bar patrol, even working the stockade. I never had more fun in my life. I mean, we used to *kick* some ass." He opened his mouth and slipped in the fresh stick.

"You should have stayed in, then we wouldn't have to listen to your gum popping all day," Arredondo said, thumbing through a *Playboy*.

"I used to smoke five packs of Luckies a day, Pancho. Maybe you'd rather be sitting here with a smoke puffer. A man who's addicted to the weed."

"He's right. Anything's better than smoking," Fordyce said without looking up from the computer keyboard.

"I still miss it. Every minute of every day. I even enjoyed lighting the fuckers. That's all part of it, you know. Ask any shrink. They'll tell you straight out."

"I saw you smoking up a storm last payday at the Rumor Control Bar," Fordyce said.

"That's because I was drinking. When I drink, I can't help but smoke. After a drink or two I say fuck it."

"But you drink almost every night," Fordyce said.

C.R. Black smiled his wide okie grin. "Nobody's perfect." He stood up from his desk and moved to the computer. "How are you doing with those red pickup trucks, Four Eyes?"

Fordyce tapped a key twice. "Not too good. There are six thousand of them registered within the zip codes that make up East L.A. And my name is Fordyce, not Four Eyes."

Arredondo held up the *Playboy* to show the Playmate of the Month, an athletic brunette with capped teeth. She was balanced uncomfortably in the lotus position on the prow of a speed boat. "How's this for some top-quality stabbing?"

Fordyce gave a momentary glance of displeasure, shook his head, and turned back to the computer screen.

Arredondo admired the magazine photo closely. "Bet you've never had anything like that in your life, C.R."

"When I was working Hollywood division, I used to shove gash like that out of my radio car, brown boy."

"I'd like break her open like a shotgun."

About five Stepanovich had completed the affidavit for the search warrant. He rubbed his eyes for a moment. Because the others were either chatting or talking on the phone and he couldn't hear himself think, he picked up the handwritten draft, stepped into Harger's vacant office, and shut the door behind him. The private cubicle was decorated with framed photographs of various Los Angeles Police Department athletic and marksmanship teams, academy graduating classes, fishing-trip group shots. On the corner of the desk was an eight-by-ten of Harger with his tanned wife and three towheaded boys posing alongside an oval swimming pool.

Stepanovich sat down at Harger's desk, made a few corrections to the affidavit, then went over it one last time. It read as follows:

I, Detective Jose Stepanovich, Ser. #613845, have been a Los Angeles police officer for nine years and am presently assigned to the CRASH Detective Bureau Gang Task Force to investigate gang-related homicides and other violent crimes. Since entering on duty as a police officer, I have participated in the investigation of numerous gang homicides and gang assaults, and have qualified in Superior Court as an expert on the methods of operation of Los Angeles street gangs.

On August 21 I received a radio call of "shots fired" and responded to Our Lady Queen of Angels Church. Upon arrival at the scene, I observed two gunshot victims: Primitivo Estrada, a wounded adult male, and Guadalupe Zuniga, a nine-year-old female pronounced dead at the scene.

Numerous witnesses (see attached police reports) stated that a male adult suspect armed with a shotgun had chased victim Estrada into the church and fired twice, striking Estrada and Zuniga. The suspect then shouted, "Eighteenth Street," and ran back out the door. One wedding guest (hereafter referred to as Source A), who wishes to remain anonymous because he fears for his life, told me that the suspect who fired the shotgun had green eyes.

In my expert opinion, shouting out the name of one's gang affiliation is the custom and practice of street gangs in the City of Los Angeles. Also, the Queen of Angels Church lies just inside the border of the area the Eighteenth Street gang claims as its gang turf. Therefore, I am led to believe that a member of the Eighteenth Street gang may be responsible for the shooting.

Continuing my investigation, I conducted a records

check of the file kept on the Eighteenth Street gang and learned that only one member of the gang, a male adult fitting the general age and description of the male described by the witnesses as the man who ran into the church and fired the shotgun, has green eyes: Pepe Gomez, a.k.a. Greenie. His arrest record shows that he has been arrested twenty-two times. Four of these arrests were for felony crimes involving the use of weapons, including one arrest for a gang-related murder in which the alleged murder weapon was a shotgun. In this case the charges against Gomez were dropped for lack of evidence.

Today, I reinterviewed Source A and showed him a spread of five photographs (see attached photos) that included Gomez's booking photograph among those of persons of similar age and description. Source A picked the photograph of Gomez from the spread of photographs as being the shotgun-wielding assailant at the Queen of Angels Church.

A recent police report bearing Gomez's name reflects his address as 2965 Eighteenth Street, Apartment 203.

It is my expert opinion that a search of the above address may recover guns, ammunition, evidence of gang affiliation, and other items of evidence relating to the August 21 murder at the Queen of Angels Church.

I request that this information remain confidential because disclosure may endanger Source A.

Satisfied that all the information he'd developed was contained in the search warrant, Stepanovich corrected a few minor typos in the draft, and went upstairs to the divisional copying machine. After waiting for a secretary to finish running off the division bowling league standings, he made the twelve copies of the search warrant required by the district attorney's office.

At six Stepanovich and Arredondo stopped by the L.A. County Courthouse, where a muscle-bound deputy marshal in a tailored uniform showed them into the chambers of the duty judge, a young red-haired woman whom Stepanovich remembered as having lost most of her cases while a city prosecutor. She reviewed the search warrant carefully, asked a couple of perfunctory questions, then signed both the search warrant and an arrest warrant for Greenie.

It was dusk when Stepanovich and Arredondo left the courthouse. As they climbed into the unmarked car, Stepanovich lifted the radio microphone from the dashboard hook and called Harger. He responded promptly.

"The warrant is signed."

"Good work."

As they were driving toward Greenie's apartment over the Third Street Bridge from downtown into East L.A., Harger's voice crackled over the police radio as he transmitted staccato instructions to the members of the task force concerning the search warrant operation.

Stepanovich turned right onto Eighteenth Street and drove slowly past rundown apartment houses and residential courts. It was now dark and the street was quiet.

At the end of the block he pulled up across the street from the Florentine Gardens housing project, a graffiti-covered cluster of pale-green cement-block apartment houses linked by outdoor clotheslines, community trash receptacles, and unmowed patches of grass. He drove along a little farther, checking the addresses painted on the curb. Stepanovich had served numerous other search warrants in the project. Familiar with its layout, he looked up to the second floor and counted apartments from east to west. Using binoculars from the glove compartment, he located the apartment listed in the search warrant as Greenie's. There was a light on.

Arredondo reached behind the passenger seat and hoisted a pump shotgun into the front seat. Keeping it aimed at the floorboard, he cranked the slide and chambered a round.

A police sedan pulled up alongside. C.R. Black was

driving and Fordyce was in the passenger seat. Both were wearing black bullet-proof vests. "Where do you want us?" Black asked.

"Take the back."

Black gave a thumbs-up gesture and drove off. With his headlamps off, he turned into a driveway leading to the rear of the building.

Stepanovich and Arredondo climbed out of the car and jogged across the street and up a flight of steps to the first landing. Stepanovich pulled out his revolver and they crept cautiously down the landing to Apartment 203. They deployed on either side of the door. Stepanovich felt his heart beating powerfully, his fingers tingling. "Police!" he yelled. Hearing the sound of running inside, he aimed a powerful kick directly at the doorknob. The door jamb splintered and the door flew open.

A woman shrieked as Stepanovich ran inside, Arredondo right behind. Pepe Gomez had one leg over the windowsill of the open rear window. "Hands up!" Stepanovich shouted, aiming his revolver at the man's chest. Gomez raised his hands. Arredondo ran into the other room.

Stepanovich thought of the little girl lying on the carpet in the church as he assumed the combat stance and aimed his Smith & Wesson directly at Pepe Gomez's kill zone. There were no witnesses present. At that moment, with his heart trying to beat its way out of his chest, he considered wasting Gomez. He could let him have it and later say Gomez had reached into his waistband for what Stepanovich believed was a gun.

There was no doubt in his mind that the shooting would be ruled justifiable and in compliance with the police manual.

His finger tightened on the trigger.

"Don't shoot!" Gomez begged. "Don't shoot. I give."

"Go ahead and jump, cocksucker!" Black shouted from below the window.

"My hands are up!" Gomez begged. "Please don't shoot."

Arredondo reentered the room dragging an obese young Mexican woman wearing only a black bra and panties. He shoved her to the floor and took a position to cover Gomez with the shotgun. "She's the only other one here."

Stepanovich holstered his revolver. Advancing to Gomez, he grabbed him by the collar and pulled him to the floor. With his knee planted between Gomez's shoulder blades, he cuffed his hands behind his back.

As Gomez lay on the floor, Stepanovich took out his wallet, removed a Miranda warning card, and read it off. Concluding, he asked, "Do you understand those rights?"

"Yeah."

"Do you wish to answer questions?"

"No. I want a lawyer."

Stepanovich and Arredondo looked at each other, and Arredondo shrugged.

Black and Fordyce entered the front door and began searching the living room.

Stepanovich left his prisoner with Fordyce and walked into the bedroom. There was a mattress on the floor and a pile of clothing in the corner. A shadeless lamp was perched on a cardboard box next to a framed photograph of Pepe Gomez and three other shirtless, unsmiling gang members standing in the living room of Pepe's apartment. Gomez was holding a pump shotgun in the port-arms position. The other three were holding revolvers.

"You OK?" Arredondo asked.

Stepanovich nodded, not taking his eyes off the picture. "I almost shot him."

"No loss to the world."

"I was halfway back on the trigger. He was unarmed and I almost let him have it."

"He's an asshole, man. He killed a kid. Anyone would want to kill him. Besides, you didn't do it.

What you were thinking is your own business."
Arredondo slapped him on the shoulder.

Stepanovich took a deep breath and exhaled. Picking up the photograph, he slammed it sharply against the edge of the dresser. The glass shattered on the floor as he pulled the photograph from the frame.

The task force detectives' search for weapons lasted until after eleven. Every piece of furniture was overturned, every drawer emptied, every piece of clothing thoroughly patted. Black even dumped the contents of the refrigerator and a brimming trash receptacle onto the kitchen floor and examined everything thoroughly.

There was no shotgun.

With the search completed, Stepanovich kicked aside some canned goods and kitchen utensils, slid a chair back from the kitchen table, and sat down. He reached into his pocket and took out a pen and the search warrant. Then, per the required legal procedure, he listed the items he'd seized as evidence on the reverse of the search warrant:

1. One 8 x 10 photograph depicting Pepe Gomez and three other males holding weapons (found in bedroom).
2. One pair tennis shoes bearing Eighteenth Street gang markings (living room).
3. Letter bearing return address of California State Prison at Chino (kitchen).
4. One shotgun shell—12 gauge (bedroom).

SIX

Stepanovich and Arredondo booked Gomez for murder at the Parker Center jail, then trudged across the street to the County Courthouse. Showing their badges to a guard at the door, they took an elevator to the district attorney's office on the fourth floor. The modern, well-furnished office was empty. A piece of typing paper taped to the reception counter read: "DEPUTY DA ON DUTY IN ROOM 210." An arrow on the sign pointed to the right.

In Room 210 a slender man whom Stepanovich figured to be about his age was sitting with his feet on a desk reading a *Model Railroader* magazine. A nameplate on the desk read "ELLSWORTH C. WEBER." Weber had neat, kinky hair and wore a wrinkled short-sleeved white shirt and a soiled necktie. Taking his feet off the desk, he hid the magazine under some papers.

"I'm Joe Stepanovich. This is my partner, Raul Arredondo. We're with LAPD CRASH. Is Howard Goldberg working tonight?"

"Why do you ask?"

"He's a friend."

"He's on nights next week. I'm in charge tonight. If you have a case you'll have to present it to me," he said, revealing a full set of braces.

Stepanovich handed Weber a stack of papers including the report of investigation at the church and the search warrant return listing the items of evidence.

"What am I supposed to do with this?" Weber said.

"We've arrested a suspect and we want to file murder charges against him."

Weber let out his breath, picked up his eyeglasses by the bridge, and blew on the lenses to clear away possible dandruff flakes. With a flourish he balanced the spectacles on his face. "Pepe Gomez. Hmmm."

Stepanovich and Arredondo sat in silence as Weber read slowly, moistening the top of his index finger with his tongue each time he turned a page. With each lick Stepanovich found himself becoming more and more annoyed. The moment he had walked into the office, in fact, he'd decided Weber was an asshole.

"Hmmmm," Weber said as he finished the final page. "Where's the motive?"

"The motive is revenge," Stepanovich said. "The tennis shoes with gang markings and the letter from prison with references to the Eighteenth Street gang prove Greenie's gang affiliation. And I have piles of police reports proving that the Eighteenth Street gang is at war with the White Fence gang. In fact, it's gone on for generations."

"Revenge," Weber said to an El Monte College of Law diploma on the wall to this left. "Very good. Now how do we prove the suspect had the means to commit the murder?"

"The crime was committed with a pump shotgun. In the photograph we found in his apartment he is standing with three other known Eighteenth Street gang members holding a pump shotgun. We found a shotgun shell in his bedroom. Also, he's been arrested twice before in possession of sawed-off shotguns—"

"But you found no shotgun during the search of his apartment."

"Didn't really expect to," Arredondo said. "In gang shootings the shooter always hands off the murder weapon to a another gang member right after a shooting. He would never keep it where he lives."

"But there's no shotgun," Weber said condescendingly.

"We found a shotgun shell," Arredondo said.

"That's not evidence of anything. What do you have that ties Gomez to the scene of the crime?"

Stepanovich crossed one leg over the other. "We have an eyewitness who picked Gomez's photograph from a spread."

"Just one?"

"Just one what?"

"Just one witness."

"That's what I said."

"How many people in the church when the shooting went down?"

"More than a hundred."

"Out of a hundred people only one person got a look at the shooter?"

"The witness was sitting in the pew nearest the door when the shooter entered."

"What assurance is there that the witness will actually show up in court and point the finger at Pepe Gomez?"

Stepanovich cleared his throat. He had a feeling of déjà vu. "The witness will show up."

"People in East L.A. know it's not healthy to testify in court against a shooter. Witnesses who we are sure are going to testify and make a big case often chicken out the day of the trial. When this happens, the prosecutor on the case is left holding the bag. I speak from experience."

"We'll personally bring him to court," Stepanovich said.

"I see here that when you arrested Gomez he refused to make a statement. No confession. No incriminating statements."

"He asked for an attorney."

Weber set the reports down and adjusted the pile. "Looks like we have a cliffhanger."

"What do you mean by that?" Stepanovich asked.

"Your witness takes the stand and says Gomez was the shooter," Weber said. "Gomez takes the stand and says he was home washing his Chevy. It's a one on one."

"If I had a lot of witnesses, I could prosecute the case myself."

Weber glared at him. "But you don't. You have one witness and a bunch of nebulous bullshit for evidence."

"I guess that means you're not going to file the murder charges."

"You guessed it."

"What should I tell my captain, that the DA said the case was a cliffhanger and we had to let a shooter go?"

"I don't care what you tell him."

"May I ask you a question?" Stepanovich said.

"Um-hm."

"If your nine-year-old daughter had been murdered and an eyewitness identified the killer, would you be satisfied with the case not being prosecuted because the DA thought the case didn't look like a sure winner?"

"It's not my daughter, and as far as I'm concerned, this is just another ghetto murder—one of six or seven I've reviewed this evening. There's not enough evidence to prosecute and that's that." Weber held out the reports and Stepanovich and Arredondo stood up to leave.

"Try reinterviewing the witnesses," Weber said as they walked out.

From the district attorney's office Stepanovich drove straight down Fourth Street to a soot-covered industrial area near the L.A. River. Parking the car in a truck space in front of a cardboard container factory, he and Arredondo walked across the wide street to the Rumor Control Bar, an establishment identified only by the letters "R.C." spray-painted above the door.

Inside, the dark bar was filled with male cops wearing loose-fitting shirts to cover off-duty iron. There was only one female in the place: Brenda Last-Name-Unknown. Barefoot, the beefy, ponytailed young woman was wearing tennis shorts and a halter top made of two large seashells cupping her breasts which was tied in back with a thick leather thong. She was perched on a stool near the middle of the bar: a seat she'd earned, as Sullivan the bartender often remarked, by blowing any and every swinging dick in the division without regard to race, creed, or rank. Stepanovich knew from the grapevine this included sucking off a platoon of motorcycle cops after the traffic-division steak fry, the entire Wilshire Division morning watch, a group of narco detectives at an on-duty swim party, and every badge-carrying male who attended last year's robbery-homicide Christmas party. Rather than being simply tolerated like other camp followers, the veteran fellatrix was a distinct source of pride to the entire division because of her consistent refusal to go down on sheriff's deputies, firemen, and officers from other police departments.

As Stepanovich and Arredondo approached the bar and ordered beers, Brenda waved at Arredondo.

Sullivan, a retired police officer with puffy eyes and habitually unruly hair that made him look as if he had just awakened with a hangover, set beer bottles on the bar. He picked a cigarette from a pack and lit it with a silver LAPD lighter. "I hear you two have been assigned to the CRASH special unit."

Stepanovich nodded as he set money on the bar.

"A Bob Harger brainstorm, right?"

"Right."

Picking up the money, Sullivan used a soiled rag to wipe the bar. "I knew Harger when he first came on the Department. We worked together at Central Division."

Arredondo swigged his beer. "What do you think of him?"

Sullivan sucked on his cigarette and gritted his teeth, inhaling smoke deep into his lungs. He turned his palm and looked at the cigarette. "First day I met him I could tell he'd make rank," he said, holding the smoke inside.

C.R. Black whistled shrilly from the other end of the bar. "Hey, Sullivan, you baggy-eyed creep! Bring some beer down here!" The bar crowd laughed.

"You're going to be working with him too, right?" Sullivan said, reaching into the cooler for a bottle of beer.

"How do you know?"

"Black wangles his way into any unit where he can earn overtime pay," Sullivan said. With a practiced motion he popped the cap and handed him the bottle.

Stepanovich and Arredondo joined Black and Fordyce at a table in the corner and Stepanovich explained what had happened at the district attorney's office. Fordyce shook his head as if he'd been informed of a death in the family. Black smiled sardonically. "I'm not surprised."

"Where do we go from here?" Fordyce asked.

"Captain Harger will start by telling us to redo the investigation," Black said before Stepanovich could answer. "While we spin wheels on a case that no one wants to prosecute, Greenie or one of his incest-bred pals will go out and kill someone else. Another investigation will start. The division will be short of detectives so the captain will disband the task force and we stop making overtime. It's what always happens."

All of them just sat glumly for a minute. "You're right," Stepanovich said finally.

Arredondo nodded toward the door and the others turned to see Harger, coatless and wearing his two guns, step inside. As he looked about, Stepanovich waved and he headed toward them.

"I heard about the DA refusing to file," Harger said, sitting down. Black headed to the bar for refills.

"The evidence is weak," Stepanovich said, shrugging with palms up. "But there's not much else we can do at this point. We've done everything we can."

Harger smiled as if he knew a secret. He leaned closer and gave Stepanovich a brotherly pat on the shoulder. "As far as I'm concerned, the investigation has been handled in a top-flight manner. You guys have done a great job. The evidence just isn't there and I accept that. But that doesn't mean we're going to go home and eat animal crackers."

Black returned to the table with beer bottles laced between his fingers. He set them down on the table and slid one to Harger. Harger picked it up, took a healthy swig, then wiped his mouth with the back of his hand. "I'm open to suggestions," he said, swiveling his head to make eye contact with each man.

"We could beat Greenie until he talks," Black said. "A confession would send him to the joint."

Harger was unfazed by the remark. "We could do that," he said. 'But there's no guarantee he'll talk."

"Maybe if we did some surveillance on the Eighteenth Street gang members, we could find the weapon used at the church," Fordyce said.

"Good idea," Harger said, though Stepanovich figured neither Harger nor anyone other than Fordyce considered it practical. "But our chances of coming up with anything would be slim, and the manpower expenditure would be too great." Harger turned to Stepanovich. "What do you think?"

"This isn't the first case where we knew who the shooter is, but can't prove it."

Harger nodded. "You're right. In that way this is like the hundreds of drive-by shootings that occur every year. Virtually no evidence. But, gentlemen, the difference is the Chief has taken a personal interest in the gang problem—and in the church shooting in particular. He's giving us the green light to move in on the pricks."

That got everyone's attention.

"Do you have something in mind, sir?" Stepanovich asked.

Harger leaned forward. "I'm thinking not just of this case, but of the the gang problem in general," he said in a conspiratorial tone. "The big picture." He turned to Stepanovich. "You know how the gangs operate. Make a prediction. What is going to happen next?"

"White Fence was hit. So their homeboys will snoop around, conduct their own investigation. When they find out Greenie was the shooter, they'll go gunning for him. This will all happen quickly—within the next few days, I'd say."

"Looking at it in those terms, we have knowledge that a crime is going to occur," Harger said.

A quizzical expression spread slowly across Black's face. "I don't see what you mean."

"I mean, we're one step ahead of the game. We know White Fence is gonna retaliate against Eighteenth Street. They'll try to kill Greenie, but if they can't, they'll settle for someone else in the gang. If that isn't convenient, they'll just drive down Eighteenth Street and shoot someone. They won't wait, that's for sure. In other words, we know a crime is going to occur on Eighteenth Street," Harger said.

"I see what you mean," Stepanovich said.

"Rather than sitting on our ass, waiting for the next drive-by shooting, we stake out Eighteenth Street twenty-four hours a day. I'm talking surveillance, pro-active."

"With Greenie as bait," Stepanovich ruminated.

"Exactly. When White Fence comes to do Greenie, we'll be waiting with a surprise party for the mother-fuckers."

"We'll get burned in ten seconds sitting on Eighteenth Street," Black said.

"We could use my motor home as a surveillance vehicle," Fordyce offered. "With dark curtains over the windows, we could park right across the street from Greenie's apartment, and no one would know the difference." He looked to Harger for a reaction.

"That's what I like to hear," Harger said, looking pleased. "If the system won't let us in the front door, then we'll go in the back."

"Let's go for it," Arredondo said.

"Sounds good," Stepanovich chimed in.

"If we see a gun, we jump out of the motor home and blow their shit away," Black said.

Harger hoisted a beer bottle for a toast. "Lock and load, gentlemen." Bottles clinked.

Later, after more beers, Harger slapped a couple of shoulders and said something about taking his kids to an early morning soccer game.

As he left the table, Stepanovich observed that Harger didn't stagger in the least on his way out of the place. Rather than matching the others drink for drink, he'd had been leaving his beer bottles half full, a trick he'd seen used by other officers who wanted to be one of the boys without risking intoxication.

With Harger gone, the discussion returned to how to manage the surveillance.

SEVEN

Sullivan came from the bar with a tray of Budweisers. Stepanovich helped him set the bottles on the table, feeling the effects of the alcohol, wishing he'd eaten something earlier that might have soaked up the booze. Sullivan picked up the empties and hurried back to the bar.

Black, his eyes red from drink and lack of sleep, unfastened his necktie and slipped it from his collar. "Harger's saying all the right things now." He folded the tie carefully and shoved it into the pocket of his suit jacket. "But I want to see him after something actually goes down. Then we'll see if he backs up his men."

You're thinking about manual section 319.5," Arredondo said.

"That's exactly what the fuck I am thinking about. The part where it says it's against regulations for an officer to fail to act when one has information that a crime is going to occur. If we go along with his plan, we're in violation of the manual."

Fordyce finished chewing a pretzel and washed it down with beer. "Personally, I believe Captain Harger will back us up. He's always kept his word to me."

Black picked up a fresh beer. "His word on what?

About getting you transferred to the records bureau? About some computer bullshit? The question is whether the man will suck heavy heat if a shooting goes down. Whether he'll testify before a board of rights hearing that we were acting on his orders. Whether he'll be a man and not leave us hanging by the dick."

"If you don't think he'll back us up on the street, you should have told him that to his face," Fordyce said.

Black leaned forward on the table. "All officers are bullshitters. Take the Chief. He had a lamp installed in his office that beams directly on him. A spotlight. What kind of a guy would do that? Only a fucking glory hound."

Arredondo's cheeks were flushed from drink. He hiccuped. "Policewomen are the real glory hounds on this job. They want a badge so bad they are willing to wear a uniform designed for men."

"Badge-carrying dykes!"

The crowd at the table erupted into laughter.

Fordyce wasn't laughing. He finished his beer and set the bottle down. "I know some women who are good cops."

"That has nothing to do with what we're talking about," Black said.

"Excuse me for living."

"Harger has a good reputation," Stepanovich said.

Black guzzled some beer and wiped his mouth. "We stake out the shooters and wait for them to get shot," Black said sarcastically. "It certainly makes sense. Hell, I like the idea on general principles."

Stepanovich took a drink from his bottle and felt the icy beer slide all the way into the beer pool in his stomach. "Harger's right. Either we make the first move or wait for the next gang shooting."

"The Mexicans have been been killing each other since L.A. was a fucking pueblo," Arredondo said, slurring his words. "They'll never stop."

"I wonder why they do it?" Fordyce asked.

"Do what?"

"Kill each other. I mean that as a serious question. Why?"

Arredondo spun an empty beer bottle on the table, then stopped it. "Because that's the way it is," he said. "They do what their older brothers do."

"Mexicans have it in their blood," Black said. "They go on the warpath like Indians."

Arredondo glared. "I'm a Mexican. You talking about me, you hillbilly cocksucker?"

Black sipped his beer. "Don't get your shit hot over nothing. I'm just talking."

"People in the Mafia kill each other," Stepanovich said. "The blacks kill each other every minute of the day. Chinamen kill each other in Chinatown. Even Samoans have hit men. Everybody's killing everybody."

"I guess we wouldn't even hear about gang murders if we weren't cops," Fordyce said.

"You have to admire the gangs for sticking together," Black said. "They defend their clan. You kill one of mine, I kill one of yours."

"That's right," Arredondo said. "They make bad enemies, but damn good friends."

Black cleared his throat. "Last year there was a drive-by shooting in El Sereno. A White Fence *veterano* got killed. The shooter was a homeboy who'd been released from San Quentin that very day. Now here's a guy who's been fucking his fist for nine years, and the first thing he does when he gets out of the joint is kill someone. We arrested him and he went back to prison without so much as getting himself a piece of ass. But the man had made a promise and kept it. You gotta respect him for that."

Arredondo finished his beer and set the bottle down. "Fuck him. He's just another stupid *chongo*."

"Whatever you say about the man, he gave up everything rather than welsh on a promise. He's tried, tested, and proven. If he was the captain in charge of this unit, we wouldn't be wondering if he'd back us up."

"Harger will back us up if we get in a jam," Fordyce said, slurring his words like everyone else at the table. "I'd put money on him."

"I've never heard anything bad about him," Stepanovich said. He was in the stage of drunkenness when voices sounded slightly distant.

"We'll find out soon enough. If we stake out Eighteenth Street, it won't be long before something goes down," Arredondo said, coming to his feet. "I have to take a leak."

Nothing was said for a while. It occurred to Stepanovich that everyone at the table could be booked for drunkenness.

"My mom and dad never wanted me to be a cop," Fordyce said, changing the subject. "They think it's like on TV, with policemen getting shot every day."

The others looked at him. Black shook his head. Arredondo returned and related the graphic details of a motel sex orgy he'd engaged in with a mother-and-daughter pair he'd picked up at a bar in North Hollywood a few weeks earlier. Stepanovich only half listened. His thoughts all evening had been on Gloria Soliz. He was mellow-drunk and at the stage of intoxication when he felt comfortable, warm, and safe.

A short while later Black left the table and walked to the middle of the bar, where Brenda Last-Name-Unknown sat in front of a tall drink. He lifted her ponytail playfully and kissed her on the neck, then whispered something to her. She climbed off her bar stool and accompanied Black back to the table. The others made room for her to sit down.

Black put his arm around her. "I told Brenda I wanted her to meet the new gang task force."

"I know all these guys," she said in what Stepanovich called a smoker's voice. "And your boss Captain Harger, too."

Black smirked. "Brenda's good people. Right, Brenda?"

Arredondo put his arm around her. "What do you really think about cops?"

"I think you're all badge-happy."

"We respect your opinion," Fordyce said in a feeble attempt to be one of the boys.

Brenda drew liquid from the clear plastic straw in her gin and tonic. She checked her wristwatch, an official LAPD timepiece the shape of a police badge— the kind sold only at the police gift shop. "It's nearly midnight and I have to go to work in the morning. So whoever wants it, let's don't waste a lot of time bullshitting."

There was a round of harsh laughter at the table.

"Brenda, if you were a man you'd have been promoted to chief by now," Arredondo said.

More strained laughter. Brenda took a swig of beer, washed it around in her mouth for a moment, and swallowed. "OK, who wants to be first?"

Black grabbed Brenda's hand and led her out the door.

Arredondo left the table and joined Brenda's friends, two women with beehive hairdos sitting in a nearby booth, and Fordyce joined Sullivan and a couple of motor cops who'd started a crap game on the floor by the jukebox.

Stepanovich felt cop fatigue, a tiredness that does not allow rest. For the life of him, he still couldn't get Gloria Soliz out of his mind. It wasn't that she reminded him of anyone, he told himself. There was something about her he couldn't put his finger on. He glanced at his wristwatch. It was shortly after midnight.

He carried his beer to the pay phone near the door, dialed information, and asked an operator for Gloria Soliz home telephone number. The operator gave him the number and he wrote it down on a cocktail napkin. Then he dropped change into the coin slot and dialed.

After three rings Gloria came on the line.

"Gloria, this is Joe Stepanovich."

"Hi, Joe."

"I know it's late, but I have this mental problem I thought you might be able to help me out with."

"Have you been drinking?"

"A little."

"I'm listening," she said.

"I have this overpowering desire for Chinese food. It's a compulsion."

"I see."

"And I can't stop myself from heading to Chinatown."

"So what's the big problem?"

"I can't stand to eat alone."

"It's midnight."

"I know a place that's open all night," he said.

"Thanks for giving me so much notice."

"Sorry, but I've been tied up with a case . . ."

"It really is kind of late," she said.

"Tomorrow is your day off."

"I guess you're not going to take no for an answer."

"I'll pick you up in ten minutes."

Outside, Stepanovich crossed the street and climbed into his car. As he drove down the street he passed Black's car, parked near the corner directly under a streetlight. Grinning fiendishly while leaning against the driver's door with one leg over the front seat Black noticed him and waved as Brenda's ponytail bobbed between his legs.

There was little traffic as he made his way the short distance on the freeway to the City Terrace offramp. He wound up a grade past homes perched precariously on hillsides, then down past some dying business establishments to a line of newly built apartment houses leading to Wabash Avenue. He checked curbside addresses until he reached a brown-stucco apartment house across the street from a mini-mall. The apartment house sign read: "TAHITIAN VILLAGE." Parking in front, he made his way past a cement-block planter lit by the kind of wrought-iron Hawaiian ceremonial torches sold in every hardware store in Southern California.

He climbed steps to the second floor and knocked on the apartment door. Gloria opened it immediately. She was wearing a curve-hugging black knit dress and pearls. Stepanovich suddenly felt a sense of anticipation and excitement welling in his loins, a feeling he hadn't experienced in years.

"Nice outfit," he said as she retrieved her purse from a chair near the door.

"I wear it on all my midnight dates," she said, moving past him.

"Sorry about not giving you more notice."

"You're forgiven."

A jumble of neon-lit pagodas and tiny Oriental gift shops nestled just below the Hill Street freeway offramp, L.A.'s Chinatown had deteriorated in recent years. Stepanovich had childhood memories of Chinatown as a thriving tourist area, but like much of the rest of downtown, it had been choked by overdevelopment and lack of parking.

The Jade Tree Inn, a cavernous, newly refurbished restaurant, was open and packed, even though it was a weeknight. The owner, Charlie Fong, leapt up to meet them as they walked through the door. He was a tall, crew-cut Chinese who'd served as a sergeant in the Taiwanese Marine Corps. He greeted Stepanovich warmly and Stepanovich introduced him to Gloria. Fong led them to a booth that provided a view of neon-lit Hill Street.

"May I bring you a drink?" Fong asked. Gloria ordered white wine, and Stepanovich said he'd have the same. Fong bowed slightly and rushed toward the bar.

For an awkward moment they found themselves staring at each other.

"I apologize for pestering you into going to breakfast with me the other day," Stepanovich said.

"I'm not sorry I joined you."

"You probably think all cops are weird."

She hung her purse on the back of the chair. "Not weird. Just different.

"I guess the job changes people."

"People choose their professions."

"I guess that means you think all cops are different to start with. That the chicken came before the egg."

"Something like that."

Charlie Fong returned to the table with drinks, set them down, and moved away.

"The man you asked about at the hospital, Mr. Estrada, is doing better. He's going to live."

Stepanovich nodded, sipping his drink.

"I'm sure you'd be more interested if he were cooperating with your investigation," she said wryly.

During a dinner of steamed fish in a garlicky black bean sauce, beef with scallops, and sauteed shrimp, he learned that she'd been a member of the woman's volleyball team when attending UCLA, had graduated with a 3.8 average, and she lived alone.

"The Army and the police department, that's the story of my life."

"Where did you meet your wife?"

"Her car was burglarized when she was working downtown at the Design Center. I was the officer sent to take the report. I asked her out and things took off from there. She moved in three weeks later and after a couple of months we decided to get married. But it was a bad match from the beginning. Nothing in common. We were never friends."

"I don't think I would live with a man unless I was married. I mean, it's great for the man, but I'd want more."

"That's why men and women don't get along anymore. They want different things."

"They don't get along when they lie to each other.

When they misjudge each other. That's when the problems start."

Charlie Fong came to the table with a small plate of almond cookies and set the plate between them.

"You've been letting me do all the talking," she said as Fong moved away. "I'd like to know something about you."

"I've told you—"

"I don't mean where you went to school. What are your goals, your dreams?"

"Goals? I'm in a new specialized anti-gang unit that has a chance of hitting the gangs like they've never been hit before. I like the guys I'm working with. They're solid cops. I'm excited about the new job."

"Always back to police work."

"The gangs are running wild."

"They don't bother me," she said, closing the subject. "What do you do in your spare time?"

"Lift a few weights, some jogging—"

"To stay in shape for your job."

"I guess you could say that. What about you?"

"On Sundays I usually go to Raider games with the other nurses. I've tried my hand at writing a textbook on nursing supervision, but gave it up. I found out I'm not much of a writer. Do you have any hobbies?"

"I put in thirty hours a week in overtime. That doesn't leave much time."

"Unpaid overtime," she said, unimpressed.

"You don't like cops, do you?"

She bit into an almond cookie. "I was raised in the barrio. Policemen weren't exactly the local heroes."

"The gang members were the heroes."

"Chicanos don't like to see their own get arrested, if that's what you mean."

"That kind of sticking together is why the gangs are ruling East L.A. and children are getting killed at weddings. Sticking together for the wrong reasons."

"You'll never stop it by arresting people," she said.

"You have a better answer?"

"Better schools and more jobs so that people can maintain their dignity," she said, looking him straight in the eye.

He met her gaze. "I'll drink to that," he said rather than pursue an argument.

On the way out of the restaurant Stepanovich shook hands with the owner, and Fong patted him on the back. "Don't stay away so long."

"I notice you didn't pay the bill," Gloria said as they walked down the street toward his Chevrolet.

Stepanovich nodded toward a small group of young Asian men loitering across the street in front of a bar. All wore styled hair, baggy trousers, and three-quarter-length silk jackets. "You can thank the Viet Ching Street gang over there," he said. "They were extorting three hundred a week from Charlie until my partner and I locked a few of them up. Now Charlie's off their collection list."

She laughed. "And on yours."

"It pays to support the local police," he said, opening the passenger door.

He drove Gloria to Monahan's bar in Pasadena, a crowded singles hangout with walls decorated with Irish kitsch and framed collages of Polaroid snapshots of the bar's yuppie habitués posing with arms around one another. They found a booth in the corner and ordered Irish coffees.

"Why haven't you ever married?" he asked.

"For a long time I was caught up in my nursing career and didn't care about anything else. And I have family responsibilities. My father passed away two years ago."

"You know, as I sit here talking to you, I feel there's a glass wall between us."

"I guess we are, uh, different."

"Is it because I'm a cop?"

"Only a police officer would ask such a question," she said without rancor.

"I guess we cops are all a little paranoid."

"As a nurse I don't try to analyze everyone I meet. But you policemen do. Your job comes first and you see the whole world in a peculiar way. It's more than an occupation for you. It's a way of life, a refuge."

"It's a matter of survival. If you don't learn the street, then the street learns you."

"That's what I mean. You never let down. I bet you have a gun on right now."

"All cops carry guns off-duty."

The waitress set their drinks on the table and moved away. Stepanovich picked one up.

"I wish things were different in the world," Gloria said as she reached for hers. "I wish East L.A. were a safe place to live."

"So do I."

"I'm glad we agree on something."

Back at her apartment, they walked arm in arm to the door. Gloria pulled a ring of keys from her purse and unlocked it.

"Look," Stepanovich said, feeling embarrassed. "I guess I haven't been the most scintillating conversationalist this evening. It's probably because I have a lot on my mind, and frankly, having been married and all, I think I've forgotten how to act on a date."

"I enjoyed myself. You didn't have to say that."

"I said it because I got the feeling that you and I just aren't . . . cutting it. And I don't want that to happen. Because I think you're a nice person."

She took his hand. "I think you're a nice person, too, Joe. And I really did have a wonderful time. Thanks."

He took her in his arms and kissed her. As his tongue found hers, he could feel her delicate hands grasp the back of his neck and prayed she wouldn't let go.

Their mouths parted. "I'd better go in," she whispered. "And you said you have to be back on the job at five."

"I don't want to leave."

"I'm not ready to go to bed with you," she said softly without looking him in the eye.

"Is there someone else?"

"No."

"I'm not much of a mind reader, Gloria. If you don't want to see me again, just say so."

She looked at him for a long, tantalizing moment. "I want to see you again."

EIGHT

Stepanovich woke early the next morning, feeling more rested than he had in months.

It was Wednesday, his mother's day off from the Dolly Madison Bakery, where she'd worked as a cake-icer for as long as he could remember and after shaving and showering he drove straight to her house.

His mother lived near the end of the block on Vega Street, a narrow dead-end street that abutted a steep, grassy hill that Stepanovich, Howard Goldberg, Freddie Mascorro, and the other neighborhood kids used to climb. At the top they would race back down full speed, finally tripping and tumbling. The downhill race had been even more exciting on bicycles. Oddly, the hill looked even steeper to him as an adult than it had as a child.

He pulled in the driveway of the tiny, well-kept home. Like the other one- and two-bedroom houses on the street it was unique, having been built shortly after World War II by family and friends rather than contractors or tract developers. Stepanovich's father, some of his fellow railroad employees, and Stepanovich's maternal Uncles Pete and Hector Elizondo, who were master carpenters, had built the place in one summer. Like all the other houses on the block, it had steel bars covering the windows. Some families had even invested in wrought-iron screen doors and burglar alarms.

His mother was waiting for him on the front porch wearing a simple flower-print blouse and skirt. Standing with her patent leather purse hooked over her arm, she was a rangy woman whose tanned Latin complexion contrasted starkly with the white hair pulled back sternly in a bun. She had piercing dark eyes and wore neither lipstick nor makeup.

He pulled up at the curb and she came to the car, walking quickly, as was her habit, as he reached over and opened the door. She climbed in and kissed him on the cheek.

"You have dark circles under your eyes, Jose," she said as he made a U-turn and headed back toward Whittier Boulevard.

"How's everything at the bakery?"

"The same. I slap on vanilla frosting and listen to gossip in the lunchroom. The women my age talk about arthritis, and the younger ones can't understand why the men they live with won't marry them."

He chuckled. "What do you tell 'em, Mom?"

"I tell 'em, 'Why should a man marry you if he's already getting what he wants?' But they don't want no advice. They think they know everything."

Five blocks away at the twenty-four-hour Safeway Market, his mother opened her purse and took out the weekly Safeway Market newspaper ad and, moving quickly down the aisles with Stepanovich pushing a grocery cart behind her, picked items from shelves. She'd been shopping at the store for more than thirty years, and knew the location of every item. Stepanovich told her three or four times not to rush, that it didn't matter if he was a few minutes late for work, but she continued to march briskly through the aisles.

They were in and out of the store and back in the car with a week's supply of groceries within twenty minutes. He noticed three Reno Street gang members standing on the corner as he pulled out of the parking lot. One, a pock-maked teenager with styled hair and a long-sleeved shirt buttoned to the collar, noticed Stepanovich in turn and made a remark to the others. The three men turned and stared at him with looks of focused enmity as he drove past. He stared back. He remembered arresting Mr. Pockmark, whose name escaped him at the moment, for possession of a gun a month or so earlier. He was pleased his mother hadn't noticed the stares.

"When you retire at the end of the year, what you ought to do is get out of the neighborhood. You could sell or rent the house and move somewhere else," he said.

"I'll think about it," she said, though he knew she wouldn't. They'd been through it a hundred times. A few months ago, he'd even offered to buy a condominium in Glendale where they could live together.

"I won't hold my breath."

"My parents and her grandparents lived and died within two blocks of here. Why should I go anywhere?"

"Because this isn't the same neighborhood. You like living behind bars?"

"Do you have time to come in for breakfast this morning?"

"I'm working on a big case, Mom. Maybe next week."

"When you have darkness under your eyes, it means you're worried about something."

"Everything's OK, Mom," he said, turning onto Vega Street. He pulled into the driveway and, leaving the engine running, carried the groceries to the house. Mrs. Stepanovich unlocked the front door and followed him inside. Having set the two bags on the sink, he gave her a hug and headed outside to the car.

"I saw those *cholos* in the parking lot staring at you," she said from the porch.

He opened the car door. "It's nothing. I arrested one of them."

Gerald Petievich

"The way you were staring back at them is why you have circles under your eyes. I don't like to see that in you."

"Call me if you need anything, Mom."

He climbed behind the wheel and pulled into the street. He waved at her as he drove away and she waved back.

At Hollenbeck Station, Stepanovich and the other members of the task force, all puffy-eyed and hungover, spent the morning in the parking lot equipping Fordyce's motor home with a police radio. As they worked, Harger dropped by now and then to see how the project was progressing.

At noon Stepanovich and the others waited in the parking lot as Fordyce drove the car over to Eighteenth Street and transmitted some test counts for a radio check. The messages were received loud and clear on the police radios in the other squad vehicles, and Stepanovich told Fordyce to return. At Arredondo's suggestion Fordyce stopped by Manuel's taco stand on the way back.

After Stepanovich and the others wolfed down a box of tacos standing in the parking lot, they followed him into the motor home. As Stepanovich spread a city map on the table inside, the others, including Harger, gathered around. Using a red marker pen, he drew a circle around the location of Greenie's apartment house. Taking his time, he selected the best places for the other surveillance units to be positioned. He drew four red dots. "Here's where we'll set up. Fordyce will be across the street inside the motor home." He pointed: "The other units will be stashed here, here, and here, away from the location until the signal is given. No one will notice the motor home parked on the street, but if they see a lot of unmarked cars dicking around the area, no one will dare make a move and we could end up sitting on Eighteenth Street until Christmas."

Harger studied the notations carefully. "I like the

setup. And keep in mind that we're only interested in gang members. If you observe someone selling dope on the street or stealing a car, you didn't see it. We're waiting for shooters and shooters only."

Fordyce cleared his throat. "I just thought of something. What if the White Fence shooters don't know it was Greenie? Like what if they actually haven't figured out that Greenie was the one who did the shootings at the church? We might be watching Eighteenth Street from now until hell freezes over."

"If we've been able to find out, they've been able to find out. You can bet on that. And if they know, they'll hit. There's no telling exactly when, but they'll hit," Stepanovich said.

Harger drummed his fingers on the map for a moment. "Because the DA refused to file the case, Greenie should be getting released from the county jail shortly after five. Let's be set up on location by kick-out time."

At five, Stepanovich cruised along a hillside road looking down on Eighteenth Street. To hide his sedan from the street below, he parked behind a growth of chaparral. He opened his city mapbook and made sure he was familiar with the streets in the area in case there was a pursuit. Though the plan was to trap the shooters on Eighteenth Street, he knew full well that all the planning in the world didn't allow for what a carload of gang shooters high on dope and cruising for blood might do. Taking binoculars from the glove compartment, he focused them and scanned Eighteenth Street.

Fordyce's motor home was parked directly across the street from Greenie's apartment. Stepanovich shifted the binoculars to the left. Black's police sedan was parked on a residential street one block north at the edge of a deserted industrial area. To the south, Arredondo sat in the driver's seat of a sedan hidden from the street behind a dumpster. Pleased with the configuration of the surveillance, Stepanovich set the binoculars down on the seat beside him.

For the next hour he killed time thumbing through a day-old copy of the L.A. *Herald Examiner*. The story about the church shooting was on page four. The article featured a photograph of the mother of the murdered child standing on on the steps of the Our Lady Queen of Angels Church clutching a doll, a pose he assumed was the news-grabbing idea of some enterprising *Herald* reporter. In the text of the article the director of the city's Community Gang Services Agency commented that the shooting was a result of the city not allocating enough money to hire ex-gang members to counsel the gangs not to kill one another. A member of the city council, whom Stepanovich knew had once been arrested by vice detectives for exposing himself in a Hollywood porno theater, suggested that the mayor was totally insensitive to the gang problem. The mayor suggested that a blue-ribbon panel be appointed to study the situation. It was the usual gang-murder newspaper story. Stepanovich turned to the sports page.

Suddenly the radio crackled. "Fordyce to all units. We have an arrival."

"Of who?" Black said irritably.

Stepanovich grabbed the binoculars and focused on the street below as a Chevrolet pulled up in front of Greenie's apartment house. Three men climbed out of the car.

"Greenie and three of his homeboys," Fordyce said over the radio. "They must have picked him up from jail. It's a Chevy. They're getting out. Greenie looks worried . . . everybody up the stairs . . . and into the apartment. One of 'em is carrying a case of beer."

Stepanovich watched the arrival through binoculars, then, to kill some time, tuned the car radio to a Spanish language station. For the next few hours he listened to Latin music interspersed with commercials for beer and immigration lawyers. He switched stations and listened for a while to a shrieking, hoarse-voiced evangelist scold the world. Leaving the radio on, Stepanovich climbed out of the car and walked about to stretch his legs. He found himself almost marching in cadence to the exhortations of the preacher. "You won't find it in greed!" the evangelist rasped. Stepanovich took a few steps. "You won't find it in liquor!" A few more steps. "You won't find it in adultery!" Continue to march. "You won't find it in homosexuality!" Stepanovich lifted his arms above his head and stretched. "You'll find it in the message of *Jesus Christ, King of kings, the one-and-only son of God, who came to this earth to die on Calvary!"*

Stepanovich opened the car door and turned off the radio. For the next couple of hours he alternated between using the binoculars and rereading the newspaper. Finally he took out his wallet and gave it a thorough cleaning. He purged it of unneeded credit-card and cash-register receipts, and pulled out an Oasis cocktail bar matchbook cover with the inscription, "MARTI (FRIEND OF JUDY) 213/912-1573," an old lottery ticket, and from a crusty inside compartment, a worn photograph of Nancy looking tanned and sexy in her tennis outfit. He tore the items into small pieces and shoved them into the dashboard ashtray.

Dusk came as a neon orange sun sank slowly into smog.

Stepanovich moved to the trunk of the sedan, opened it, and fished among some empty ammunition boxes and roadway flares. He found the night-viewing binoculars he always brought on surveillances and tested them by focusing on the apartment house. Because of the infrared lens, everything appeared illuminated in shades of green. Panning the binoculars slowly to the right, he focused on the bay window of a small house south of Greenie's apartment. A man and woman, like mannequins, were slumped in front of the flickering light of a television. Stepanovich wondered what program they were watching.

The man was eating. Because Stepanovich was hungry, he imagined him enjoying a thick salami sandwich on French bread, heavy with mayonnaise and mustard.

The sound of static coming from the radio startled him.

"Homeboy exiting," Fordyce said.

Stepanovich steadied the binoculars on the apartment house. A young man wearing a baseball cap was descending the steps in front of Greenie's apartment. He looked about, then crossed the small patch of lawn to a customized Chevrolet. Under the illumination of a streetlight, the man stopped, looked around, then climbed behind the wheel.

"Homeboy into his ride," Fordyce said via radio.

The Chevrolet pulled away from the curb and cruised slowly down Eighteenth Street toward Whittier Boulevard.

"Should we follow him?" Black said via radio.

Stepanovich glanced at his wristwatch. He picked up the microphone and pressed the transmit button. "Let him go."

"That's a roger."

A few minutes later the radio crackled again. "Homeboy returning," Fordyce said.

Stepanovich checked his wristwatch. The man had been gone exactly fourteen minutes. Stepanovich climbed onto the hood of the police sedan to use his binoculars knowing that no one below would be able to see him in the dark. The Chevrolet was pulling up to the curb in front of the apartment. The man climbed out the driver's door and walked to the trunk.

"Homeboy unloading from the trunk," Fordyce said via radio.

The man opened the trunk and removed a box. He closed the trunk and headed toward the apartment.

"All units be advised this was nothing but a beer run," Fordyce said. "He's carrying beer back into the apartment."

"What are they drinking?" Arredondo said.

"Coors—two cases."

"They're having a party to celebrate Greenie beating the rap," Black said.

There was the distinct sound of a beer can being opened over the radio, which Stepanovich recognized as Arredondo's mimicry.

About eleven, Stepanovich leaned back in the driver's seat and closed his eyes. The hillside was alive with the sound of crickets, and the air earthy and pungent with nightfall. It reminded Stepanovich of Vietnam.

He remembered lying in jungle darkness on a thin, waterproof ground cover separating him from soil rich and wet, moldy earth mixed with the remains of dead leaves, rodents, and as he used to imagine it, carefully buried Vietcong bodies.

He'd dropped out of college his second semester and enlisted in the regular Army because he would have never been able to face Uncle Nick or his mother if he'd obtained a fraudulent medical deferment or joined the National Guard to avoid Vietnam service, like so many of his classmates at East Los Angeles Junior College. Though enlisting required that he serve three years rather than the two years draftees served, he was able to pick his branch of the Army. Acting on Uncle Nick's advice, he selected the intelligence corps. Nick claimed that the former Los Angeles Chief of Police, William H. Parker, had once told him he'd organized the department's command structure on what he learned while serving as an Army spook. Nick respected Parker for coming up through the ranks as a two-fisted cop. He was not a brown nose or a professional test taker.

As an Army intelligence sergeant in Vietnam, Stepanovich's first assignment had been at MACV headquarters in Saigon, analyzing stacks of intelligence reports about enemy sightings. Like most Army administrative jobs, his duties seemed fruitless, particularly when it became clear to him that most of the reports were fabricated by low-level sources scrambling for favors or a few bucks in confidential funds or by enemy double agents.

The war became more real to Stepanovich when the Ling Hoc Hotel, where he and the other members of the intelligence unit were billeted, was blown up by a Vietcong satchel charge, and he fell from the second floor into the lobby as the building crumbled. Miraculously, his only injury was a two-inch cut on his back.

Seeing men he knew killed, he volunteered for the field rather than remain in Saigon, where he knew he could stay for the rest of his combat tour.

At a base camp outside of Duc Loc, he had interrogated prisoners and prepared reports like the ones he'd been analyzing in Saigon. There, he'd been as brutal as the other interrogators in getting information out of the Vietcong prisoners because it was the only way to get back at the enemy. Also, as foolish as it sounded to him now, he believed in the mission. At the time he believed the president and the Congress wouldn't have sent him all the way across the world if the cause wasn't just. Though a loyal, hardworking spook, he also recognized even then that few of the intelligence reports he was sending forward could be relied upon because neither he, nor, as far as he was concerned, any other American in Vietnam, could figure out what the hell was going on at any given time.

His three-year tour of duty completed, he'd been discharged just before the fall of Saigon.

Suddenly there was the sound of radio static.

"What's up out there?" Harger said after giving Stepanovich's call sign.

Stepanovich picked up the microphone. "No activity. They're drinking beer inside."

"Keep me advised. I want you to stay on it. If nothing happens, I'll get some Metro officers to relieve you tomorrow afternoon."

"That's a roger."

Stepanovich climbed out of the car and walked around awhile to stay awake. Around two Fordyce reported that the lights had been turned off in Greenie's apartment. Stepanovich used his night binoculars to check the television watchers. The man was still sitting in his easy chair staring at the tube.

For the rest of the night Stepanovich alternated between taking catnaps in the car and walking about on the hillside road. As the sun came up the next morning, he gained something like a second wind.

It was four the next afternoon by the time he and the others were relieved by officers from Metropolitan Division.

Back at his apartment, the exhausted Stepanovich stripped and climbed into a hot shower. He soaped up his entire body, scrubbed, and rinsed thoroughly. He stepped out of the shower, dried off on the only clean towel he could find in the apartment, then dropped into bed. Lying there, he thought about Gloria until his eyes closed.

NINE

At 5:00 A.M., on his way back to the surveillance, Gloria was still on his mind. He stopped at an all-night convenience market on Brooklyn Avenue and purchased a package of salami, three French rolls, a jar of pickles, a handful of Snickers bars, and a six-pack of Coke—provisions he figured would last him for the day. Because of the light traffic, it took him less than fifteen minutes to arrive at the hillside road above Eighteenth Street. He parked his sedan in exactly the same place as the day before.

During the next hour he exchanged bits of radio conversation with the other members of the task force. After a few transmissions he was confident the surveillance was again in place. Nothing more was said. Everyone had accepted another day of police ennui: sitting in a car in one place waiting for crime to happen as the bad guys drank beer, played pool, slept, or knocked off a piece of ass. For Stepanovich it certainly wasn't the first time. He remembered hiding in the woods above Elysian Park for a three-day holiday weekend waiting for a rumored gang assassination. As families picnicked, lovers necked, teenagers drank beer and played softball in the crowded park, he had watched and waited, feeling somehow detached and excluded, as if holidays were only for others.

He and the other members of that surveillance team had made up for the isolated weekend at the Rumor Control Bar drinking heavily through the night.

The day passed slowly. Stepanovich moved his car every couple of hours to keep it in the shade of the eucalyptus trees protecting him from being seen by anyone on Eighteenth Street. At two he climbed out of the car and did some stretching exercises. Then, in a clear area under the trees, he dropped down and did a hundred push-ups, counting them out loud. Feeling refreshed after the exercise, he ate his lunch.

In the afternoon, the meticulous Fordyce reported via radio that men were coming and going from Greenie's apartment. Stepanovich figured they were Eighteenth Street gang members just dropping by to talk about Greenie's arrest and release.

As dusk came, Eighteenth Street was bathed in a gray, weakening light. Because it was summer, darkness didn't come until almost nine. With the absence of sun, Stepanovich felt a chill on his neck and figured he had a slight sunburn from being out of the car so much during the day.

For the next couple of hours he listened to a female radio talk-show host with a heavy New York accent give advice to troubled callers. "Walk away from your husband," she advised the wife of a man who preferred carving wooden ducks in his garage to showing her affection and sharing his day. "Move out," she instructed a young woman living with a fry cook who didn't want to get married.

When he tired of the radio fare, he used his night binoculars for a while to spy on the couple he'd watched the night before through the bay window ensconced in front of their television. They were in their respective couch-potato positions in their living room. The man would leave the room every twenty minutes or so and return with something to eat. Again Stepanovich tried to guess what programs they were watching for a few minutes, but that only held off the boredom for a few minutes. He closed his eyes and relived his date with Gloria. After lengthy consideration he decided that, though aloof and independent, she probably was as interested in him as he was in her. Otherwise, he told himself, she wouldn't have agreed to got out with him in the first place.

The rest of the night passed uneventfully.

At nine, he and the other squad members were relieved by some officers from Metro Division. After a short meeting at Manuel's taco stand with the others, he drove directly to Gloria's residence. He parked his car in the parking lot and climbed the stairs to her apartment. The lights were off and there was no sound coming from inside. Figuring that she'd gotten off at midnight and had had time to get a full night's sleep, he rapped on the door. A few moments later, the peephole opened and closed. The door opened from the inside. Gloria was wearing a pink silk robe and her hair was neatly pulled back with a barrette.

"I hope I didn't wake you."

"I've been up. I thought you were on twenty-four-hour surveillance."

"I just got off."

"You look like you can use some coffee."

She opened the door wide and Stepanovich stepped inside. He shoved the door closed behind him and followed her into the kitchen.

"I hope you like instant."

"Fine."

Gloria spun the cap off a coffee jar. "Must be exciting, watching someone all night."

"It's boring."

"I'd probably fall asleep."

Stepanovich crossed the kitchen to be close to her. "I was thinking about you all night."

She spilled a spoonful of coffee on the sink. Setting

94

the spoon down, she turned to him and their eyes met. "And I've been thinking about you."

He took her in his arms.

"No," she whispered as he covered her mouth with his. He could feel her teeth softly bite his lower lip. His hands slid to her firm breasts, then cupped her buttocks.

As she breathed heavily, her nurse's hands were on him, unbuttoning his shirt, tugging his belt, then his zipper. Suddenly the whole world consisted only of them undressing each other. She took his hand and led him into a bedroom that smelled faintly of a female fragrance—lilac? In the streetlight shining through sheer curtains, she led him onto the bed. Grasping him firmly, efficiently, she took him without reservation fully into her mouth. Lost in a sexual trance, Stepanovich maneuvered to touch her erect nipples, her wetness, and she moaned with pleasure. Feverishly he arranged her dark, silken legs. His tongue found her and he was lost in her taste and the sound of her long moans of pleasure.

Finally he was in her: thrusting, dissolving, submitting to the rocking violence of sex for what seemed like an eternity, and her fingernails dug deeply into his shoulders as to punish him for resisting orgasm. Then her breath unexpectedly started, and with a cry she arched to him rapidly. Unable to restrain himself a moment longer, he surged to an almost painful pleasure. All at once he was giver, taker, killer, and protector.

Later, as they lay on the bed with arms around each other, he could tell from the rhythm of her breathing she'd fallen asleep. But rather than the fatigue he should have felt because of the sleep he'd lost in recent days, he felt rejuvenated.

In the afternoon, he awoke alone in the bed. There was a note on the nightstand that read:

Good morning Jose Stepanovich,
I didn't wake you up to say good-bye because you were

sleeping like the dead. I had to go in early to fill in for an emergency room supervisor who called in sick. But I'll be off tonight.

I'll be thinking about you all day.

Gloria

P.S Please help yourself to the contents of the refrigerator.

He was on duty at his surveillance post above Eighteenth Street less than an hour later. All during the day and into the next evening he found himself reliving his time with Gloria. A couple of times during the day he even almost talked himself into leaving the surveillance position to phone her, but he figured that the way things were going, with nothing much happening at Greenie's place, he would get relieved by Metro officers again and would be able to see her.

As evening came and he began to survey Eighteenth Street with the night-vision binoculars, he opened a bag and nibbled on a chunk of French bread left over from the day before, then washed it down with a can of Diet Coke. He ate the last candy bar for dessert, deciding at this point he was sick of junk food.

At about eleven Stepanovich was leaning back in the seat with his eyes shut when suddenly the police radio came alive. "Fordyce to Stepanovich." There was tension in Fordyce's voice.

Stepanovich grabbed the microphone. "Go."

"Four lowriders in a blue Chevy just made a slow pass. They're hawking the location."

Stepanovich grabbed the binoculars. The Chevrolet, tinged an eerie green, continued past Greenie's apartment and turned right at the corner. Safely out of sight from Greenie's place, the car pulled slowly to the curb. Holding the binoculars with one hand, Stepanovich picked up the radio microphone and brought it close to his lips as he pressed the transmit button. "This is Stepanovich to all units. Stand by. The Chevy is one block south of the location."

Keeping his eyes on the Chevrolet, Stepanovich wondered how many times in his career he'd been alerted to possible danger and had his heart race, as it was right at this minute, only to determine it was only a false alarm. Hell, for all anyone actually knew, the Chevrolet could be simply pulling over to check a flat tire. But, nevertheless, his policeman's sixth sense was telling him danger was present.

The Chevrolet pulled away from the curb, made a U-turn, and cruised slowly back in the direction of the apartment house. As it passed under a bright street lamp, Stepanovich focused the binoculars. The man in the passenger seat was Smokey Salazar. "This is Stepanovich," he said, keying the microphone. "We have visitors. Repeat. Visitors. Meet me at location one."

Stepanovich dropped the microphone on the seat and started the ignition. He slammed the car into gear, stepped on the accelerator and, to avoid drawing the attention of anyone on the street below, sped downhill without headlights. At the bottom of the grade he swerved into a service alley running parallel with Eighteenth Street. He stopped his car about a hundred feet from the rear of Greenie's apartment house. Quickly he clipped the walkie-talkie to his belt, then reached into the backseat, and grabbed his shotgun and bullet-proof vest. He climbed out of the car.

Changing the shotgun from hand to hand, he shrugged on the thick vest. Then, aiming the shotgun at the ground, he cranked the beavertail and chambered a round.

Arredondo and Black jogged up to him from the darkness. Both held shotguns in the port-arms position and were wearing bullet-proof vests.

"I got a look at the driver when they cruised past me," Arredondo said, catching his breath. "I think it was Payaso, the one who got shot at the church."

Stepanovich's walkie-talkie came alive. "The Chevy is pulling up in front," Fordyce said with a quavering voice. "They're parking. Repeat. *They are parking.*"

Stepanovich unsnapped the walkie-talkie from the holder on his belt and pressed the button. "Stay where you are and tell us what they are doing."

"Roger."

"They're here for blood," Black said, thumbing green shells into the magazine of his shotgun.

Arredondo drew his revolver and snapped open the chamber to check the load. With a flick of the wrist he clicked the chamber shut.

There was the sound of radio static coming from the walkie-talkie. "They're getting out of the car," Fordyce said. "The driver is staying behind the wheel."

"They've got their balls up. They're gonna do it," Arredondo said.

Stepanovich said nothing, motioning to the others to follow him down the walkway leading toward the front of the apartment house. "We'll take 'em before they go upstairs."

Black didn't move. "Arrest 'em now and they'll be home before we finish writing the report."

Stepanovich stopped.

"C.R.'s right," Arredondo said. "Greenie killed a little girl. Let White Fence give him some of his own medicine."

Stepanovich, keyed-up for the arrest, suddenly had another feeling—an excitement akin to a kid playing hide-and-seek when the seekers are getting closer—the stifled urge to both piss and yell at the top of his lungs at the same time.

"They're headed toward the steps," Fordyce said via radio, "Repeat. *They are gonna do it.*"

Stepanovich slowly pulled the walkie-talkie from his belt, hesitating before pressing the transmit button. "Stepanovich to Fordyce. We're getting set up," he said, then released the button.

"You'd better hurry . . . they're at the steps . . . going up," Fordyce replied. "They're prowling."

Stepanovich lowered the volume on the walkie-talkie a few notches and clipped the radio back on his belt.

"They have to come down the same way," Stepanovich said. "We'll set up at the bottom of the stairs."

Using the shadows for cover, Black and Arredondo followed Stepanovich along a six-foot cinder-block wall adjoining Greenie's apartment house. As the wall's elevation dropped a foot or so, Stepanovich could see Smokey Salazar and the others creeping along the dimly lit second-floor landing and into a shadow where Greenie's apartment was situated.

"They're trying to figure out which apartment is Greenie's," Arredondo whispered.

Salazar's Chevy was parked in front of the apartment building next door, just out of sight of Greenie's apartment. There was a driver sitting behind the wheel. Stepanovich stopped the others and pointed to him. Crouching low, holding his shotgun balanced in one hand, he crept in the darkness along a row of Italian cypress trees leading to the curb. Peeking from behind the shrubbery, he could see Payaso staring straight ahead.

Without hesitation, Stepanovich moved across the parkway, keeping down out of Payaso's view, and around the car to the driver's side. Arredondo was behind him.

Stepanovich poked the barrel of the shotgun in the driver's window and touched Payaso's temple. "Police, motherfucker," he whispered. "Keep your mouth shut."

Payaso raised his hands slowly and Stepanovich adjusted the shotgun slightly to allow Arredondo to open the door. Arredondo's left hand cupped Payaso's mouth. He pulled him out of the car and to the asphalt.

Arredondo handcuffed Payaso quickly, then with a knee in his back, held his revolver to his head to keep him quiet.

Stepanovich immediately hurried back to the wall. Quickly he and Black climbed over it and, staying close to the apartment building for cover, edged toward the stairs leading to the second-floor walkway.

The bottom few steps were illuminated by the harsh light of an outdoor fixture attached to the corner of the building. He stopped. "Right here," he whispered. "They'll have to come down into the light." He motioned and Black, keeping his eyes on the well-lit target area, moved a few feet away from him so they wouldn't shoot each other by accident.

From the second-floor landing there was suddenly the unmistakable crack of rapid gunshots, screams, breaking glass, and male shouts of "White Fence!"

A thunder of frantic footsteps came along the landing and down the stairs.

Stepanovich, standing in the darkness a few feet from the steps, raised his shotgun to shoulder level and aimed. Smokey Salazar and two other men, all carrying guns, rushed down the stairs into the harsh illumination.

For a millisecond after Salazar spotted him, Stepanovich thought he detected a look of recognition on his face. Salazar's eyes opened wide and his jaw dropped. He could have been any creature in flight suddenly confronted by impending doom.

Stepanovich pulled the trigger. "One," he shouted to himself as he'd been trained to do at the police academy. The sound of shotgun blast mixed with that of human shrieks. He cranked the slide. "Two" and the world became muzzle flashes and deafening blasts as Stepanovich worked the action of his shotgun. Black was firing rapidly. "Three."

Bodies tumbled down the cement steps.

Black dropped his empty shotgun and it clattered to his feet. He pulled his revolver and advanced forward, firing alternately at the prostrate shooters.

"Hold it!" Stepanovich yelled.

Black stopped firing. The air was filled with the odor of gunsmoke. Stepanovich dropped his shotgun and pulled his revolver. Holding it in the two-handed combat position, he moved closer.

The light was glaring on the three victims. Smokey

Salazar was convulsing, holding his groin. The other two men were lying askew, unmoving. They had almost bloodless holes in their respective faces and chests. Stepanovich remembered the homicide school axiom: dead bodies don't bleed.

"Ahhhh," Salazar moaned. He was crying, whimpering.

Black holstered his revolver and knelt beside him. He pulled Salazar's hands behind him and ratcheted handcuffs onto his wrists. "Don't cry, fuckface," he said.

Fordyce's nervous falsetto voice came through the walkie-talkie. "Shots fired! Man down! Eighteenth and Toberman. Requesting paramedics and a field supervisor."

From upstairs there was the sound of a woman moaning.

Stepanovich raced past the dead and wounded and up the steps. Moving cautiously along the landing, he made his way to Greenie's apartment. There was shattered glass on the landing in front of the open door. He stepped inside. Greenie was on the carpet holding a blood-soaked towel to his wife's head. A man was lying in a fetal position on the kitchen floor. Another man, shirtless and bloody, his eyes wide, was crawling across the floor. There was the wail of sirens in the distance.

Greenie looked up at Stepanovich. "My wife."

Stepanovich stood there, breathing hard, saying nothing. His left hand inadvertently touched the burning barrel of his shotgun and he yanked it away. He moved to a telephone hidden on the bare floor among empty beer cans. His hand was shaking as he picked up the receiver and began dialing Harger's number. Then he thought better of it and set the receiver down.

Retreating out the door, he hurried down the steps a few feet past the bodies to Black. Arredondo approached from the car, dragging the handcuffed Payaso.

Payaso's shirt was torn open and his torso was covered with bandages.

"Those are my homeboys," Payaso cried. "You killed my homeboys."

Arredondo shoved Payaso facedown in the middle of the lawn facing away from the bodies. He moved closer to Stepanovich.

Stepanovich turned to Arredondo. "Your prisoner," he whispered. "What did he see?"

Arredondo shook his head. "Nothing. He was facedown in the street when the shooting occurred."

Fordyce hurried toward them from the motor home. Suddenly he stopped, staring at the bodies.

"What did you see?" Stepanovich said.

Fordyce couldn't take his eyes off the men lying on the steps. Stepanovich grabbed his arm. "Did you hear what I said?"

"I saw you guys move toward the steps and the shooters coming down," Fordyce whispered back. "Then all hell broke loose."

A police car, siren wailing, pulled up at the curb, but the detectives ignored it.

"You heard us yell, 'Police,' right?" Black asked.

Arredondo nodded. "That's the way I remember it, amigo."

Stepanovich turned to Fordyce. "And you couldn't hear anything because you were using the radio at the time."

Fordyce was still staring at the bodies. Stepanovich touched his arm. "Isn't that right?"

A police car with flashing lights and siren blaring squealed its brakes as it came to a stop in front of the apartment house.

"I won't contradict what you say," Fordyce said.

"Black and I are the only ones who know what happened at the steps," Stepanovich said to the others. "Now and forever. Is that understood?"

Arredondo, then Fordyce nodded.

Two uniformed officers with drawn revolvers rushed

across the lawn. They stopped and stared at the bodies.

"CRASH special unit," Stepanovich said. "We've had an officer-involved shooting." He pointed to Payaso: "Put this prisoner in your car, then block off the street."

By the time the ambulances arrived, occupants of the other apartments in the area were outside gawking, and a crowd of onlookers two-deep had formed across the street.

Stepanovich noticed Fordyce, with head bowed, move away from the others to the cypress trees, lean at the waist, and loudly vomit.

TEN

Harger arrived as Smokey Salazar and Greenie's wife were being taken away in ambulances. Eighteenth Street was a maze of flashing red lights, traffic stanchions, and yellow evidence tape.

Stepanovich met Harger at the curb and led him under evidence tape to the bodies. The captain made a point of examining the dead closely, then came to his feet.

"Do we have any problems?" he said, keeping his voice low enough so that even other policemen standing nearby couldn't hear.

"They fired at Black and me. We fired back," Stepanovich said.

"The shooting team will ask you why you fired so many times," Harger said. "Those people look like hamburger."

"They kept moving as if trying to shoot, so we continued to fire," Stepanovich lied.

Harger gave him a brotherly slap on the shoulder. "Very good," he said. "Keep it simple."

Later, with the area sealed off for investigation, paramedics and coroner's deputies milled about. A station wagon pulled to the curb near where Stepanovich was standing. A television camera crew and a young

TV reporter, a curly-haired blond man who looked like a male model, climbed out and approached Harger. Camera lights were turned on as the reporter held a microphone close to Harger's mouth and asked what had happened.

Harger cleared his throat. "Officers of the L.A. Police CRASH Gang Task Force were on routine patrol when they heard gunshots and observed men with-guns running from a residence. At that time the officers identified themselves as police officers and were fired on by three armed males. The officers returned fire. Two of the suspects were killed and one was wounded. We are not releasing the names of the dead and wounded until next of kin are notified."

Later that night, the task force's basement office was a maelstrom of activity—phones ringing and being answered, Harger escorting command-level officers into his office for briefings, the robbery-homicide division shooting-team investigators interviewing the members of the task force one at a time. As all that went on about him, Stepanovich sat at his desk writing and editing his report, making sure it was concise and free of any equivocal language that could be attacked later by the money-hungry attorneys whom he knew would represent the families of the deceased in suits against the police department. When completed, the report read as follows:

SOURCE OF ACTIVITY:
    Acting on information received from a confidential informant, officers of the Hollenbeck Division CRASH Gang Task Force were routinely deployed in a gang crime prevention detail near the 2900 block of Eighteenth Street, a known gang area.

ACTIVITY:
    At approximately 1910 hours officers observed known gang member Arturo Salazar, a.k.a. Smokey, and two

males (later identified as Hernandez, Ralph and Nunez, Luis) approach Apartment 203 at the location carrying handguns. Believing that a crime was in progress, Officers Stepanovich, Jose, Serial #613845, and Black, C. R., Serial #992318, approached the location to investigate. At this time, shots were heard and the suspects attempted to run from the location. Believing that a crime had occurred, the officers immediately identified themselves to the suspects as police officers. The suspects opened fire on the investigating officers. Officers Stepanovich and Black returned fire, hitting all three suspects.

Hernandez and Nunez were pronounced dead at the scene.

Salazar was transported to the jail ward of the L.A. County General Hospital with multiple gunshot wounds.

(signed)
Stepanovich, Jose
Serial #613845

Stepanovich realized Harger was looking over his shoulder.

"Fine report," Harger whispered. "Short and sweet."

As Stepanovich turned to face him, Harger rested a brotherly hand on his shoulder. "The shooting team is ready for you now. I've talked with the Chief. He's very pleased with what went down, but he doesn't want it to look like the task force was staked out waiting for a crime to occur. You were staked out, but it was for the purpose of crime prevention. Prevention is the key word." He winked and cuffed Stepanovich on the shoulder.

Stepanovich opened the door to the interview room and stepped inside. A diminutive bald man with rheumy eyes and a flaky, sun-spotted scalp was sitting behind a table in front of a portable tape recorder. Stenciled on its side was: "SHOOTING INVESTIGATION TEAM." Houlihan wore a brown polyester suit and a yellowish necktie that matched the color of his teeth. He turned on the tape recorder and motioned Stepanovich toward a chair.

"I'm Lieutenant Jack Houlihan from the shooting team," the man said as he shuffled some papers in front of him, though the men knew each other from working patrol in Wilshire Division a few years before. Houlihan had once studied to be a Roman Catholic priest and was well-known in department circles as a consummate ass-kisser. As a patrolman with less than a year on the job, he had taken out a loan from the Police Credit Union to pay the initiation fee at the Los Angeles Tennis Club in order to play singles with then-Wilshire Division Captain Seth Leyva, an easily influenced dolt who promoted those officers whose names he could remember.

Houlihan picked up a sheet of paper, slipped on half-frame reading glasses, and read off the Miranda:

"Before I ask you any questions you must understand your rights. You have the right to remain silent. Anything you say can and will be used against you. You have the right to talk to a lawyer. If you decide to answer questions, you can stop the questioning at any time to consult with a lawyer. If you want a lawyer and cannot afford one, one will be appointed to you.

"Do you understand those rights?"

Stepanovich fidgeted in his seat. "Yes."

"Do you wish to waive your rights and answer questions?" Houlihan said in an emotionless tone.

Without answering, Stepanovich took out his wallet. He removed his Police Protective League Membership card. From the reverse of the card he read: "If I refuse to answer questions, may I be subjected to discipline?"

"Yes," Houlihan said without looking up from his notes.

Stepanovich cleared his throat, continued to read. "Could that discipline be as much as discharge or removal from office?"

"Yes."

"In other words, my statement will be for internal administrative purposes only and will not be used in any way in any criminal investigation or prosecution?"

Houlihan uttered another routine yes.

"Then for those reasons, and those reasons alone," Stepanovich read, "I will give you a statement." He returned the card to his wallet and shoved it into his right rear trouser pocket.

"First shooting?" Houlihan asked.

Stepanovich shook his head. "I was in one when I first came on the department. A liquor store robbery."

"Then you should be familiar with the procedure. I ask questions. You can take all the time you want to answer."

Houlihan touched Stepanovich's report on the table. "Your report is a little skimpy."

"Like how?"

"It doesn't explain why you were staked out on the location."

"We were in the Eighteenth Street gang turf to prevent crime. Shooters from Eighteenth hit a White Fence wedding a few days ago, and we figured Eighteenth was due for retaliation."

"So you saturated the area."

"I thought the Eighteenth Street area was the best place to patrol because of the gang tension."

"What did you tell the other members of the task force in the briefing?"

"To keep their eyes open for members of the White Fence gang."

"Officer Fordyce told me he spotted Salazar and the other White Fence gang members climbing out of their car with guns and reported that to you via radio."

"That's correct."

Houlihan smiled wryly. "It seems like a lot of time went by between spotting the guns and moving in to investigate. What took so long?"

"I had to move to the location and deploy the men properly."

"And as you were doing that you heard gunshots."

Stepanovich nodded. "Yes."

"Then the suspects came running out of the apartment."

"Right."

"Who shot first?"

"They did."

"Which one?"

"It was dark. There was a fire flash and a blast. We shot back."

For a moment Stepanovich relived rushing into Greenie's apartment and seeing Greenie on the carpet with his wounded wife. If he'd stopped the White Fencers before they reached the apartment, she wouldn't have been shot. And afterward in court, if the judge had found him justified in believing a crime was going to occur and thus had acted legally, he would have sentenced them to a couple of months in county jail for carrying concealed weapons. When they had been released, they would surely return to Greenie's apartment and the same thing would have happened. Besides, Stepanovich told himself, Greenie and the White Fencers brought it all on themselves. A little girl had been killed.

Nevertheless, for the first time since the shooting had occurred, Stepanovich felt the same revulsion he had experienced during his first days in the interrogation tent in Duc Loc. Master Sergeant Herb Longacre, a deliberate, taciturn man, with a neat crew cut, had hooked up a young Vietcong prisoner's testicles to an electric generator to make him tell the location of his base unit. The prisoner took six terrific jolts without saying a word and then died. Longacre quietly dragged the body out the back of the tent and buried it in the jungle. Though the incident was never mentioned again, every time Stepanovich saw Longacre he'd recall the incident. If Longacre so much as came into the mess hall when Stepanovich was eating, he'd stop eating and leave. Finally, though, by the end of Stepanovich's combat tour, Stepanovich had gotten used to Longacre. He disliked him but found he could accept him because even if he was a ghoul, he had survived six combat tours in Vietnam, had come to understand the Vietcong and be able to predict their actions. No one was as effective as Longacre at gathering intelligence and thus saving American lives. And in Vietnam, nothing else had any meaning except survival.

"Looking back at the situation from the point of view of an LAPD supervisor, is there anything you would do differently, knowing what you know now?"

"No," Stepanovich answered to the well-known trick question.

Houlihan made some notes on a police-issue yellow pad. Then he asked the same questions over again, phrasing each in a slightly different way. Stepanovich took care to answer each question exactly as he'd answered it previously. With the questions completed, Houlihan reached into his shirt pocket and took out a tube of lip balm. "Didn't you say Officer Fordyce and Officer Arredondo were in the street when the shooting occurred?"

"I believe so."

"So they should have been able to see who shot first."

"You'll have to ask them," Stepanovich said.

"I did. They said they couldn't tell."

Houlihan took a handkerchief from his suit jacket pocket. He unfolded it and blew his nose loudly. His index finger ran down a page and stopped on some notes. "The suspect who survived said you and Black failed to identify yourselves as police officers before you opened fire." Stepanovich maintained eye contact with Houlihan, but didn't answer. "Did you hear what I said?"

"What's the question?"

Houlihan coughed nervously. "Did you identify yourselves . . . ?"

"I identified myself by shouting, 'Police officers! Drop your weapons!' "

"And Black?"

"Is that a question?"

Houlihan's face turned an Irish-pissed-off red. "Did Officer Black identify himself before . . . ?"

"I don't recall what he said. At that moment people were shooting at me, and I was in fear of my life and firing back with a shotgun."

Houlihan smirked. "It takes both hands to fire a shotgun. How did you show your badge and fire your weapon at the same time?"

"My badge was in plain sight, clipped to my belt as I recall. So was Black's."

Houlihan looked like it was Christmas morning and there was nothing under the tree. As he returned to his notes, Stepanovich glanced at his wristwatch. He'd been in the interview room for more than an hour.

"Is there anything you wish to add?" Houlihan asked.

Stepanovich said no.

Houlihan turned off the tape recorder. "I remember you from Wilshire Division."

"It's been a long time."

"Just between you and me, this shooting looks like it's within policy guidelines."

Because Stepanovich didn't trust Houlihan any farther than he could throw him, he just nodded amiably rather than reply and thus have his reply recorded.

"So I'd say you have nothing to worry about."

"Is there anything else?"

"Off the record," Houlihan said in a conspiratorial tone, "I take my hat off to you for wasting those assholes."

Without acknowledging the remark in any way, Stepanovich stood up and left the room.

Payaso was sitting in the interrogation room with his right hand handcuffed to a reinforced eyebolt protruding from a heavy wooden table. He'd been released from the county hospital earlier in the day, and the bandages covering his wounds were itching furiously under his black Sir Guy shirt. To alleviate this suffering, he'd tried sniffing some paint Smokey had brought with him, but rather than perking him up, it had only made him lightheaded.

Across the table sat a pig-eyed cop who'd introduced himself as Detective Black.

As Black filled in the blanks on an arrest-report form, Payaso stared at a large mirror on the facing wall. Because he'd heard whispers coming from behind the mirror during the booking and interviewing process of previous arrests, he assumed the mirror was made of one-way glass so the cops could watch one another mind-fuck the people they arrested. For this reason he stared at the mirror and made a face.

"There's nobody behind the mirror," Black said without looking up from the paperwork.

"If there is," Payaso said to the mirror, "they can kiss my motherfuckin' ass."

"When was the last time you were arrested?" Black asked in a fatherly tone.

"I don't remember."

"Who is your nearest relative?"

"All that shit is in my package. I been arrested twenty-three times."

Black looked up at him with a hooded glance. "Whose idea was it to hit Greenie today?" he said in a nonthreatening manner.

"I don't know nothing about hitting no motherfucker," Payaso said. "My homeboys and me was just riding around, and one of 'em asked to stop to see somebody. So that's what I did."

"Which one asked to stop?"

"I don't remember."

"Who were the homeboys in the car with you?"

"You killed 'em. Take their fingerprints."

"What were their names?" Black said calmly. Payaso could tell he was starting to lose his temper.

"I only know 'em by nicknames."

"What are the nicknames?"

"I forget."

"Why did you stop on Eighteenth Street in front of Greenie's apartment?"

"To pick up a baseball mitt. We was going to Hazard Park to play some baseball."

"I guess it must have been a real shock to you when all the shooting started."

"Like for real," Payaso said, fingering the handcuff on his wrist.

Black took out a package of Camels and offered Payaso one. Payaso shook his head. Black tapped the pack on the heel of his palm and lifted out a smoke. "How long have you been out of the hospital?" he said, lighting up.

"Since this afternoon."

Black turned his head and expelled smoke. "If someone had shot me, I'd get back at 'em. I have the *huevos* to go after them. No matter what. That's just the way I am. I'd go up against 'em the minute I got out of the hospital."

Payaso knew enough not to reply.

"I'd get me some boys and go running. If a man won't stick up for his rights, he's nothing but a goddamn *puto*. Right?"

"Like for real."

"Who furnished the guns?"

"I don't know nothing about no guns."

"Whether you believe this or not, I respect you and your homeboys for going up against Greenie. He's a rotten prick."

Payaso remained expressionless.

"There's no need to be uptight," Black said. "You have nothing to worry about. See, what happened is history. It's over and done, and there's not a damn thing anyone can do to change it. You may not believe it, I'm only asking these questions because I'm curious. I swear to God."

"You're asking because you want to put a case on me."

"Wrong. You didn't shoot anybody. And there's no law against driving a Chevrolet."

Payaso felt anger welling inside him, oozing from under his bandages. The cop sitting across the table was suddenly all the cops who'd arrested him from the time he was nine years old: white cops, black cops, juvie cops, Chicano shit-eating Catholic School mother's-boy cops—the uniformed prick robots who frisked him, handcuffed him, led him about from cell to interrogation room, from courtroom lockup to the sheriff's sour-smelling felony bus, to the van that took him to Chino prison. They were the ones who made him eat Los Angeles County Jail watery oatmeal, beat him for talking back, beat him for not talking, and beat him for talking out of the corner of his mouth to the dude in the next cell. "You know what I mean," he said, holding his temper in check. "Like for real."

Black turned his fingers and looked at his cigarette longingly, waiting to take another puff. "No, actually I don't," he said. "I'm sitting here trying to treat you civilly and you want to give me shit. No one is trying to trick you or get you to incriminate yourself. I just have to fill out the required forms and get a brief statement from you. Then you're free to go. Like for real."

"Bullshit."

Black reached into his shirt pocket and took out a handcuff key. He leaned across the table and unlocked the handcuff. Payaso rubbed the deep red indentation in his wrist.

"You're reading me wrong," Black said, looking him directly in the eye.

"You're cold, man," Payaso said as the picture of Smokey and the others lying on the steps flashed through his mind. "You killed my people, but you're still not satisfied. Cold. Like for real."

"This is just a job to me. Look, what happened on

114

the street is just . . . a coincidence." Black turned the report form around and shoved it carefully across the table toward him. "I have no reason to lie to you."

Payaso picked up the report form. On it the following had been printed by the detective:

I, PRIMITIVO ESTRADA (a.k.a. Payaso) WISH TO MAKE THE FOLLOWING STATEMENT OF MY OWN FREE WILL AND ACCORD: Today, Smokey Salazar, Luis Nunez, Ralph Hernandez, and I talked about getting back at Greenie from the Eighteenth Street gang. Greenie was the one who shot me at the Our Lady Queen of Angels Church three weeks ago. We agreed to do it. We all got in my Chevrolet and I drove the others over to Greenie's apartment on Eighteenth Street. I waited in the car and the others went up to Greenie's apartment and did the shooting. I kept the motor running so we could get away after we killed Greenie. THIS STATEMENT IS TRUE AND CORRECT TO THE BEST OF MY KNOWLEDGE AND BELIEF.

Payaso felt his face growing ever redder with embarrassment as he took endless minutes to read the statement.

Black reached over and set a ballpoint pen next to his hand. "Just sign right under the word 'belief,' " he said. "This is just paperwork."

Payaso set the paper down on the table and shook his head.

Black furrowed his brow in annoyance, quickly checked himself, and forced another smile. "This is what you need to sign so you can go home. Just a formality."

"I ain't signing shit."

"Why?"

"The only way you can get me is to have me say I knew the other dudes were gonna shoot. You're trying to put a conspiracy on me."

"If you'll sign it you can walk right out the door. That's a promise."

Payaso looked up at the cop and shook his head. "You're sending me straight to the county jail. You ain't gonna let me go."

"It's best if you sign the paper. See, it'll show you got nothing to hide. I'm talking to you man to man now, son."

"You ain't a man. You're a pig."

Black picked up the report form and slowly tore it in half, then fourths, and dropped the pieces into a wastebasket. "It's too bad the way it worked out on the street. A damn shame."

"What's that supposed to mean?"

"You being in the car."

"What is this, a riddle? Like for real."

"I mean, I wish I had had the chance to send you up yonder to the land of the dead *cholos* along with your incest-bred *compadres.*"

"You don't scare me, *cabron*. I ain't no punk."

Glaring, Black pulled his chair around close to Payaso. He straddled it so they were face-to-face.

"You're real slick, *cholo,*" he hissed with tobacco breath. "But if you stay on the street, someday we'll surprise you just like we did your buddies. We're gonna pull the plug on you, cocksucker."

ELEVEN

Feeling relieved after the interview with Houlihan, Stepanovich shuffled out the back door of Hollenbeck Station into the parking lot. Fordyce's camper was parked near the door, and a television was on inside.

"We've been waiting for you, homeboy," Black said, playfully pulling him in the door. The odor of whiskey was overpowering.

Arredondo, sitting in the passenger seat, slapped Stepanovich on the back as he entered and handed him a half-empty bottle of Jack Daniel's. Fordyce was tuning a ten-inch television resting on the utility table.

Stepanovich drank directly from the bottle. Feeling the booze warm his mouth and throat, he handed the bottle back to Arredondo. "What happened with Payaso?"

"He wouldn't sign a statement," Black replied. "Says his homeboys stopped by Greenie's to pick up a baseball mitt."

Stepanovich turned to Fordyce. "What about Smokey?"

"I interviewed him at the hospital. He's not wounded that bad. His story is he was invited to a party at Greenie's, and when he got there Greenie pulled a gun. So he pulled his own gun and defended himself."

"And Greenie and the others in the apartment won't say anything and will never testify," Stepanovich said.

"I already called the DA," Arredondo said. "He says that without a confession, we can't prove Payaso drove to Greenie's with the specific intent of committing murder. And since Smokey has his own bullshit story and his other homeboys are dead, there's not enough evidence to file a case. I asked him about filing misdemeanor weapons charges on Smokey, and he feels that since we already killed two of the assholes it would be a waste of time."

"But take heart, gentlemen," Black said. "There are two less gangbangers in East L.A. So who really gives a shit whether the DA files charges?"

Stepanovich nodded.

On the television screen the blond TV newsman of earlier was standing on Eighteenth Street, bathed in artificial light. "From what I've been able to gather from police department sources," he said, "the officers involved in this shooting are assigned to an elite gang-suppression detail that's been in operation for only a short time."

Black held up the bottle. "Here's to the elite," he said. He took a swig and passed the bottle to Arredondo. He took a long pull and offered the bottle to Stepanovich.

As Stepanovich took the bottle, he noticed a framed five-by-eight photograph on the wall depicting Fordyce standing with his arms around his parents. The three were wearing Levis and plaid shirts. Behind them was the motor home and snow-capped mountains. Stepanovich drank and wiped his mouth with the back of his hand. "Houlihan said the shooting is good," he said.

Black reached for the bottle. "Houlihan couldn't find his asshole with a flashlight."

Fordyce drank from the bottle, coughed, and caught his breath. "He told me the same thing. That the shooting was within department policy. We have nothing to worry about." He handed the bottle to Stepanovich.

Stepanovich took another sip. He could feel the effect of the liquor already. "What did he press you on?"

"That from where I was, I should have been able to see who shot first. But I just kept telling him I didn't see anything."

"Fordyce, you're a man among men," Black said. "Salt of the fucking earth." He was drunk.

"Is that supposed to be a joke or something?"

"When those fuckers were coming down the steps, it was them or us. Their balls were up and they were high on blood. We're lucky they didn't get us," Black said.

"It's too bad Smokey is still alive," Arredondo said. "He's an asshole."

"If we had gone by the book, we'd be dead," Stepanovich said. "We'd be at the morgue right now getting filleted instead of those homeboys."

Black took another drink from the bottle, then stared at the label for a moment. "It's kinda comical when you think about it. These fuckers shooting up Greenie's place and running down the stairs." He laughed, a genuine belly laugh that the others didn't join. "They thought they were shittin' behind tall cotton. And the look on their faces—"

"It sounded like the shooting range on the last day of the month," Arredondo laughed.

"We did it and we came through," Stepanovich said. "White Fence asked for it."

Fordyce emitted a peculiar chuckle that he often used to introduce what he was going to say. "It's funny, we were investigating Eighteenth for shooting up White Fence and we ended up shooting White Fence."

"Gangbangers are gangbangers," Black said, glaring at Fordyce. "We shoot 'em where we find 'em."

"Don't take that in the wrong way," Fordyce said. "I'm just pointing out an interesting fact."

"Fuck your interesting facts."

"I stood up like everybody else here," Fordyce said.

"You're solid," Stepanovich said. "We're all solid."

Black laughed again. "Right about now every gang *cholo* in this town is wondering where we'll show up next."

"Hey, *ese*," Arredondo said in his best East L.A. gang accent. "The pigs are lowriding. They want to kill us, *ese*."

"Let's head for the Rumor Control," Black said. "Brenda is bringing some of her friends."

During the ten-minute ride they finished off the bottle, and Black opened the door and tossed it out. There was the sound of the bottle shattering in the street. Moments later, a police car with red lights flashing pulled up next to them. Black leaned out the window and waved. The officer driving the police car recognized him immediately and gave an abrupt salute before turning off his red lights and making a U-turn.

Fordyce parked directly in front of the Rumor Control Bar. From inside came the sounds of jukebox music and booze-confident voices—a stark contrast to the surrounding industrial ghost town. The shooting party was already underway.

Inside, the place was filled with laughter, loud voices, and cigarette smoke. It seemed to Stepanovich as if every drinker in the division had shown up.

Harger threw an arm around him. "The gunfighters!" he shouted as the task force sauntered in the front door. The crowd cheered and applauded.

Sullivan leaned across the bar and handed Stepanovich a beer. "Nice going, Joe."

Black rushed forward to put his arms around Brenda and a woman standing with a high beehive hairdo. He gave a rebel yell. "Two down and one on the machine!" he yelled. There was a burst of shrill laughter and some applause and whistles.

"If anyone here wants to join a gang, both White Fence and Eighteenth have openings," Fordyce yelled.

Harger took Stepanovich aside. "I just talked spoke

with the Chief, and he's assured me the shooting will come back clean. He told me he's overjoyed that the gangs got a taste of the blade for once. Don't you love that, 'a taste of the blade.' Those were his exact words." Harger touched his cocktail glass to Stepanovich's beer bottle and they tipped bottoms up. "The Chief knows your gang expertise helped make the Eighteenth Street caper successful. This could mean a promotion for you down the line."

"I'm not looking to be promoted. I'm happy working the street."

"I respect the fact that you aren't fighting for the limelight," Harger said. "But mark this day. The first step in destroying the power of the gangs has been taken and you were there."

"It's not always going to be this easy," Stepanovich said. "Without luck, we might have had to continue the stakeout on Eighteenth Street for a month or two before anything happened."

"We make our luck," Harger said, throwing an arm around him.

"If you could call it that."

Harger threw his head back and took in some cocktail ice. He chewed loudly, then swallowed. "Are you OK?"

"Of course."

"I don't think you realize what you and the squad have done. We have two less gang shooters in L.A. tonight. The whole department is talking about it. You guys are heroes." Smiling broadly, he moved toward the bar and threw an arm around Black and Arredondo.

By four, Stepanovich was the only one left at the bar. Brenda and her beehived friend were in the corner slow-dancing with Black and Arredondo to "Harbor Lights," playing for the umpteenth time on the jukebox. Arredondo was convinced the tune was an irresistible aphrodisiac to, in his words, "all women from virgin coeds to executive stockbroker cunt."

Fordyce was curled up asleep in the corner booth.

Sullivan dipped a sponge and squeezed soapy water onto the bar. "I wonder if the bad guys have a party when they shoot a cop," he said in a diffident tone than indicated that he didn't care if he got an answer.

"Probably," Stepanovich said to a half-empty glass of Jack Daniel's.

Sullivan wrapped a napkin around two fingers to wipe out a dirty ashtray and dropped the napkin behind the bar. "Funny," he said, "when a cop gets killed, the shooting team investigates to find out what *he* did wrong. They re-create the scene with videotape to show what a stupid asshole he was to get himself shot. Then a month after the funeral everybody forgets his name. But it's different with the gangbangers. A guy gets his ass blown away and he gains respect. Everybody in the turf talks about him. 'Loco was a cool dude. Loco wasn't afraid of shit,' they say."

"It's a different culture."

"It's fucked. That's what it is."

"You don't have to tell me. I grew up here."

Sullivan squeezed his sponge and gray water dribbled into the sink. "You're just as much of a *cholo* as the punks in White Fence."

"Sullivan, you'd do anything to start an argument—"

"The gangbangers don't know anything outside their chickenshit little turf and neither do you."

"I know the players."

"I've heard prison guards say the same thing."

"O.K., I'll admit it. I like putting gangbangers in jail. So maybe I'm crazy."

"You can kill a hundred gang shooters tomorrow, and their baby brothers would just take their places. It wouldn't change jack shit." He tossed the sponge in the sink. Reaching behind him, he picked up a bottle of Old Granddad and filled a shot glass. With one hand holding the bar, he threw back the shot quickly, then made a smacking sound. "The idea of stopping gang murders is a dream," he said, dropping the shot glass into soapy water. With a practiced motion he set the Granddad back in its place.

"I still believe in the Department," Stepanovich said.

"The Department? Who are we talking about? The Chief? The slick-sleeve who directs traffic at First and Main?"

"Harger. I believe in Harger."

Sullivan smiled wryly and nodded his head. "When I was a kid, I believed in the Lone Ranger and Tonto."

"Harger's a solid guy from what I've seen."

"That's because you haven't seen shit."

"Just what is that supposed to mean?"

"Someday you'll start putting in your eight hours without taking everything so serious. You'll be more concerned with where you can score a free lunch than who you're gonna arrest. It'll happen all at once. You'll be begging some mushmouth deputy DA to file a case, or you'll be working overtime to arrest the same mope the ninth or tenth time for the same offense, and all of a sudden you'll hear this little voice in the back of your head. It will say, *'Stepanovich, you're spinning your wheels in this shit.'* From then on, until the day you retire you'll see yourself for what you are: a drone, a lackey for that half-baked city politician calling himself the chief of police who is a drone for the mayor who is a drone for his rich, thieving friends eating caviar and fucking one another in the ass up in Beverly Hills. Right at that very moment when you realize that you've been breaking your balls to do nothing more than keep Leroy and Chuey from committing burglary in Beverly Hills, you'll change from a hotdog detective to a blue-suit burnout. The job won't be interesting any longer, and you'll spend your the rest of your time on the job avoiding all the nastiness you thrived on. You'll hate coming to work, but you'll eat like a king and . . . you'll sleep better."

"I'll quit first."

Sullivan picked up an ashtray and dumped its contents in a waste can behind the bar. "You'll stay," he said, setting the ashtray back on the bar. "On the other hand, if the job doesn't burn you out, it'll eat you alive." He turned to the others in the place. "Last call, you people. I'm outa here."

Black stopped dancing and swaggered behind the bar. Lifting a case of Budweiser from the cooler and balancing it on his head, he headed toward the front door.

Sullivan glared at him.

"One case of Bud on credit, you baggy-eyed fuckhead," Black said on his way out.

Accompanied by Brenda, they adjourned to Fordyce's motor home. At Black's suggestion, they sat around the tiny dinette table and played poker. Brenda, like a dutiful geisha, kibitzed and served beer.

Black began to laugh. "The look on their faces when they got to the bottom of the stairs." He dropped his jaw histrionically. "*EEEE Ho Laaaa.*" He aimed a simulated shotgun. "Boom! Boom!" He doubled up in a fit of laughter.

The others joined in and the motor home rocked with barracks-style, all-night-drinking male laughter that reminded Stepanovich of Nam.

"You dudes are crazy," Brenda said after the laughter subsided. Lifting a leg and sitting on Arredondo's lap, she took the beer bottle from his hand. "And your boss Bob Harger is crazy too. I know him from when he worked Newton Division. This was before he made sergeant."

"How was he?" Black asked with a leer. Everyone laughed.

"I don't talk about the men I . . . date. How would you like me talking about all of you?"

"C'mon, Brenda," Arredondo said. "We'll never say anything."

"He used to come over to my house."

"That doesn't answer the question," Arredondo said.

"Lieutenant Harger is a very visual person," she

said with a wry smile. "He used to bring his Polaroid and take pictures. He would set the timer and then jump on the bed and we would be doing it. I still have some of the shots. He has a cute butt."

"The man likes exposure!" Black shouted into the din of laughter.

During what was left of the night, the cops continued the poker game and drank heavily. Brenda, who seemed pleased at having been invited to the gathering, either listened in awe as the detectives recounted the shooting over and over again, served beer, or administered efficient blow jobs to whoever led her to the semi-privacy of the upper bunk at the rear of the motor home. Perhaps because Black and Arredondo made two trips each, no one noticed that Stepanovich hadn't availed himself.

As the sun was coming up, everyone was at that point of inebriation where every utterance sounded profound and utter nonsense was defended as perfectly logical.

"We need some fucking T-shirts that say CRASH," Arredondo said.

Stepanovich, who'd folded his cards earlier, sat in the passenger seat with his eyes closed, thinking of Gloria. He had considered leaving more than once during the long night, but he didn't want to be the one to break up the party.

"Belt buckles," Fordyce said, slurring his words. "I know a guy who makes specialty belt buckles."

Black guzzled beer and belched. "Silk jackets. That's what we need. Black ones with CRASH written on the back." Everyone laughed.

Arredondo finished his beer and tossed the empty can into a cardboard box. "We're outa beer. *No mas cervesa.*"

Fordyce climbed behind the wheel. "I know a place that's open," he said, starting the engine and slamming the car into gear. The motor home lurched as he steered over a curb and into the street and past dingy warehouses and loading docks.

"How about a medallion?" Brenda said proudly. "I like medallions. Like the ones from that place that advertises on TV. They make 'em to order."

"What the fuck you talking about?" Black said.

Brenda sipped beer. "You guys remember the Lone Wolf? The TV detective? He would solve the case and leave this wolf medallion. It was pure silver."

"How do you know it was pure silver?" Black said.

"Do you always have to be such a jerk?"

"Yeah," Arredondo said, "at the end of the show some whipdick would find the medallion and hold it up and say: 'It's the sign of the Lone Wolf.' "

Black popped another beer. "If I was the whipdick who found it, I'd just shove it in my pocket and shag ass to the nearest pawnshop."

"We need some fucking medallions," Fordyce said. His eyes were rimmed with red.

Black belched loudly. "I got your medallions hanging."

"Keep your eyes on the road, amigo."

Brenda moved to Stepanovich and sat heavily on his lap. "Why are you so quiet tonight?" Smelling her cheap perfume, he shrugged.

"Brenda's got a pair of medallions," Fordyce said.

Black shoved open the door and tossed out an empty. "Fuck the Los Angeles Police Department right in its dirty ass."

"If it wasn't for the police department you'd be shoveling shit on a farm," Arredondo said, discovering one last beer in a six-pack container. He popped open the can. "You wouldn't be shit."

"And you'd be right there working for me, homeboy."

"Where are we going?" Brenda said as they reached the Fourth Street Bridge.

As they crossed it, someone suggested tattoos. Though later Stepanovich was unable to remember whether it had been before or after they stopped at a liquor store and purchased more beer and a quart of whiskey, he was relatively certain it was Black who came up with the idea.

"We need some homeboy tattoos," he said.

Popping fresh cans of beer, they weaved past a backdrop of narrow, sooty streets lined with factory buildings and brick-front flophouses to the very pit of Los Angeles: Main Street. Lying in the shadow of L.A. City Hall, the street was lined with secondhand clothing stores, peep shows, fruit bars, grimy fast-food outlets, and shoe shine stands. A mixture of ex-cons, elderly poor, sickly winos, bag ladies, Mexican illegal aliens, and Marines on weekend leave from Camp Twenty-Nine Palms to roll queers, wandered up and down the street killing time.

Fordyce parked in a no-parking zone directly in front of a tattoo parlor he said he remembered from his first year on the job when he'd walked the Main Street police beat accompanied by a training officer. The tattoo parlor was a fading, hutlike structure interposed between an abandoned movie theater and a dingy cocktail lounge called The Circus. Stepanovich and the others popped cans of beer as they climbed out of the motor home and barged into the place. The walls were covered with colorful tattoo-size designs, and there was an overpowering medicinal smell.

"You guys cops?" said the owner, an intimidated tattoo artist with a ragged goatee and a pack of smokes rolled up in the sleeve of his dingy T-shirt. His face, the only part of visible skin that wasn't tattooed, was etched with lines. Stepanovich's sixth sense told him he was an ex-convict.

Black emitted a beer belch. "That's right, my man. We're the men from CRASH, so dig out some nice fresh needles."

"And women," Brenda said.

"Huh?"

"CRASH," Black said. "You've heard of the FBI and the CIA? Well, that ain't diddly squat compared to CRASH—Community Resources Against Street Hoodlums. We kill gangbangers."

"We knock their dicks in the dirt," Fordyce said.

"Whether they like it or not," Arredondo added.

The men laughed. The tattoo artist said his name was Slim and recited the prices for tattoos.

"This is really stupid," said Brenda, downing a can of beer.

Black negotiated price as Fordyce, like an art connoisseur, took his time scanning the walls for an appropriate tattoo.

Because Stepanovich was drunk, he had trouble focusing on the various tattoos. One in a frame and much larger than the others depicted a smiling human skeleton waving a checkered racing flag. The inscription below the flag read: "THE WINNER." Probably because he was drunk, he suddenly had an overpowering sense of déjà vu. He felt as if he'd seen the tattoo on the wrists of a thousand people he'd arrested.

Fordyce pointed to a design. "Here it is."

Slim lifted the design from the wall and the others gathered around. It was a three-dimensional crucifix, the kind favored by East L.A. gang members. Everyone readily agreed it was the perfect unit logo. As Slim readied needle and ink, Black, stripping off his shirt, insisted on being the first to be tattooed.

"I want a tattoo on my butt," Brenda said.

To Stepanovich it seemed they were in the stuffy parlor for an eternity.

TWELVE

That evening, Stepanovich woke up in his apartment lying fully clothed on his mattress.

He craned his neck to look at the clock radio. It was after ten and his bladder was full. Coming to his feet, he walked to the bathroom to relieve himself. At a dull ache throbbing from his ankle, he looked down. Then he held it up to the mirror on the back of the door. There, in an area he remembered that the tattoo artist had shaved with an electric razor, was a swollen, scabby green tattoo: the letters CRASH above a three-dimensional Latin crucifix.

Hazy, lightheaded from the beer and whiskey, he staggered back to bed. Lying there with his mouth dry and his ankle aching, he tried to remember how he'd gotten home. His mind wandered through a boozy haze to the image of Brenda lying nude from the waist down on a long table as Slim worked on her alabaster right buttock with his electric needle/Black, shirtless and tattooed, unashamedly pissing on the sidewalk in front of the place/Fordyce passed out on the floor of the motor home/Arredondo walking around the tattoo parlor in his underwear with beer cans in both hands.

Later, to ease his growling stomach, Stepanovich made his way into the kitchen and opened the refrigerator. It was empty except for a head of lettuce and a tomato. Using two heels of bread he found in the bread drawer, he prepared a tomato-and-lettuce sandwich with lots of mayonnaise. He gobbled down the vegetarian repast in a few bites, then returned to bed.

He slept fitfully for what was left of the night and awoke the next morning with a vivid picture of Greenie holding a bloody towel to his wife's head. He rubbed his eyes for a long time, as though to massage the thought away. Then remembering that it was Gloria's day off, he climbed out of bed and picked up the phone. The other end of the line clicked and he listened as a tape recording of Gloria's voice asked him to leave a message. At the sound of the tone, he recited his name and phone number, and set the receiver down. Then, realizing he was nearly late for work, he showered quickly and dressed.

On his way to the gang unit office at Hollenbeck Station he was stopped several times by other officers and congratulated on the shooting. He made his way down the stairs. There was no one else in the gang unit squad room.

The phone rang. It was his mother. In the background squeaked a metal conveyer belt.

"I saw the television," she said.

"I'm OK, Mom. There's nothing to worry about."

"I could tell something was bothering you. You've been acting like you did when you came home from Vietnam."

"Television always blows things up."

"You're in some kind of trouble, aren't you? I can tell by the tone of your voice."

"They had an shooting investigation, but that's normal."

"It's not normal to shoot people. I want you to get out of that gang unit. You can be a teacher at the police academy and get paid the same money. Let them find someone else to do that gang crap. You've been there long enough."

"I'll come over when I get a chance and we can talk."

"Don't treat me like one of your girlfriends. I'm your mother and I know what's good for my son."

"I know you're frightened because of what you saw on TV, but everything is OK, Mom. There is nothing to worry about," he said, staring at the desk.

There was the sound of a horn in the background. "I have to get back on the line," she said. "I'm going to go to church tonight and pray for you. Please be careful, son, I love you."

The phone clicked. Slowly Stepanovich set the receiver back on the cradle.

Harger stepped out of his office and motioned Stepanovich inside. As Harger closed the door behind them, Stepanovich saw on it a framed photo of Harger dressed in police SWAT team gear holding an M-16 rifle at port arms.

"How are you feeling?" Harger asked, moving to the hot plate in the corner of the room. He picked up a glass coffee pot, filled a styrofoam cup, and handed it to Stepanovich.

"Still a little hungover."

Harger filled another cup. "I just spoke with the Chief. He wanted me to extend unofficial congratulations to you and the others. He insisted I write all of you up for medals of valor. I've never seen him so positive and upbeat."

"And the shooting investigation is OK?"

"The Chief made sure you and the others came out clean in the final report," Harger said with a wry grin. "He's the angel watching over the gang unit." Without warning, Harger's expression suddenly turned hard. "Gimme one sentence on the effect of the shooting, Joe. Just between you and me. What does it mean on the street?"

"Both Eighteenth and White Fence lost face," Stepanovich said.

Harger sipped his coffee. "What's next? Give me the street gang big picture."

"Because of the shooting, they'll probably lay low for a while."

"Then what?"

"It's hard to say."

"I want you to look into that crystal ball for me. You know how these gang assholes think. What's their order of battle?"

Stepanovich sipped the bitter coffee as he reflected. "With Greenie's wife in the hospital, Eighteenth Street will be after blood. When the time is right, they'll come into White Fence's turf for a payback."

"How? What will they do . . . and where?"

"Their shooters will cruise Hazard Park. The first White Fence member they see gets blown up. If no gang members are around, they'll shoot whoever is there."

"Why Hazard Park?"

"White Fence turf is small and mostly residential— lots of cul de sacs. It's an easy place to get trapped after they shoot someone. On the other hand, Hazard Park is at the edge of their territory. They can open fire and speed onto the freeway. That's where they'll hit."

"A drive-by shooting," Harger mused on the way to his desk. With a furrowed brow he pulled his chair back and sat down. He made eye contact with Stepanovich. "I want you to be at Hazard Park waiting for them."

"The park'll be hard to cover."

Harger used an index finger to wipe a design in the moisture coating his coffee cup. "You'll manage," he said smugly.

"If we keep this up, eventually the gangs will figure out what we're up to."

"Then we'll change tacks, but until that time we're going to set up one trap after another. We're going to keep the heavy heat on 'em until every time they cruise for blood, they'll be worrying as much about us as the gang they are going to hit. I want to give them nightmares, then make the nightmares come true."

Back in the squad room, the others members had arrived and Stepanovich related what Harger had told him. As he spoke he noticed how pale and hungover everyone looked. Having completed the briefing, he stepped to the wall map of East Los Angeles posted above the copying machine. He pointed to a small green square on the left side of the chart representing Hazard Park. "If it's gonna be a drive-by shooting, they have to drive down Breed Street," he said, running his index finger along a black line on the north side of the park. "They'll either come off the freeway and make a left turn, or approach from Fickett."

Arredondo pointed at the map. "There's a wall right here."

"Right. If they're going to open fire they'll have to be at this end of the street. If so, afterward there's only one logical way to escape."

"You're right," Black said, studying the map.

"We'll never be able to mount surveillance on Hazard Park," Arredondo said. "The homeboys know that any stranger in the neighborhood has to be a cop."

"We could stake out near the freeway," Fordyce suggested.

Concentrating on the problem, Stepanovich leaned against the copying machine. Perhaps because of his hangover, the colors on the map—a thick red line for the freeway, the blue rectangle designating a housing project near the park—seemed harsh. He closed his eyes for a moment, picturing the park where he'd played as a child. He opened his eyes. "The freeway is too far away. If a shooting goes down we need to be close enough to respond. Otherwise, there's no point being there in the first place."

"We can use my motor home," Fordyce said.

"I'm afraid you're right. It's the only way we can

watch the park without the gangbangers knowing what we're up to," Stepanovich said.

Stepanovich and the others spent the rest of the day cleaning weapons, checking out equipment, and completing overdue reports. Though they hardly talked, Stepanovich felt a sense of anticipation among them, a sense of oneness he'd experienced only with his platoon in Vietnam. Because of the shoot-out and the wild night afterward, they shared a bond that no one on the outside would ever understand.

Around six they loaded the equipment into the motor home. Stepanovich informed the others to meet him in the station parking lot the next morning at five, and everyone headed for home. Concerned that Gloria hadn't returned his call, he picked up the phone and dialed her number. She answered on the sixth ring.

"Did you get my message?"

"No, I, uh, just got home."

"How would you like to go to dinner with a nice policeman?"

"I'm busy tonight," she said in a tone that told him there was something wrong.

"I thought this was your night off."

"Yes, but, I, uh, have a lot to do."

"Is everything OK?"

There was a long moment of silence. "We'll talk sometime."

"We're starting a surveillance tomorrow. I may not be able to call you."

"I have to go," she said softly. "Bye."

The phone clicked.

Stepanovich set the receiver down and left the office. The drive to Gloria's apartment took about five minutes. "What's wrong?" he asked as she turned away from the opened door. Closing it behind him, he followed her.

Gloria picked a newspaper off the coffee table and handed it to him. The headline read: "GANG COPS KILL

TWO." Below the headline was a poorly lit photograph of the front lawn of the Florentine Gardens city housing project. Lying on the steps leading from Greenie's apartment were two sheet-covered corpses. In the background, he, Arredondo, and Black were conferring together on the lawn. Because of the distance and the lighting in the photograph, their faces were blurry.

Gloria pointed at him in the photo. "Is that you?"

He nodded.

"One of the men you killed was a friend of mine," she said, her voice cracking. "Luis Nunez."

"Jesus."

"He and his family lived next door to me when I was growing up—"

"I had no idea who he was when it happened," Stepanovich interrupted. "We were on a stakeout."

"He'd been involved with the White Fence gang since he was ten years old. His whole family was involved with the gang." She walked to the window. "I always figured Luis would end up this way. Strange, isn't it? Luis, who's never held a job, who spent his whole life hanging on street corners and getting in trouble—never accomplished anything in his entire life—will now be a hero. All because he got himself killed by the police." She shook her head. "It's so sick."

"He and the others had guns—"

"Guns and shootings and gangs. Violence. I grew up with all that. It turns my stomach, Joe."

"Do you think I like it?" he said after a while.

Gloria brushed her eyes quickly with the back of her hand. "I think it's better if we don't see each other anymore," she said without looking at him.

"This is just—just something that happened," he said, "a one in a million chance—"

She turned to him. "This is what always happens. You're the one who chose to be 'out there on the street,' as you call it. It's the same thing the gangbangers say."

"It's my job."

"What kind of job is it to shoot people?"

"You act like we're from different worlds," he said angrily. "Don't forget, I was raised here too. This isn't Disneyland. This is East L.A. Your friend Luis and his homeboys shot three people."

"There's something you should know," Gloria said. "When I was growing up, the White Fencers were always around the house. My stepbrother Johnny ran with the gang. He was tough. He had a lowered Mustang and his nickname was Spider." She stormed toward him, her index finger touching the tiny scar close to the corner of her right eye. "See this? It used to be a teardrop tattoo before I had plastic surgery to remove it. I was a White Fence girl. A *cholita.*"

"I don't care about that."

"But then Johnny killed somebody from the Clover gang. He was convicted of first-degree murder and sent to San Quentin for the rest of his life. Just like that, Johnny was gone. I remember my mother, who'd begged him not to hang around with the gang, sold his car and gave away his clothes. Johnny'd been devoured by the neighborhood, by White Fence machismo. From that day on, I never spoke to another gang member. In high school I kept to myself. That's how much I hate the violence."

"Then why stay here in the old neighborhood?" Stepanovich said. "Why not move out and work at a hospital in Palm Springs or Beverly Hills?"

"Because the people in Palm Springs and Beverly Hills aren't my people. I'm a Chicana. My people are here: the bad and the good."

"Your kind of people shot a little girl in church the other day."

"I'm staying here to help."

"What do you think I'm doing? If it weren't for the Department, East L.A. would have killed itself years ago. I'm not going to apologize for being a cop."

There were tears in her eyes. "You're in it for revenge, not for the law. You're a *veterano*—like my brother Johnny and the man he killed. Shooters and victims—vengeance going all the way back to God knows when."

Stepanovich moved close to her. When she looked up at him, her eyes showed a weary anguish he'd seen on the faces of a hundred women who'd lost men to violence. He could see them, generations of mantilla-draped Mexican widows comforting each other at the cramped gravesites of Evergreen Cemetery. He touched her cheek. "What happened two nights ago has nothing to do with us," Stepanovich said.

"My brother was drawn into the darkness," she said. Stepanovich tried to embrace her, but she held him away. "You're just like him."

"There's nothing we can do about the past."

Soberly she wiped tears from her eyes. "I don't want to be consumed by the violence and hatred of this neighborhood."

"I can't help who I am," Stepanovich whispered.

"Being a policeman is more important than anything else to you. It's because when you're a cop, you're always in control."

"Do you want me to leave?"

"Yes," she said, her voice cracking.

THIRTEEN

Though it was sweltering outside, the air conditioner kept the motor home relatively comfortable. Stepanovich held the binoculars up to the opening in the black curtain covering the side window, and slowly he scanned the half block of brown-spotted lawn that was Hazard Park: a baseball diamond, a windowless cement-block public restroom, a swimming pool protected by a high chain-link fence, the all-day shadow cast over the eastern corner of the park by an elevated section of the freeway. The cement stanchions upholding it, the walls of the swimming pool, the aluminum bleachers behind home plate, the trunks of the park's eight trees, and every inch of sidewalk was sullied with spray-can gang graffiti.

Black was lying on his side in the motor home's upper bunk eating a sandwich. He wadded the clear plastic sandwich wrapper and tossed it at Fordyce. The missile hit him on the top of the head and bounced to the floor.

"Thanks, fella."

"Next time get something other than deviled egg."

Fordyce yawned. "You guys said get whatever I wanted. Well, I like deviled-egg sandwiches. When I was a kid I always ate egg sandwiches. My mom thought I was crazy—"

"Egg's good for you," Arredondo said, sitting across the table from Fordyce. He popped open an aluminum can of Coke. "It puts lead in the *chingas.*"

"Fordye doesn't need any extra bullets," Black said. "He can already hit the shower curtain."

The others laughed, but Stepanovich didn't join in.

"I'm tired of being the butt of every one of your stupid jokes," Fordyce said.

Black formed his mouth into an O and belched stridently.

"Do you have to do that in here?" Fordyce pleaded.

For the next few hours they took turns at the window watching a group of twelve-year-olds play baseball. At one point Arredondo spent what seemed like a full half hour announcing the events on the field as if he were a sports announcer.

Though he knew violence could erupt at any time, Stepanovich had difficulty keeping his mind on anything but Gloria. Over and over he reviewed their first meeting at the county hospital, their dinner at the Jade Tree Inn, their night together. He could feel her hands on the back of his neck. Finally he convinced himself it was better to do nothing. Hell, she would call him eventually.

That night at midnight, when the last park visitors had left and the lights in the park had been extinguished, Fordyce crawled from the motor home shell into the cab and started the engine. He drove to Hollenbeck Station, where they decided by mutual consent that they would separate to get a few hours' rest and be back at Hazard Park by the first light to avoid being noticed by the people living in the area.

The only message on his answering machine when Stepanovich arrived back at his apartment was one from the local cleaners telling him to pick up a sports coat that had been there for two weeks.

The second day of the surveillance he still couldn't get her out of his mind. She still hadn't called.

During the afternoon of the third day he realized that she was never going to call him. She was as stubborn as he was. If he was ever going to see her again, he would have to initiate the contact. That night, after concluding the surveillance, he drove straight to her apartment.

He knocked lightly on the door. No answer. He knocked louder. A light came on inside, followed by the sound of footsteps. The door opened. Gloria, dressed in a robe, was holding a book in her hands.

"I know it's late, but I'd like to talk."

She stood there for a moment without saying anything, then stepped back to allow him inside.

"If you don't want to see me anymore, I understand. But before that happens, I want to get something off my chest."

She motioned him to the sofa. When he sat down, she took a seat at the opposite end.

"I've been doing a lot of thinking for the past couple of days," he said. "I'm not here to change the way you feel about what happened. In fact, if the situations were reversed, I probably wouldn't want to see you again either. But I want you to know that the last thing in the world I would ever do is knowingly hurt you. I'm sorry about what happened."

"Thanks, Joe."

"I guess that's about it," he said after a pause. He rose to his feet and retreated slowly toward the door.

"I've been thinking about you too," she said.

"My job has always been more important to me than anything else . . . until the last few days."

"Joe, I gave up the values of the barrio a long time ago. But you didn't. That's what is standing between us."

"Values change."

"Can you change?"

"I'm not sure. But I'm willing to try."

Gloria stood up and came to him. She put her arms around him and nestled her head in his shoulder. "I don't want to be hurt."

"I'll never do anything to harm you." His lips moved to hers and suddenly he was lost in her softness, the smell of her hair, the sensation of her body close to his. "Since the day we met, I haven't been able to get you off my mind," he said when their mouths parted for a moment.

He carried her into the bedroom and they undressed quickly. Without hesitating, she took him and firmly guided him into her, and they rocked for a long, long time until they were both liberated from every care in the world.

Afterward, lying in bed with his arms around her, Stepanovich could feel the tingle of perspiration evaporating slowly from his neck and back.

"Let's go somewhere this weekend," she whispered. "I don't care where."

"I'm stuck on a stakeout," Stepanovich said softly.

"When will it be over?"

"There's no way of telling. We're expecting trouble at Hazard Park."

"There's always trouble in East L.A. The way to stop it is to change the conditions causing it."

"Let's not argue, Gloria."

"If the gangs would just leave each other alone. If the violence could stop . . . just for a while . . . maybe things would change."

"Maybe.

Soon he found himself aroused again and drew her close. Her velvety-smooth brown legs saddled him, and they were face-to-face, breathing hard, lost in each other.

Later, they showered together and dressed. In the kitchen Stepanovich helped Gloria as she prepared an elaborate Mexican meal, and they sat down to a quiet dinner of *steak picado, quesadillas,* and refried beans.

The next morning he woke early with Gloria in his

arms. His first thought was relief that she hadn't noticed the CRASH tattoo on his ankle. Or had she just chosen to ignore it?

Quietly disengaging himself from her arms, he slid out of bed. Into the bathroom he tiptoed for a long shower. Back in the bedroom, watchig her sleep, he picked up his holstered revolver from the dresser table where he'd placed it the night before and slid it onto his belt. Having carefully arranged it in the cross-draw position, he moved quietly to the side of the bed and knelt down. He kissed her on the cheek. Her eyes opened.

"I have to go to work."

Her hand touched his cheek. "Please be careful."

Outside, as he climbed in his car, he looked up. Gloria, wearing a white robe that seemed almost fluorescent in the morning sunlight, was standing at her bedroom window looking down at him. She waved and he waved back.

Driving off, he checked the rearview mirror. She was still watching him.

On the way to Hazard Park a female dispatcher cackled East L.A. emergency calls over the police radio: " . . . group with guns, possible gang activity. Fifteen sixteen Crusado Lane. 459 suspect there now at 2642 Drew Street. Suspect described as a male Hispanic, brown khaki pants, white T-shirt attempting to enter residence through rear window. PR is in a car across street from the location. Ambulance cutting: 3200 North Broadway at the gas station. Vandalism suspects spray-painting a garage door. Any unit in the vicinity, gang activity, possible narcotics involved at Pecan Playground First Street and Pecan. All units and Four Adam One, a shooting in progress, 2932 Greenwood Street, Apartment B . . ." Rather than listening closely to the transmissions as he was supposed to, Stepanovich was caught up in reliving his night with Gloria.

* * *

EARTH ANGELS

By the ninth day of the surveillance, the incessant metallic hum of the motor home's air conditioner had become an unending source of irritation to Stepanovich. For what seemed like the thousandth time, he used the binoculars to check the park. By this time he'd become an authority on the park and everything around it. Hell, he could diagram every inch of the place . . . or write a book about it. Because nothing had happened in nine full surveillance shifts, he knew the book would rank among the most boring in history . . . until today.

Today, he could tell, something was wrong.

The only people in the park were a couple of elderly Mexican men playing checkers on a park bench and a group of young boys tossing a football.

"It's Saturday," Stepanovich ruminated. "There should be a lot more people in the park."

Fordyce, who was sitting at the table resting his head on his arms, stirred and sat up.

"Something's up," Stepanovich said. "I can feel it."

Fordyce rose and joined him at the window. "I don't see anything out of the ordinary."

"There should be a lot of picnickers here by this time of day."

Black climbed off the bunk and checked outside. "Maybe they all went to the Dodgers game," he said.

"The Dodgers are playing in New York," Arredondo said, tugging back the curtain to check for himself.

"Maybe the gangbangers know we're here," Stepanovich said.

"There wasn't a soul on the street when we parked here this morning," Fordyce said. "It was dark. Besides, there are other motor homes parked on the street. We don't look out of place."

Nothing else was said for what seemed like a long time. Black opened a can of Coke and guzzled it. Arredondo took his time unwrapping a second sandwich. Then he chuckled. Stepanovich recognized the chuckle as a signal he was going to tell a cock story.

"Last night Christine and Gilda joined the beaver club," he said.

"What's that supposed to mean?"

"They came over to my apartment and they went down on each other."

"Bullshit," Fordyce said.

"I swear to God."

"Let's hear the details," Black said.

"A coupla weeks ago I'm having a few drinks with Christine. She's drunk and we're just talking shit and I asked if she would let a broad go down on her. Like it's a theoretical question. Not that she would have to do anything, but just if she would lay there and let another broad eat her pussy—"

"You're sick," Fordyce interrupted. "Really sick."

"Let him finish, goddammit."

Arredondo sipped his Coke. "Good 'ol Christine kind of laughs and says maybe. Right then I knew I had her. 'Maybe' means they've been dreaming about it. Then last night Gilda comes over to my apartment after work. I ask her the same question. She says maybe. So when Gilda makes a trip to the john, I hop on the phone to Christine and invite her over. It was a little strained at first, but I make the introduction and mix a couple of drinks. Pretty soon they're talking real nice. When Christine is out of the room for a minute, I tell Gilda that Christine begged me to call her." He laughed.

"Don't stop there, cowboy," Black said.

"By midnight the three of us are in bed, and I have Earth Angel playing on the ol' tape player. It was all tits and clits, a real circus act. They were really chowing down on beaver. I'm talking hair-pie frenzy. Then they took turns blowing me and when I reached my rocks I came all over their faces and they lapped it up like a couple of dogs."

"Sick," Fordyce said. "Warped."

"Sounds like good clean fun to me," Black said.

"The bitches were really working out," Arredondo said.

Black cleared his throat. "The only problem, amigo, is that I saw Gilda at the Rumor Control last night. She was there until two."

Arredondo coughed nervously. "This happened the night before."

"You know, you've got some great stories. But come to think of it, I've never seen you with a broad."

Arredondo's face was flushed. "Just what is that supposed to mean?"

"Nothing."

"You calling me a liar?"

"It's just that for a guy who claims to be the king of the dicks, no one's ever seen you with a woman."

"Except Brenda," Fordyce said.

Black laughed sharply. "And she doesn't count because she'd fuck the Ayatollah Khomeini if he showed her a badge."

Stepanovich, choosing to avoid the discussion, turned toward the window. Just at that moment a black four-door Chevrolet slipped slowly around the corner and drove past the motor home. The windows of the car were tinted, eerily masking the driver and any passengers from view. The Chevrolet cruised slowly down Hazard Street to the other end of the park, near some metal swing sets and slides, then made a U-turn and pulled in at the curb facing back down the street. Stepanovich picked up the binoculars and checked the car. "Lowriders in a black Chevy," he said. "They've parked down the street facing this way."

Fordyce sidled next to Stepanovich in order to get a better look. "Tinted windows."

Stepanovich adjusted the binoculars to focus on the front of the car. "No front license plate." He felt his abdominal muscles tighten.

Now Arredondo took a look. "Probably just some White Fence homeboys out to smoke a little weed.

'Let's go down to the park and smoke some shit, man,' " he said, mimicking the *barrio* dialect.

Black moved to the small rectangular window in the bunk area and thumbed the curtain back. "Don't worry. Eighteenth Street shooters wouldn't dare park around here."

Stepanovich's eyes were riveted on the Chevrolet. The windows, reflecting the August sun, were rolled up all the way. He felt his senses quicken: the familiar, inarticulable feeling that meant danger.

Black leaned close to the port hole. "It could be some White Fence bangers toking up before hitting Eighteenth. Getting their balls up for a drive-by shooting."

Fordyce chuckled nervously. "That'd be all we need. We're sitting here waiting for Eighteenth to hit White Fence, and White Fence cruises over and hits Eighteenth."

Stepanovich checked his wristwatch. Only two minutes had elapsed since the Chevy had arrived. He swung the binoculars to the opposite side of the park. The group of boys who'd been playing baseball were hurrying out of the north end of the park toward the housing project across the street, looking back toward the Chevrolet. They climbed onto bicycles and pedaled away.

"Something's wrong," Stepanovich said.

There was the sound of Black clicking open the chamber of his service revolver to check the load. He snapped the cylinder shut.

Suddenly the Chevy began to move slowly in their direction. "The Chevy's moving . . . this way," Stepanovich said. The others crowded next to him to get a look out the window. He could hear the others breathing. "Something's up."

Staying close to the curb, the Chevy cruised slowly along the curb line parallel to the park. As it came closer, Stepanovich's binoculars caused his vision to blur. He pulled them away to get a better view.

At that moment the Chevy accelerated and swerved directly toward the motor home. The barrel of an automatic weapon extended from the left rear passenger window.

"Gun!" Stepanovich shouted, but the sound of his voice was swallowed by a heavy burst of automatic fire ripping through the thin aluminum and wood walls.

Fordyce shrieked. Stepanovich was struggling to pull his gun and get low at the same time. Shouts of "White Fence! White Fence!" came from outside.

Stepanovich slapped the door handle downward and propelled himself out the rear door, holding his gun in both hands. The Chevy was nearing the corner. He dropped to his knees and, aiming low to account for windage, fired all six rounds as the car made a right turn at high speed. From beside him came popping gunfire as Black and Arredondo also emptied their revolvers.

The car disappeared down Third Street.

Stepanovich, his ears ringing from the gunfire, hurried back to the motor home. Inside, Fordyce was lying on his back with his hands covering his stomach. His complexion was gray and his expression one Stepanovich had seen too many times before: the glassy-eyed, pleading grimace that meant impending death. Stepanovich knelt close to him.

Like a child, the speechless Fordyce lifted his hands from his torso for a moment to reveal a silver-dollar-sized blood spot spreading under his rib cage. "Don't let me die," he said. There were tears in his eyes.

Out of breath, Arredondo used the walkie-talkie to transmit a request for an ambulance. The dispatcher immediately acknowledged the request.

Fordyce coughed harshly and arched in a spasm of pain. Stepanovich took his hand. "You're gonna be OK," he said, though it was clear to him the opposite was more likely.

"The paramedics are on the way," Arredondo said.

Black pulled a blanket from the bunk, folded it into

a pillow, and placed it under Fordyce's feet. As Fordyce coughed a few more times, Stepanovich lifted his neck to keep his airway clear, as he'd been taught in the emergency first-aid course at the police academy. Fordyce continued coughing and Stepanovich, overwhelmed by a sense of helplessness, looked up at Arredondo and Black.

Fordyce's breathing became labored. His mouth opened and he began to gasp uncontrollably. Eyes wide, his tongue protruded and he retched violently and disgorged a mouthful of dark, foamy blood. Quickly his skin took on a bluish-gray tinge, a color Stepanovich associated with many of the soldiers he'd helped load onto Medevac choppers in Vietnam, with heart-attack victims and gunshot victims he'd helped since becoming a cop. It was the cast of death.

The sound of a screaming siren drew closer and two paramedics, a young black man and a husky woman, rushed into the motor home and began to work on Fordyce. Stepanovich stepped out onto the street, which was in the process of being barricaded from both ends by arriving patrol cars.

After conferring with a uniformed officer, Black turned to Stepanovich. "A priest is on the way."

Stepanovich nodded. Suddenly feeling lightheaded, he turned toward a crowd of Mexicans gathered on both sides of the street. He wanted to fight, to cry, to chase them away.

FOURTEEN

At L.A. County General Hospital, Harger was waiting for him at the emergency room door. Stepanovich briefed him on what had occurred, and Harger hurried to a phone. Suddenly a police squad car driven by a young uniformed officer sped up the ramp leading to the emergency entrance and came to an abrupt stop. Stepanovich opened the passenger door and Father Mendoza, an overweight Roman Catholic priest with thinning hair swirled to cover his balding pate, stepped out. Stepanovich introduced himself and led Mendoza through hospital doors, down a hallway, and into a crowded emergency room, where medics were ministering to Fordyce. Without saying a word, Mendoza kissed his tippet, draped it around his neck, and edged in between two green-gowned nurses to lisp the sacrament of the last rites.

Before he'd finished, Fordyce's terrified parents, a well-groomed, gray-haired couple who looked like brother and sister, were ushered into the emergency room by Arredondo. As they stood there holding hands, clutching one another, Stepanovich noticed, God knows why, that they were wearing the same walking shoes as in the photo inside Fordyce's motor home. Trapped in the tiled room with the sounds of scissors and ripping cloth, an Oriental doctor's commands in broken English, the clank of metal instruments, the crackle of needles being freed from sterile wrappings, of Mendoza's Latin chants, of the Fordyces crying, Stepanovich felt like he was suffocating. He found himself escaping out the doors and into the hallway. Black and Arredondo were standing in front of a vending machine.

"We should have realized White Fence might figure out what we were up to," Black said, handing him a can of Coke.

"We had no way of knowing."

"Somebody must have noticed the motor home parked at Greenie's place and figured we were using it," Arredondo said.

Black took out a package of filter cigarettes and ripped off the cellophane. "Doesn't matter how they knew we were there," he said. "The point is, we killed their homeboys and they came gunning for us. I give 'em credit for having balls. They have to know what this means."

Stepanovich knew that his face and neck must be bright red. He could feel the heat of his anger.

Harger stepped out of the emergency room. Advancing to the men, he spoke in a subdued, official tone. "Because this is an officer-involved shooting, major crimes division is in charge of the investigation."

"Fuck major crimes," Black said.

"They don't know shit about solving a gang case," Arredondo said.

Harger cleared his throat. "In my position, I can't really make any official comment. But you men know how I feel. Fordyce is one of us. This should be our case."

"We can put this case together on our own without interference from a bunch of third-floor prima donnas," Stepanovich said.

Harger put an arm around Stepanovich and led him away from the others.

"I've spoken with the Chief," he said as they walked.

"He wants CRASH to stay on this as long as it takes—but unofficially. If you guys come up with the shooters before major crimes does, then so be it."

"That means the Chief is giving us the go ahead?"

"His exact words to me were: 'Bob, in the old days, when an officer was shot we had an unwritten code about what to do when we found the shooter.' Need I say more?"

"You're saying he wants us to catch 'em and kill 'em?"

"That's a ten-four. He feels that if the gangs get away with this one, no policeman is safe in this city. He's not talking a few arrests and a long trial to clear the books. He wants notches on the gun."

"There's always a risk in this kind of thing."

"I'm well aware of that. And I'll certainly understand if you don't think you can handle it."

"That's not what I'm saying," Stepanovich said, restraining his emotions.

Harger put his arm around him. "Of course. I apologize for coming on so strong."

"I'm ready and the others are ready, but I just want to know whether we're going to be on our own or with help from the top."

"I'm standing here as a man telling you the chief of police will back anything you think you have to do to get the fuckers that shot Fordyce. If heat comes down, the Chief and I will be there to take it with you. This city is in a war and he intends to win."

"This can't be done without some heavy moves."

"Do whatever you have to."

Their eyes met for a moment. Then Harger slapped Stepanovich on the shoulder and headed down the hallway toward a cluster of uniformed officers, detectives, and hospital employees.

Someone touched Stepanovich and he whirled about. It was Gloria. There were tears in her eyes and she looked visibly shaken. As they embraced, she said, "I saw all the policemen and thought you were the one who'd been shot."

He wanted her arms around him forever. "I love you," he whispered.

"I've missed you so much."

"I'll have some time off, soon."

"What's wrong?"

She shook her head.

"There's nothing to worry about."

"Sometimes I wish I'd never met you," she said.

"You're just upset. We're all upset. But this isn't for you. It's just . . ." His words sounded hollow to himself, and he could tell they sounded the same to her.

She turned away, using a Kleenex to wipe her eyes. The tiny scar near her eye seemed a deeper red. There was a look of defeat in her eyes . . . or was it fear? He reached out to touch her, then thought better of it.

"I have to get back to my ward," she said. "When will we be able to have some time together?"

"Soon. This will all be over soon."

She nodded gloomily and walked away to answer a call from the nurses' station. She returned to be with him as she continued her duties during the day and later obtained permission for him, Black, and Arredondo to wait in the staff lounge rather than the hallway.

Around five, Stepanovich left the room and found a water fountain in the hall outside the emergency room. When he leaned down to take a drink, the water was cold and hurt his teeth.

Suddenly the emergency room door swished open, and out drifted a rush of hospital air, carrying the awful odor of alcohol, Lysol, and nervous perspiration. The young Oriental doctor, dressed in a green surgical gown, stepped outside and looked about for a moment. Then he spotted Mr. and Mrs. Fordyce.

Silence descended on the hallway as he walked toward them. "I'm very sorry, but your son has expired," he said. Mrs. Fordyce's knees buckled, and she and Mr. Fordyce broke into loud, uncontrollable sobs. Harger and the doctor helped them to a bench.

Stepanovich felt his eyes glaze with tears. He, Black, and Arredondo threw arms around one another. Harger joined them in the mutual embrace, and Stepanovich could feel the strength of Harger's hand grasping the back of his neck and smell the tobacco odor on Black's coat.

Later, in the hospital parking lot, Stepanovich, Arredondo, and Black huddled next to a police car. As Stepanovich used a hand to shield his eyes from the harsh pink light of dusk, he asked, "What do we have at the scene?"

"The shell casings in the street are nine-millimeter parabellum," Arredondo said. "They probably shot at us with a Uzi."

"There's no record of any White Fence member having access to a submachine gun," Black said.

"And no one in the gang drives a black Chevy," Stepanovich ruminated.

Black lit a cigarette and exhaled some smoke. "No one. I checked the file."

"That means they have a caper car stashed somewhere," Stepanovich said. "Without it we have nothing."

"A black Chevy with bullet holes," Black said. "I'm sure we hit it at least once."

"The word from the Chief is if we find the shooters before major crimes, we own 'em," Stepanovich said. "This is with full backing from the top."

Arredondo slammed fist into palm. *"All right."*

"Let's go for it," Black said.

Stepanovich turned away from the dying sun and ran his hands through his hair. "We have to find the Chevy."

Black took a long drag on his cigarette. "My guess is the wheels are still right here in East L.A."

"It's where we start looking," Stepanovich said, reaching into the driver's window of the police sedan for a city mapbook lying on the front seat. He dropped it on the hood of the car and flipped pages to a map of East L.A. He reached into his pocket for a pen and marked the map into three areas. "These are the places White Fence has been known to stash caper cars."

"It'll take us all night to cover—"

"We're going to split up to save time," Stepanovich interrupted, pointing to the map. "Black, you take City Terrace and this area all the way to Eastern Avenue. Raul, handle from Diamond Street all the way to Sunset. I'll cover the Gardens and the stash areas along the freeways."

"And if we spot the car?" Arredondo said.

"Just stake it until all of us get there. If you complete your search area and find nothing, head for Manuel's taco stand. We'll meet there. And stay off the radio unless you have an emergency. I don't want everyone in the Department knowing what we're up to."

Stepanovich drove them to Hollenbeck Station, where they picked up two more police sedans from a sleepy garage attendant. With little else said, the three men climbed into their cars and drove out of the station lot.

Stepanovich began his search on a dirt road paralleling the freeway near Wabash Avenue. He'd once found a stolen pickup truck used in three drive-by shootings here below the freeway. The road was deserted and the air seemed to vibrate with the sound of trucks and cars whizzing by overhead. Near where the road merged with a paved street, he parked and climbed out of his sedan. Using his flashlight to guide him, he walked hesitantly in the darkness to a shallow gully behind some magnolia trees, a place so hidden from cursory view of any passing police patrol car he would have picked it himself for a stash location.

There was nothing in the gully but trash.

Stepanovich, cold and invisible in darkness, returned to the sedan. At the sound of a car backfiring on the freeway he recalled himself in the motor home, trapped among the others as it was being pierced by gunfire. Then Fordyce was looking up at him, taking his hands away from his chest to show his mortal wound.

With the bitter warmth of tears in his throat, Stepanovich reached out to the sedan to steady himself. He shuddered and a sob came from his lips—an alien, embarrassing sound. He lifted his hands from the car and slammed them down violently on the fender, stinging his palms. After a moment he took out a handkerchief and blew his nose, took a few deep breaths, and climbed back in the sedan. He sped along streets in his search area like a robot, stopping now and then to make sure the black Chevy wasn't hidden behind trees or shrubbery.

It was two by the time he completed his part of the search. Manuel's taco stand was nearly deserted. He swerved into the small parking lot and pulled his sedan into a space directly between Black's and Arredondo's sedans.

They were prudently sitting at one of the wooden picnic tables behind the stand rather than at the sidewalk tables, where they would be a target for shooters. Stepanovich advanced to the counter and ordered three tacos from Manuel, who prepared the order and placed them in a small gray cardboard tray. Stepanovich made a show of trying to pay, but as he expected, Manuel refused to accept payment and said in Spanish not to insult him. When Stepanovich had brought the tacos to the table and took a seat, he didn't have to ask if the others had found the caper car.

"If it was me," Black said as Stepanovich dug into his first taco, "I'd stash my caper wheels outside the city—in Pomona or Bakersfield or Uncle Chuey's garage in Tijuana. On the other hand, if I was a real smart *chongo,* I'd drive the fuckin' car out of town and set a match to it . . . or maybe drive it over a cliff."

Arredondo spun the cap off a small bottle of bright red Pio Pico hot sauce and reached across the table for one of Stepanovich's tacos. "A gangbanger would never torch his car," he said, thumbing open the taco and drenching it with Pio Pico.

"I agree," Stepanovich said. "The car is probably still somewhere in East L.A."

Black finished his Coke. "We've looked everywhere."

"If I was a White Fencer and my wheels were hot, I might head out of my own turf to stash," Stepanovich offered.

Black nodded as if he liked the idea. "After killing a cop there's no telling what they might do."

"White Fence has been getting along with the Happy Valley gang for the last few months," Stepanovich said. "That's where I'd go."

After they finished eating, Stepanovich followed the others back to the motor pool, where they dropped off their sedans. They climbed in Stepanovich's car and he took a shortcut down Griffin Avenue to Lincoln Heights. He cruised past Lincoln High School and made a right turn into the area known as Happy Valley: a residential vicinity comprised of older wood-frame dwellings and stucco apartment houses tied together by alleys, sluiceways, and power lines. He shifted down into low gear and steered the police sedan to a winding snail track of a road leading past deteriorating cracker-box homes jutting from the hillsides.

Stepanovich drove carefully in the morning darkness, stopping three times to check out dark-colored Chevrolets. As they climbed, he felt exhaustion creeping up on him, and because the conversation in the car had dwindled to nothing more than a grunt when someone spotted a car, he could tell the others were just as used up as he was.

By four Stepanovich had traversed every street in Happy Valley. The rim of Happy Valley leading to the east had a view of chapparal-covered hills separating the valley itself from the teeming suburb of El Sereno, and there he drove beyond the paved street and onto a level dirt road recently formed when earth-moving machines had scraped off the crest of the hill. If he remembered correctly, an article in the *Los Angeles Times* said the road had been built by a developer who'd promised to deliver low-cost housing to the city, but had flown to the Cayman Islands with the allocated city housing funds shortly after the grading was completed.

At a wall of high grass marking the end of the road, Stepanoich stopped the car and set the emergency brake. Leaving the headlights and ignition on, he stepped out of the sedan and was met by the aroma of damp earth and grass. To the southwest the lights of the city meshed into a carpet of white dots extending to a bank of downtown high-rise structures. Even farther in the distance, a tiny flashing red light protected the top of the Los Angeles City Hall from being sheared off by low-flying aircraft.

"This is where lowriders like to bring their women," Arredondo said, following him out of the sedan with Black. "You know. Lean back on the front seat of the old Chevy and watch the city lights while Concha eats the standing rib roast."

Black yawned. "Inspiration point."

Stepanovich used his flashlight to check the soft dirt of the clearing. There were indentations that could have been made by tires. He stepped a few feet to the end of the cleared area and moved the light slowly along the edge of the grass. The circle of yellow picked up some broken branches on the ground and two heavy indentations that seemed to enter the grass. He leaned down for a closer inspection. "Tire tracks."

Stepanovich kicked the branches aside. The tracks led directly into low chapparal.

Keeping their flashlights trained on the ground in front of them, the three pressed forward, following the path of the tires through the underbrush. In the midst of his exhaustion Stepanovich felt a surge of adrenaline.

Just where the path began to lead downward, it turned behind a wall of cypress trees to a gouge in the earth—neatly hidden from view of the street below.

The beams from three flashlights danced on shiny black steel.

"Hijo fucking *la,"* Arredondo said in awe.

In the recess was a black Chevrolet with tinted windows. The front bumper had no license plate.

Before approaching the car, Stepanovich and the others circled the Chevrolet, using their flashlights to painstakingly check the ground for clues. This search went on for a long time, but they found absolutely nothing of value: no weapon, no scrap of paper. And because of the heavy brush and dry, sandy soil, not even so much as a footprint.

With the exterior search completed, Stepanovich stepped down into the shallow ditch to get closer to the car.

Black aimed the beam of his flashlight on the trunk. It had three bullet holes. "We hit him."

Noticing that the front passenger window was down a few inches, Stepanovich beamed his flashlight into the interior of the car. There was nothing visible on the seats or the floorboard. He reached into his pocket and took out a ballpoint pen. Carefully, in order to preserve any fingerprints, he touched the pen to the door lock and pushed firmly. The lock made a snap sound and he pulled the door open. Inside, the glove compartment door was open but empty. There was no dust or smudges on the dashboard. He leaned down to the floorboard and used the flashlight to check under the seat. Nothing.

At the corner of the dashboard he located the tiny aluminum strip bearing the vehicle's identification number. Using the pen and a scrap of paper he dug from his trouser pocket, he copied it carefully. Arredondo, who was standing in the doorway watching him, took the paper out of his hand and headed back toward the police sedan.

"It's clean," he said, coming to his feet.

Black was checking the backseat area. "That's a ten-four." He said. "Nothing back here either."

As Stepanovich and Black removed both the front and rear seats of the car and continued to search, they heard the distant sound of Arredondo's voice transmitting the car's identification number via the police radio.

With the interior search completed, Stepanovich rounded to the trunk of the Chevrolet. Using a handkerchief, he opened the trunk and held up the lid. The trunk area, including the indentation for the spare tire, was completely empty. "Looks like they cleaned up before they left," he said.

Arredondo returned from the police sedan. "This car is a Hollenbeck stolen—taken from Sears and Roebuck parking lot over a year ago. It's a caper car all right."

"Call Sparky's tow," Stepanovich said. "We'll have it towed in for prints."

As Arredondo headed back to the police radio and Black began filling out a vehicle-impound report, Stepanovich suddenly felt exhausted, and the steel police-issue flashlight he was holding seemed inordinately heavy. He rubbed his eyes for a moment, opened them. Just then he spotted something in the bushes a few feet away and advanced closer to get a better look. It was a spray can of Four-Star spray lacquer.

"Looks like the homeboys were sucking some fumes before they did their thing," Black said, joining him.

Stepanovich carefully lifted the aerosol can by its plastic nozzle and carried it to the police sedan. He took a clear plastic bag from the evidence kit in the backseat and dropped the can into it. Using his ballpoint pen, he marked the bag with his initials and the date.

By the time the tow truck arrived, morning light was coloring the sky.

Sparky, the tow-truck driver, a fortyish man with a beer barrel, a walrus mustache, and a mask of motorgrease blackheads covering his nose and cheeks, climbed out of the cab. The grayish T-shirt he was wearing bore the words "SOLDIER OF FORTUNE" and a depiction of a human skull wearing a U.S. Army green beret emblazoned across it. "Sorry about Fordyce," he said to Stepanovich.

Stepanovich nodded. "We think this is the car they used in the drive-by. Latent prints will meet us at the tow yard. I want it stored in the garage out of sight so the gangbangers won't know we have it."

"Yes sir."

As Sparky went about attaching a tow chain to the undercarriage of the Chevrolet, Stepanovich noticed that Black and Arredondo, obviously as exhausted as he, were standing at the edge of the slope just staring down into Los Angeles.

Sparky's towing-service and vehicle-impound yard, the largest in a row of dingy auto-salvage businesses lining Mission Road, was protected by a tall chain-link gate. Above the entrance a large metal sign read: "SPARKY'S OFFICIAL POLICE TOW." The silver police badge logo on the sign was a crude, hand-painted job, as was the lettering on the sign itself. Behind the fence the auto graveyard's oil-soaked ground was crowded with red-tagged vehicles, automobile engines on blocks, stacks of axles, transmissions, doors, and hubcaps of all kinds.

As police fingerprint technician Maxine Brown worked on the Chevrolet, Stepanovich, Black, and Arredondo were sitting on oil-stained folding chairs eating candy bars and watching. It occurred to Stepanovich that Brown, an obese, coffee-skinned woman with wide breasts and an unhealthy paunch, was wearing the same threadbare red sweater and baggy black trousers Stepanovich had seen her in for months. Unfashionable perhaps, but quite practical, he said to himself. Why maintain a large wardrobe to scrutinize blood-spattered bathrooms, dingy hallways, and automobiles?

Using a small feather brush, fingerprint powder, and clear tape, she painstakingly moved about the car in an almost automatic pattern. Methodically, without regard for time, she worked her way across the front seat, dusting the dashboard, then, lying prone on the seat for a while with her sweater inched up and revealing abdominal stretch marks, she worked on the steering column itself. Outside the car, she balanced on the running board to do the roof, then dropped heavily to her knees next to the car for the fenders and doors. Working on the bumpers, she maintained a sitting position, dipping dust and brushing with a rapid, sweeping motion like an artist painting sky. She crept sideways on her ample buttocks, working from end to end without regard to either modesty or the fact that she was on sticky, oil-stained cement.

By the time she finished, it was after two.

"Somebody wiped this car down real well," she said, coming to her feet. "Scrubbed the heck out of it. I couldn't even come up with a partial."

Stepanovich felt coldness in the pit of his stomach—and seething anger. "So there's nothing?"

"I didn't say that," she said, holding out a three-by-five card bearing a patent fingerprint affixed under a piece of clear tape. "I lifted a fingerprint from the aerosol paint can you found. It looks to me like a thumb. It's a partial—doesn't have enough points to testify on—but if you have suspects, it would certainly tell you which one did it."

"I want you to check it against the prints of every White Fence gang member in the bureau index."

"How many members they be having?"

"The White Fence gang has a thousand members, but you can start with the ones that are listed as shooters and work from there."

"I be working on it," she said, closing her attaché case. "Just as soon as I wash up and get me some lunch. But don't be calling the lab every five minutes to waste my time. Just soon as I get me a make, I'll get back to you."

"You can find me at—"

"I know where to find you," she interrupted on her

way out the door. "And if all else fails, I'll check at the Rumor Control." Then she climbed into a compact car with a City of Los Angeles seal on the door. She used a tissue to wipe her face, applied lipstick, and checked her appearance in the rearview mirror. She started the engine and drove slowly out of the lot and west on Mission Road toward downtown.

FIFTEEN

Back at his apartment, Stepanovich pulled the handful of letters and advertising pamphlets from his mailbox and carried it into his apartment. He opened a window to get some fresh air, then flopped down on the bean-bag chair. He touched the PLAY button on his telephone answering machine and heard the following message:

"This is Gloria. If you call my place and don't get an answer, I haven't disappeared. I'm working a double shift at the hospital. Love you. Bye."

Just the thought of her stirred a sexual excitement more powerful than his exhaustion.

The telephone rang. "Harger here. I'm going over to fill in the Chief, and I have a couple of questions."

"Shoot."

"Number one. Were there any clues in the car? Anything at all?"

"The only clue is a thumbprint on a spray can I found near the car."

"But it wasn't inside the vehicle."

"That's a roger."

"So it could belong to some painthead who left it there God knows when?" Harger said.

"I'm afraid so."

"What happened? The gang scenario as you see it."

"The Chevy is a caper car they keep hidden and use for drive-by shootings. They picked it up, drove to Hazard Park, and opened fire, then returned it to Happy Valley, wiped it down for prints, and left in their own car, taking their weapons with them."

"You're positive the Chevy is the right vehicle?"

"The car has our bullet holes: freshly made with no rust," Stepanovich said. "It's the one."

"Good work. Gotta run. The Chief is waiting."

The phone clicked.

Stepanovich set the receiver on the cradle and leaned back to thumb through the stack of letters. He yawned and closed his eyes for what he thought was just a moment.

When he opened his eyes, it was eight o'clock and he was leaning back in the chair with the letters on his lap. He'd slept almost five hours. He rubbed his eyes, then stripped off his sour-smelling clothes, and made his way into the bathroom.

After taking a long shower, he dried off with the last clean towel in the cupboard. He pulled on a clean pair of slacks, threaded his belt through the loop in his holster, and arranged it in cross-draw position. In the closet he found a freshly dry-cleaned sports coat, one of the three he owned, and freed it from its clear plastic laundry bag.

On his way through the living room he gathered up the stack of mail on the sofa and dug out an envelope he recognized as the monthly electric bill. That he put on top of the refrigerator, which was the only way, he knew from past experience, he'd ever remember to pay it.

Fordyce's funeral was held at the spacious St. Felicitas Roman Catholic Church in the suburban city of San Fernando, where Fordyce had lived with his parents. The semicircle of pews in the well-lit sanctuary faced a sacrament table centered on a carpeted platform. A shiny bronze coffin that Stepanovich assumed was made of some kind of durable plastic, was resting in front of the platform. Like other police funerals Stepanovich had attended, the chapel was filled to capacity with men and women in uniform. The silver LAPD police shields of the detectives, including the members of the CRASH unit and other officers in civilian clothes, were all shrouded in the same manner: a strip of black electrician's tape slanted diagonally across the badge's face and were pinned conspicuously to their jackets. The chief of police himself, a steel-eyed, athletic-looking sixty-year-old black man with distinguished streaks of gray in his frizzy hair, was sitting in the front row next to Harger.

After a young priest and two altar boys had made their ritual circuits around the sacrament table, Harger came to the lectern and, without notes of any kind, gave the eulogy. As he repeatedly used the words "service, dedication, and selflessness," Stepanovich relived the shooting over and over again, closing his eyes and picturing the black Chevrolet approaching the motor home to see if somehow he could drag an image of the driver or passengers from his memory.

It didn't do any good.

After the service, Stepanovich, Black, Arredondo, Harger, and a couple of Fordyce's male cousins acted as pallbearers. The casket was secured in a shiny black hearse, and it followed the police ceremonial motorcycle unit and a cavalcade of police vehicles with flashing red lights from the church to the nearby Rose Hills Cemetery.

There, in the heat of the day, the pallbearers carried the casket from hearse to graveside. By the time the priest had finished chanting in Latin and Fordyce's mother and father had cringed at the police rifle unit firing the required ceremonial rounds, everyone was drenched with perspiration.

At the conclusion of the service, Stepanovich joined a line leading to Mr. and Mrs. Fordyce, and expressed his sympathy again. After embracing them, he filed along with the crowd of cops heading toward the line of air-conditioned police vehicles. Stepanovich felt an overpowering rage. From the moment of the shooting, everything seemed a blur of flashing images: the hospital and church and funeral procession and Fordyce, now a corpse in a black uniform lowered into a trench.

Harger, standing in the shade of the only tree in sight, motioned to him. "Houlihan has been assigned the case by central bureau," he said furtively.

"A detective from internal affairs division handling a police homicide?" Stepanovich replied.

"Captain Ratliff assigned him the case," Harger said, speaking rapidly, keeping his eyes on the crowd of departing mourners. "Ratliff has support on the police commission and is making a move for the deputy chief's job. He sees the gang problem and Fordyce's murder as a sure way to get some publicity. Houlihan and Ratliff used to work Vice together."

"What do I say if Houlihan asks about our part in the investigation?"

"Don't tell him shit," Harger said as he looked past Stepanovich at the departing mourners. "The Chief wants *us* to make this case in our way. You have the complete backing of the Chief in keeping Houlihan out of the investigation." With a quick shoulder jab, signifying the end of the conversation, Harger moved away and greeted a group of high-ranking deputy sheriffs.

Someone called Stepanovich's name just as he reached his sedan. Recognizing Houlihan's voice, he felt the hair on his neck tingle. "I guess by now you've heard I've been assigned the Fordyce case out of major crimes," Houlihan said, slightly out of breath from hurrying to catch up.

"As a matter of fact, I hadn't."

"I know you CRASH fellas are out there beating the bushes on your own. I have no objection to that. After all, you're the gang experts . . . but I want to be kept informed."

"I'll keep that in mind."

"Have you come up with anything so far?"

Stepanovich shook his head.

Houlihan used the back of his hand to wipe perspiration from his upper lip. "We're all working toward the same goal," he said, waiting for a reply.

"I agree."

"The last thing I want is to have department politics get in the way of this kind of an investigation."

"Right." Stepanovich opened the driver's door of his sedan and climbed in.

Houlihan leaned down to the window. "Have you come up with anything so far? Anything at all?"

"Nothing. How about you?"

"We should probably get together to coordinate the investigation," Houlihan said. "You know, to avoid stepping on each other's toes."

"You'll have to take that up with Harger."

"Look, I know I'm a lieutenant and you're a sergeant, but we can speak man-to-man, can't we?"

"Certainly," Stepanovich said, looking him blankly in the eye.

Houlihan let out his breath in exasperation, then turned and walked away shaking his head.

Stepanovich pulled into the driveway at his mother's house. He entered without knocking, and Mrs. Stepanovich, wearing an apron, came from the kitchen and hugged him.

"I'm sorry about your friend," she said.

Because he could tell that emotion would choke his voice, he just shrugged and turned away. She followed him through a tiny living room decorated with obviously worn but spotless furniture: a sofa, a recliner chair, and a small oak coffee table that she refused to replace. As she herself put it, "Who am I trying to impress?" In the kitchen he opened the refrigerator, took out a beer, and popped the top. "Fordyce was a good policeman," he said.

"That doesn't matter to his mother. She doesn't care what he was. He was her son."

"What's that supposed to mean?"

"Every day you were in Vietnam I prayed for you. And when you came home, I thanked God and the angel that watched over you. I knew that nothing bad could ever happen if my son returned home safely from the war. God spared you and I was thankful."

"That was a long time ago, Mom."

"If you'd been killed, it wouldn't have mattered why."

"Fordyce died doing something he believed in—"

"He died for nothing!" she cried.

"I know you're upset, but I didn't come over here to argue."

"I don't want you fighting the gangs anymore," she said, rubbing her hands together nervously. "It's too dangerous."

"It's my job. We're working directly for the chief of police."

"Is it your job to get shot and lose your life? That's what the big shots said about Vietnam. They said it was worth dying for—as long as their boys weren't the ones getting killed. Vietnam was all for nothing and your friend Fordyce died for nothing. Piss on the chief of police! The son of a bitch!"

Stepanovich put his arm around her. "Don't cry, Mom."

She pulled away from him and ripped a paper towel from a cylindrical rack under the sink and dabbed her eyes. "I didn't raise you to get killed by *cholos.*"

"I want to introduce you to Gloria Soliz, a woman I've been going out with," he said as she blew her nose. "I was thinking Gloria and you and I can drive up to Jack Mornarich's ranch in Oregon when you get your vacation."

Pulling away from him, she opened the refrigerator, though he protested he wasn't hungry. Ignoring him, she served him a meal of fried ham, corn bread, and a green salad. They spoke little while eating.

"I know you're going to go after the ones who did it. I can tell by that look in your eye," she said as he took his plate to the sink.

"I've gotta get going, Mom. Thanks for the meal." He kissed her on the cheek and headed to the door.

"God could have never given me a better son," she said. "That's why I don't want anything to happen to you."

He opened the door and left.

At the Rumor Control Bar, Sullivan was sitting alone on a bar stool watching television. On the screen a lanky cowboy sauntered into a blacksmith's shop. Though there were no customers in the bar yet, the place would soon fill up as it did after every police funeral.

Stepanovich walked behind the bar and filled a cocktail glass with ice and scotch. Jiggling the glass for a moment to chill the booze, he took a big gulp. He felt the liquor's warmth descend in his throat.

"Actors," Sullivan said with his eyes fixed on the television screen.

From the way Sullivan pronounced the word, Stepanovich could tell he was drunk. "What about actors?" he asked.

Sullivan pointed to the television. "No normal man could. Dress up in chaps and a toy gun . . . and wear makeup—probably even lipstick."

"Actors make a lot of money."

"Millions of dollars," Sullivan gloomily agreed. "People worship them, they buy their diet books, put their pictures on the bedroom wall. Actors are some of the most powerful people on earth. They get elected president."

"So what's the point?"

"The point is: what kind of man would want to play dress-up for a living? Actually put on Maybelline eye shadow and strut around on a stage?"

"You'd have to be a little different, I guess."

Still staring at the television screen, Sullivan sipped his drink. "That guy on TV right there is probably a Hollywood queen: a daisy-chain tough guy. A weight-lifting, jizz-gurgling fruit."

"What the hell got into you?"

Sullivan hoisted his glass and threw his head back. The ice stuck in the bottom of the glass for a moment, then slid to his lips. Chewing it, he set the glass down and wiped his mouth with a cocktail napkin. "Fordyce was a believer," he said.

"You're drunk."

"I already know all the details of the shooting. You know how? Because half the station was in here after they cleared the scene. The divisional dicks sat right here and second-guessed your whole operation. They bad-mouthed the shit out of the CRASH special unit."

"They weren't there," Stepanovich said angrily.

"But don't let this bother you," Sullivan said with emphasis. "Cops talk about everybody. They like it when someone else fucks up. It makes them feel better about themselves. Gossiping. Backstabbing. It's part of police work."

"You've never heard me second-guess another cop," Stepanovich said.

"That's because you believe cops are better than everyone else. That they can save the world." He finished his drink. "You're a true believer like Fordyce."

"Let's change the subject."

"Fordyce was cannon fodder, a cog in the machine."

The sense of rage that had been swelling inside Stepanovich reached the back of his throat. His lips and face tingled with it. "Why don't you just shut the fuck up?"

Sullivan motioned in a threatening manner. "C'mon, copper. Make the bartender shut up. Pretend you're John Wayne like that asshole on TV. You gonna shoot me?"

Stepanovich reached across the bar and snatched

Sullivan with both hands. "I told you to shut your goddamn mouth."

Sullivan tossed his drink and Stepanovich felt ice and watery booze hit his eyes and nose. He yanked Sullivan over the bar and cocktail glasses broke. They struggled fiercely, slamming against racks of bottles and the sink. Then, suddenly, as Stepanovich stared at Sullivan's straining, bug-eyed alcoholic face, he realized what he was doing and released his grip.

Sullivan pulled away and stood there glaring at him.

"I didn't mean to do that," Stepanovich heard himself saying in embarrassment. "I'm sorry."

Sullivan, breathing hard, leaned back against the bar cupboard to steady himself. He unzipped his trousers and began tucking in his shirt. "Fordyce told me that when Harger picked him for the gang unit, it was the greatest thing that had ever happened to him in his entire life," Sullivan said, grabbing a clean chimney glass and dipping it into ice. "Before that, he thought everyone considered him a bookworm—a wimp."

Stepanovich grabbed some napkins and dried his face and the front of his shirt.

"Fordyce told me his mother and father were proud of him because he was a cop," Sullivan said combatively. Using his index finger, he gave the cocktail a quick stir, then took a sip. "That's what it's all about, isn't it? Making the family proud . . . status, authority . . . being one of the guys . . . carrying a piece, showing off for the neighbors—everybody has his own reason for being a cop. His own goddamn fucking deficiency."

Stepanovich moved from behind the bar and picked up his drink. Sullivan was drunk, but he wasn't crazy.

"Harger's probably trying to increase the size of the CRASH unit right now, having his secretary write the memo for him while he fucks her in his office. Two-gun Bob Harger, Mr. LAPD. Mr. Metro Division. Mr. Police Olympics."

"I thought you two were friends."

"I said we worked together," Sullivan said, leaning

171

against the bar stool. "That don't mean we're friends. It means I got to know the man."

"And you think he's a prick?"

"No," Sullivan answered, staggering from behind the bar to confront Stepanovich. "A prick is part of a man. Harger is a dildo. A rubber dick. A phony. A three-dollar bill. Ever heard the story about him overpowering a suspect and shooting him in the face? It's bullshit. The guy was a lunatic and killed himself by grabbing Harger's gun."

"So? That doesn't mean any—"

Sullivan fondled his drink like a chalice. "Heard about Harger being a big Vietnam hero?" he said. "More bullshit. He was in the Natonal Guard. How do I know? Because I know the guy who did the background investigation on him before he was hired. Harger is the ultimate bureaucrat—a tap dancer transferring from division to division, getting his career ticket punched along the way. He gets off on having everyone think he's the Chief's right-hand man." Sullivan finished his drink and spat ice back into the glass. Setting his glass down, he folded his arms and put his head down on the bar.

Though Sullivan was drunk, Stepanovich knew what he was saying was true. Unlike others he knew who would make up lies to get back at someone with whom they had a grudge to settle, Sullivan either said nothing or told the truth—depending on his degree of drunkenness. This, Stepanovich decided, was probably why Sullivan was chronically depressed. Or, hell, was it the other way around?

A group of detectives, including Black and Arredondo, entered the bar.

"Wake up, Sullivan, you sorry-assed-wino-beeroholic-fuckhead," Black shouted.

The phone rang.

Stepanovich reached over the bar and picked up the receiver. "Rumor Control."

172

"This is Brown from latent prints. Does Stepanovich be there?"

Stepanovich put a finger in his other ear to block the bar noise. "It's me, Maxine," he said, feeling a twinge of excitement. "Do you have something?"

"That partial thumbprint on the spray-paint can. It was made by the right thumb of a White Fence gang member named"—there was the sound of papers shuffling—"Primitivo Estrada, a.k.a. Payaso. I got his fingerprint card sitting right here."

"Can you testify to that?"

"There ain't enough points of identification on the print for me to take witness stand and say it be him and no other motherfucker on this planet Earth. But it be his print sure as shit. I pulled the boy's package. He's been arrested quite a few times."

"I know the name. Is there a current address in the file?"

She yawned. "Nothing current. Says here he was a victim of a shooting at the Queen of Angels Church—"

"I know about that, too."

"I hope this helps you."

"It sure does. And thanks for putting in the extra time."

"When an officer gets shot, I be working night *and* day," she said. "It doesn't bother me a bit. Now you be careful out there. Hear?"

Stepanovich said thanks again and set the receiver in the cradle. Motioning to Arredondo and Black, he took them aside.

"Maxine found a print on the spray can. It's Payaso."

"White Fence's Payaso?" Black said.

"That's a ten-four. I need to run a couple of things out on my own before we move. I'll call you here."

SIXTEEN

At the district attorney's office, Stepanovich located Howard Goldberg in the law library just off the reception area. Howard's wheelchair was pulled up close to a table piled with law books. A husky, bearded man, he wore a short-sleeved white shirt with two pockets filled with pens, pencils, and highlighting markers. His faded paisley necktie was dotted with a handcuff tie tack. He had heavy wire-rimmed eyeglasses with eye-magnifying lenses and wore a black yarmulke. Holding a bulging black-bread sandwich with both hands, he was leaning close to an open law book, nibbling as he read.

After the accident, Stepanovich remembered, while he had been pushing the wheelchair-bound Howard from his house to and from Carver Elementary School on Third Street each day, Howard would always be reading a book. He had the ability to carry on a full conversation and read at the same time.

Howard looked up, squinting because his eyesight was limited. "Joe Stepanovich?"

"None other."

Howard smiled broadly. "I hope you're not going to make me write some six-hour search warrant."

"I'm working on Fordyce's murder and I need some advice."

"Sit down, friend."

Stepanovich took a seat across the table.

Howard stared at him for a few moments. "You look awful," he said. He immediately reached into his black metal lunch pail and took out a sandwich wrapped neatly in clear plastic. He leaned across the wide table and set it in front of Stepanovich.

"No thanks."

Howard turned the lunch pail to display its contents. "Miriam sends four sandwiches to work with me every day. No matter what I say, it's always four. Rather than argue with her, I give three of them away. Take the sandwich."

"Really—"

"Take the sandwich. Unless you don't like liverwurst."

Stepanovich shrugged and said thanks. Only when he unwrapped the sandwich and took a bite did he realize how hungry he was. The liverwurst and tomato and onion seemed like the best sandwich he'd ever tasted. "I'd like to run something past you unofficially," he said.

"Prosecutors get in trouble giving out unofficial advice."

"You're the best deputy district attorney in L.A. County, Howard. I just want your gut feeling on something."

Howard squinted at Stepanovich for a moment. Suddenly he wheeled his chair away from the table, punched the door closed, and wheeled back. "No one will know we've talked," he said, taking off his glasses. "You have my word."

"A hypothetical situation—" Stepanovich began, not sure how to best protect his friend.

"Fuck hypothetical. Just talk."

"A drive-by shooting, a caper car is found a few miles away and near it—not in it, mind you, but near it—lying on the ground, is a spray can with a partial fingerprint of a known gang member."

Howard tugged his beard. "That's all?"

"There's no witness evidence because the caper car has smoked windows. No one got a look at the shooters."

"The gang member whose fingerprint was found," Howard said. "Can you tie him to a motive?"

"Fairly well."

"Guns?"

"No guns," Stepanovich said with his mouth full.

"You need a confession from Mr. Fingerprint."

"But Mr. Fingerprint isn't a singer."

"But, on the other hand, he might sing like Caruso if I charged him with murder and he faced sitting down in the gas chamber."

"Nothing short of that will get his attention," Stepanovich said, continuing to eat.

Howard lifted his glasses from his face and blew gently on the lenses. Rubbing the deep, reddish indentations on the bridge of his nose, he said, "So you want to know, even though the case is weak, whether you can get a court filing against the suspect in order to squeeze him for the names of the other shooters."

Stepanovich nodded solemnly.

When Howard set the glasses back on, the lenses caused his kindly blue eyes to appear tiny and deep-set in his eye sockets. "If an officer were to bring such a case in, I would have to tell him there was enough probable cause to arrest the suspect whose fingerprint was found, but not enough to hold him. Even if a friendly DA tried to file the case to help the investigating officer, he could never get it past Weber, my filing supervisor, whose only concern in life is to keep the office's conviction record high. I'm willing to help, but it won't work."

Stepanovich sat there for a moment. "Thanks, Howard. I'd appreciate it if you wouldn't mention I came in."

176

"We've known each other since grammar school. You don't have to say that to me."

Stepanovich felt somewhat abashed. "Sorry," he said, standing up to leave. "I didn't mean that—"

"Do you feel all right?"

"I'm OK."

"Your eyes look like two burnt holes in a blanket."

"Thanks again."

"I can imagine how you feel after what happened to Fordyce, but people make poor decisions when they're emotionally involved," Howard said as Stepanovich walked toward the door. "Sometimes it's better to take some time off."

In the courthouse underground parking lot, Stepanovich climbed behind the wheel of the police sedan and sat there for a few minutes, considering the alternatives. Then he started the engine and accelerated out the exit and into the street. In a trance of anger and frustration, he drove slowly, aimlessly. At a stoplight on Olympic Boulevard he found himself staring at a large advertising billboard depicting a small island in the middle of an enormous aqua blue ocean. Above the island were the words: "CATALINA IS TWENTY-SIX MILES ACROSS THE SEA." He stared at it until the car behind him tooted its horn. With his decision made, he swung a U-turn and stepped on the gas.

It took him less than ten minutes to get to the county hospital. Stepanovich moved briskly along the dimly lit hallways. Unlike the frenetic atmosphere during the day, the hospital corridors were empty except for a few clean-up men disdainfully mopping sections of hallway here and there. At the intensive care ward he pushed the swinging door open a few inches. Gloria was standing in front of a heart monitor machine with another nurse. She saw him and motioned to her colleague to take over. As she stepped into the hallway, he tried to kiss her, but she responded only politely. He noticed deep circles under her eyes.

"You get off in a few minutes, right?" he said.

"Yes."

"Catalina Island."

"What about it?"

"We're going to have dinner there."

"You're crazy."

"I'm driving you home to change, and we're heading to San Pedro to catch a boat."

"We'll never get on without reservations."

"Then we can take a helicopter."

"I really can't. I have too many things to do."

He took her by the arm and led her to the nurses' station.

After she had grabbed her purse and signed out, he drove her to her apartment, where, still protesting, she changed into a dinner dress. They were at the Catalina Island cruise boat dock in San Pedro within an hour, but Gloria had been right, the boat was full, so they were forced to take an expensive helicopter flight from the nearby Ports of Call village departure pad. Stepanovich was thankful they accepted credit cards.

Twelve minutes after taking off, they arrived at Catalina's Avalon Bay. It was dusk and as they descended, the island seemed to glow with its own peculiar richness: white cliffside homes looking down at a harbor faced by a street of ship-shape hotels and artificially weathered storefronts. At the end of town a curving esplanade led to the Greek-columned Catalina Casino and Ballroom, an impressive domed landmark from the thirties.

Climbing off the airship onto a long wooden pier, the youthful chopper pilot told them the last flight from the island was at eleven-thirty.

They walked along the pier to a narrow thoroughfare running between the beach and a line of hotels and shops facing the ocean. Meandering slowly along the strand, feeling the salt air and gently lapping waves and Gloria's arm in his, Stepanovich felt tension starting to leave him.

"I had forgotten how peaceful it is over here," she said.

"Thanks for coming with me. I had to get away."

"Getting away is part of it. But talking about your problems is what really helps."

They passed a candy shop with a taffy-pulling machine working endlessly in the window, a souvenir shop, a doorless bar filled with tanned young beer drinkers wearing shorts and T-shirts.

"It's not like you're the most forthcoming person in the world either," he said.

"Maybe I'm not," she said, without looking him in the eye. "But I guess we can't help the way we are."

He shrugged.

"Or can we?" she asked.

"What are you getting at?"

"Is it actually possible for you and me to change—to give up everything and live differently?"

"I'm not sure," he said.

"It all depends on what's important to you. Look at the people who live here. They gave up everything to live a peaceful life on an island."

"I could do that."

"I don't think so. I don't think you could ever leave your job."

They had dinner in a small Italian restaurant and were lucky to be seated before a window that offered them a view of the entire harbor. As they sipped Chianti, two sailboats beat the settling darkness, racing from beyond the rocks at the edge of the harbor and mooring in choppy water near the casino ballroom.

A spindly middle-aged waiter wearing an apron and a bow tie, who said he'd come to the island three years ago for a weekend and had never returned, served them solicitously all evening and soon they were stuffed.

"I'm sorry," Stepanovich said.

"About what?"

"I'm sorry for pulling you away from everything at such short notice."

"It's not that."

"Then should I ask?"

She leaned close and kissed him. "I don't want anything to come between us," she said, then put her head on his shoulder.

After dinner, they walked arm in arm along the boardwalk near the casino ballroom. A balmy ocean breeze wafted from the leeward side of the island and the bay itself, filled with swaying pleasure craft hiding from the blackness farther out to sea, glimmered metallic gray.

"It's after eleven," Stepanovich said, checking his wristwatch as they passed under a boardwalk street lamp. "We'd better get back to the helicopter."

"It seems like we just got here. What a wonderful evening."

He stopped and took her in his arms. "It doesn't have to end. We can stay here."

"But I have to be at work at ten tommorow."

He kissed her neck. "We can take the eight o'clock boat."

"We'll never get a room this late."

"It's Monday. We'll find one." He did not want to start looking just yet, though. Not taking his eyes from hers, he said, "I love you."

"I love you too."

They spent the night at the Sea Crest Lodge, a small hotel a block from the beach. The next morning they woke late because they had made love most of the night and missed the early boat. They had to take the helicopter again.

It was almost ten by the time they made it to the county hospital. Stepanovich parked in Gloria's spot in the employee parking area and walked in with her because he needed to use the telephone.

Having phoned Black and Arredondo from the nurses' station in Gloria's ward, a thought occurred to him. "I'd like to look at the medical records on Primitivo Estrada," he said after she came out of the nurses' lounge wearing her uniform. "The one who was shot at the church."

"I can get fired for giving out medical records," she whispered.

"I wouldn't ask if it wasn't important."

Her eyes focused on the filing cabinet in the corner. "Someone could walk in here any minute."

"Fordyce is dead. I need this."

"Go ahead, I guess," Gloria said mournfully.

A tall nurse with stringy blond hair stepped into the nurses' station. "Gloria, we need you in 301."

Stepanovich waited for Gloria to leave the room with the other woman and listened to the retreating footsteps down the hallway. He stepped from behind the counter and looked both ways. The hallway was empty. He advanced to the file cabinet and began pulling open drawers. The third drawer was filled with thick manila folders indexed with plastic tags with names and file numbers. One of the tags was marked: "ESTRADA, PRIMITIVO." He opened the file, flipping through pages of scribbled doctors reports until he found the patient information sheet. Estrada's home address was listed in the upper left-hand corner: 442 E. Ortega Street.

Stepanovich grabbed a ballpoint pen from the desk and copied the address onto a note tablet. He tore off the sheet of paper and shoved it in his pocket, then closed the file and replaced it exactly where he'd found it in the drawer.

In the hospital parking lot, he climbed into his sedan and drove directly to Ortega Street. Cruising at a moderate speed so as not to draw attention in the gang neighborhood, he eyed the bungalow where Payaso lived. Like the other rundown homes on the block, the tiny one-story structure was situated on a narrow lot with a patch of lawn in front. Like a seedy dollhouse, a couple of steps led to a tiny front porch supported by two painted wooden columns. Sitting in a chair on the front porch was a dumpy, heavily made-up Mexican woman whose hair hung to her waist. Stepanovich estimated her age at forty.

Rather than make another pass down the street and risk drawing the woman's attention, he made a left turn at the end of the block and drove away.

A few minutes later, Stepanovich steered into the well-lit Hollenbeck Station parking lot and pulled up beside Arredondo and Black, who, puffy-eyed from lack of sleep, were leaning against the side of a patrol car sipping coffee from vending machine cups.

"Payaso lives at 442 East Ortega Street," he said, climbing out of the sedan.

Arredondo blew steam from his cup. "Right in the heart of White Fence territory."

"I made a pass-by. There was a woman sitting on the porch."

"If we arrest him there, the whole neighborhood will know he's down," Black said, slurping the hot brew loudly.

"There's no case unless we get him to confess and give us the names of the shooters," Stepanovich said.

"Payaso's not a talker," Black said. "He's solid. He'll just sit there and hold his shit."

"Then I'll beat it out of him," Arredondo said.

"He'll take the beating, but he still won't hand up his homeboys. A dumb son of a bitch, but tough. He's a man."

Exasperated, Arredondo let out his breath angrily. He turned to Black. "You sound like a friend of his."

Black's mouth formed a sour smile. "I don't have any Mexican friends, *compadre.*"

As they stood there glaring at each other, Stepanovich stepped between them. "Look," he said, "I know we're all tired, but there's just the three of us carrying the weight. Let's forget the bullshit until we find out who killed Fordyce."

The two stopped glaring. Stepanovich went to the

sedan and reached in the open window to pick up a clipboard and pencil lying on the front seat. Then he began to sketch a rough diagram of the four-hundred block of Ortega Street.

SEVENTEEN

The lights in Smokey Salazar's crowded apartment were low and a cassette player resting on a card table in the bare living room was playing Puppet's favorite tune: "Earth Angel." Payaso could tell that the party might last through the night because though it had been going for only an hour or so, the homeboys had already gone through a case of Budweiser.

Though they all knew what happened because they'd all been in the car, he, Loco, Gordo, and Lyncho were huddled in a corner, listening to Smokey's version of what had happened. Retelling the details from the respective points of view of the shooters was a ritual Payaso was used to. There was always such repetitive conversation at a party after a "ride." Finally Smokey completed his account.

With this break in the conversation, Payaso, who'd been the driver during the ride, took a final acrid, tongue-burning drag from the joint he'd been smoking. He sucked in enough confidence to begin his version. "I was doing some heavy wheeling," he said, feeling secure in the homey atmosphere. "And when we got hit, the first thing I was thinking was 'I hope they didn't hit the gas tank,' " he said, though in reality he had been too frightened to be cognizant of such details when it was happening.

"We're gonna call you Speedy Gonzales," Gordo said, slapping him on the back, and the others laughed.

"Speedy Gonzales," Lyncho echoed. "Payaso is the Speedy Gonzales of White Fence."

Payaso smiled and shrugged. With the help of the marijuana, he easily imagined the Saturday morning cartoon character Speedy Gonzales: a long-nosed mouse wearing a sombrero and a serape. Good 'ol Speedy was only a mouse, but he was loved without qualification by both adults and children. Speedy was accepted by all for what he was. Payaso had never missed the Speedy show as a child. In fact, though hesitant to admit it even to his homeboys, he still watched the show regularly.

Holding the diminished roach with his fingertips, Payaso took a final puff and held the burning smoke in his lungs. He grabbed a cold can of beer from the case on the coffee table and popped a top. Throwing his head back, he gulped from the can until it was empty. As the effects of the roach and the chaser consumed him, he ascended to a state of utter relaxation.

As Lyncho began to tell the story of the shooting from his point of view, Payaso came to his feet and shuffled to the cassette player. The door to the tiny kitchen was open and the homegirls, Sleepy, Flaca, Sad Eyes, and Smokey's bride, Parrot, were sitting around a Formica-top table preparing tamales, laughing, and chatting in English and Spanish. All of them, even Parrot, were wearing tight-fitting blouses and pants.

Though Payaso knew Smokey would kill him if he ever said so, Parrot, with her skinny bird legs and bloated torso, looked like a pony keg on stilts. As usual, she was talking about what women always talked about—in fact, the only thing they ever seemed to talk about—men.

"Except for the days he was in the hospital, Smokey

hasn't left me alone since the day we got married,"
Parrot said. "I tell him, hey gimme a break, *cabron*.
I'm sore down there. But that don't mean nothing to
him. When he wants it he wants it. I mean like right
there on the floor in front of the television. I got rug
burns." The women laughed.

Perhaps, Payaso decided, all women were capable
of talking about was men. But it was different because
they avoided talking about men graphically as men
talked about women. Instead of saying "fuck," they
always said "we were doing it" or "he was down
there" or he wanted "some."

"He always wants it," Parrot said reproachfully.

Payaso turned to the window. Below, the well-lit
courtyard of the housing project was deserted because
everyone suspected the cops would be on the warpath
after the shooting. Feeling momentarily overpowered
by the combined effects of smoke and booze, he grasped
the windowsill with both hands to steady himself. Across
the courtyard, past some littered clotheslines, a primi-
tive mural covered the side of the apartment building:
a smiling, purple-robed Madonna riding in a customized Chevy convertible. Come to think of it, the
Chevy, right down to the moon hubcaps and pinstriping,
looked like the one he owned.

At that moment the cassette player made a clicking
sound and "Earth Angel" began to play again. Though
for the life of him he'd never been able to memorize
the words, he found himself swaying softly to the beat.
"Earth angel, Earth angel, will you be mine? My
darling dear, love you all the time. I'm just a fool. A
fool in love with you." Feeling an urge to get even
higher, Payaso considered popping some reds, then
suddenly remembered he'd taken the few remaining
pills he had left shortly before making the cruise to
Hazard Park to shoot the cops.

Hell, maybe he'd run down to the store for a can of
spray paint.

Sleepy came out of the kitchen. Payaso had always

been attracted to her big, healthy tits, black lipstick, heavy eye makeup, and long black hair ratted high. And he knew the feeling was mutual because since he'd been shot, she'd been hanging around him a lot. She'd accompanied Smokey and the others to visit him in his hospital room, and Payaso remembered the way she had sat on the edge of the bed and took his hand, allowing it to brush against her *chi chis* as they chatted. As a matter of fact, he'd been more than thankful neither she nor the others had noticed his hard-on bulging under the sheet.

"Are you hungry?" Sleepy said, flexing tit. Though high, Payaso noticed the others in the kitchen had stopped talking to eavesdrop.

"I never eat when I'm getting high," Payaso said, maintaining a stern macho expression.

"You should eat something. You lost weight in the hospital."

"Getting shot is nothing," he said in heavy barrio dialect. "I mean, it's like shit to me."

"Smokey said you were the driver two nights ago."

He nodded. "The pigs went down into the dirt. We rode on the pigs."

Avoiding eye contact, she sidled next to him. As he stood there, looking down at the courtyard and feeling high as a motherfucker, Payaso felt her hesitantly place her arm around his waist.

" 'Earth Angel' is your favorite song, isn't it?" she said.

"How did you know?"

"Because you been playing it so many times, homey," she said, taking his hand and placing it on her shoulder as to dance. He stopped himself from refusing, as he usually did because he considered himself clumsy. Instead he began to move slowly with the beat. Her tits, restricted in a tight black brassiere he detected easily under her sheer blouse, were close against him and his hands dropped low to hold her ample but firm waist. As they danced, almost as an invocation, he repeated the words of the song: "I fell for you. And I knew the vision of your love's loveliness. I hope and I pray, that someday I'll be the vision of your happiness." He imagined Sleepy as his *ruka*, sitting next to him in his Chevy, riding low, riding in fine style with just his fingertips guiding the steering wheel, cruising smoothly, with only green lights all the way down Whittier Boulevard and out of the barrio and down to the Pacific Ocean. At the end of the song he continued to stand there holding her, and she didn't try to move away.

As the homeboys continued to guzzle beer and the women en masse wandered hesitantly into the room and begged them to dance, he lit another joint and offered it to Sleepy. She cupped her hands around the joint and took a puff, then handed it back to him. He felt his cock growing between his legs.

Later, at her insistence, she fixed a plate of tamales for him.

By three, when the party was starting to break up, he took Sleepy's hand and led her down the stairs to his car, parked on the street in an unlighted spot.

In the backseat they necked for a while and he reached inside her blouse to massage her breasts. As her nipples hardened and she began to breathe harder, a momentary fear passed through his mind that because of the mixture of booze and dope, he might not be able to get a full hard-on. As though she were reading his mind, her hands slipped between his legs and unzipped his trousers. His cock was out and she was stroking him gently. By the time the windows were steamed over, he was as rigid as a steel bar and Sleepy was moaning with desire.

Suddenly straightening her legs, she arched her back. Reaching behind her, she unzipped her tight-fitting leather pants and yanked them and her bikini panties down and off. He lifted her onto him and felt her warm, slippery wetness. She moaned fiercely. Then

Payaso was in her and the car began to rock with the rhythm of sex.

"Fuck me, homes," she said. "Fuck me. Fuck me. Give it to me. Come in me. I want you to come in me." Payaso, his clumsy feet planted firmly on the floorboard for leverage, coiled powerfully into her.

Afterward, with the windows steamy and the interior of the car smelling of sex, they necked for a while. Then she told him she had to get home because she was only sixteen and every time she got home late her father always kicked the shit out of her.

They dressed and climbed into the front seat. Payaso sat low in his Chevy and Sleepy sat close to him on the way to her home. When he pulled up in front of the house, they kissed and he felt her hand caress him between the legs. "I love you, homes," she said.

"I want you to be my woman."

"I am your woman, homes," she said, kissing him.

"If you get pregnant from tonight I'll get married to you."

She put her head on his shoulder and hugged him tightly. Then the lights came on in her house and she sat up. She slid across the seat, climbed out, and hurried toward the house. Her tits jiggled as she waved at him.

He waved back.

During the short drive home he relived being in the backseat with her and felt his cock coming to life again. It felt good to have his own woman.

Payaso turned into the dirt alley leading behind the houses on Ortega Street and crunched slowly down a gravel driveway to a space next to a dilapidated garage where he always parked his car. He turned off the engine, pulled the door handle, and stepped out of the car.

Suddenly someone grabbed him from behind. His neck was in the crook of an arm and he was being choked. He tried to scream, but nothing came out. He kicked frantically as he was pulled backward toward the driveway.

"Keep your mouth shut, motherfucker," Stepanovich hissed into Payaso's ear, pulling him backward in a secure choke hold.

A police sedan driven by Black sped down the driveway and skidded on the gravel to a stop. The passenger door flew open and Arredondo jumped out.

Stepanovich lifted his knee sharply into the small of Payaso's back, dropping him to his knees. As Stepanovich continued to choke, Arredondo twisted his arm into a hammer lock and ratcheted handcuffs onto his wrists.

Rapidly Stepanovich and Arredondo dragged Payaso, still kicking, the last few feet to the car. As Arredondo opened the door, Stepanovich pulled Payaso inside. Arredondo slammed the door and climbed quickly in the front seat. Black slammed the car into gear and sped down the driveway and into the street.

Stepanovich released his hold and Payaso gasped for air.

"I didn't do nothing," he said.

Neither Stepanovich nor the others said a word. Stepanovich felt his heart pounding, and he was slightly out of breath.

"Where are we going?"

Black turned the corner onto Soto Street. Because of the hour, the road was deserted. Two blocks away at the freeway, he entered the onramp and accelerated into the stream of traffic.

Stepanovich could feel a slight vibration on the car seat. It was Payaso shaking with fear.

"Am I under arrest?"

A minute or so later, Black swerved off the freeway at the Vignes Street exit and entered an industrial area that, because of the hour and the poor street lighting, appeared cavernous. Turning frequently, he wound past the shadows of a brewery, a soap plant, and some huddled industrial warehouses. Finally turning off the headlights, he steered slowly along a dirt road leading to a wide cement border stretching along the edge of the Los Angeles River. The car lurched slightly as the front wheels bumped slowly over the edge and hummed down a steep cement bank. Stepanovich remembered having driven over the edge on his bicycle as a child. There was a lurch as it reached the flat cement bed of the river, which was the color of blued steel in the moonlight. There was only the sound of tires rolling on the waterless plain as Black continued to the middle of the riverbed.

Then the car stopped.

Black opened the car door and pulled Payaso out and away from the car. Arredondo followed and grabbed Payaso's arms roughly. He unlocked and removed the handcuffs.

Stepanovich stepped out of the car. "How did you know we were set up at Hazard Park?" he said, hearing his voice echoing along the man-made riverbed.

Payaso, his complexion a metallic bronze in the dimness, returned his glare.

Black moved closer to him. "Who told you we were going to be there?"

Payaso, realizing he was within punching distance of the three men, cringed visibly. "I don't know nothing," he said, his voice cracking.

Stepanovich stepped closer. "You knew we were set up at Hazard Park, and you and your homeboys rode on us," he said calmly, in his best cop-out-and-save-yourself fatherly tone. "There's nothing anyone can do to change that. But right now, it's time to do the right thing. It's time to help Payaso."

"I didn't shoot nobody," Payaso said.

"A policeman was killed," Stepanovich said. "You know we aren't just going home without finding out who the shooters are."

"I don't know nothing about no drive-by. I don't know nothing about no ride."

"We're all alone here tonight," Stepanovich said as

a come-on. "Your homeboys never have to know what you tell us."

"I ain't gonna tell you pigs nothing. I ain't no *rata.*"

"You're alone, *ese,*" Arredondo said. "There are no homeboys to protect you."

"You ain't got shit on me."

Stepanovich felt his fists double up involuntarily. His limbs tingled. He was ready to fight.

Black punched Payaso in the stomach and there was the unmistakable sound of air being knocked from human lungs. Payaso dropped to his knees, gasping.

"The party's over, fuckface," Black hissed. "Now we're gonna kill you."

As Payaso staggered slowly to his feet, Stepanovich grabbed him by the hair. "Who fingered us, *vato?* How did you know we were at the park?"

There was animal's fear in Payaso's eyes as he shook his head. His arms covered his stomach in anticipation of another blow.

Arredondo punched Payaso squarely in the throat, throwing him backward. His back made a hollow thud as it slammed against the cement.

Payaso gasped for breath. "Fuck you pigs," he cried, scrambling to his feet and lunging at Stepanovich. He merely sidestepped and punched Payaso solidly in the ribs to avoid leaving marks. Payaso fought back wildly, but Stepanovich countered the punches, catching him solidly with heavy blows to the kidneys and ribs. Payaso went down again and curled into the fetal position.

Stepanovich, breathing hard, restrained the surge of adrenaline inside him that demanded to kill. He squatted next to him. "We want names, homeboy. We want to know who was with you."

Payaso shook his head.

Arredondo came forward quickly. Shifting his balance onto his left foot and extending his arms outward like a punter, he kicked Payaso fully between the legs. Payaso cried out and doubled up. Now Black was kicking him. Stepanovich, his face burning with the heat of uncontrollable rage, joined in and there was a flurry aimed everywhere on Payaso's body except his face. Under the rain of kicks Payaso made little grunts at first that changed quickly to breathless cries.

Stepanovich at last regained control of himself, but the others kept on kicking. "That's enough!" he shouted, shoving them away.

Everyone was breathing hard. Payaso was sobbing.

Stepanovich reached down, grabbed Payaso by the hair, and pulled him to his feet. The cowering youth covered his groin with both hands.

"You wanna die, homeboy?"

Payaso shook his head.

"Then you'd better start jacking your jaws."

Payaso just stood there cringing in the darkness, waiting for the next blow.

Black panted as he pulled his revolver. "Let's kill the cocksucker," he said, aiming at Payaso's head.

Payaso, with his hands up protectively, slowly backed away. There was a click as Black cocked his revolver. Though the night was warm, Stepanovich felt a sudden chill.

"Let him have it," Arredondo said. "Kill him."

"OK," Payaso said, crying and gasping for breath, "I'll tell you how we knew you were at the park."

Stepanovich stepped forward and touched Black's gun hand. Black lowered the weapon.

"We're listening," Stepanovich said.

"Your *puta* told us," he shrieked. "How's that, pig? I bet your homeboys didn't know that! Your woman did a number on you."

Stepanovich felt his stomach tighten. The others turned to him. "Who *is* my woman?" he said.

"Gloria Soliz."

Stepanovich's insides swelled with nausea. "That's a goddamn lie," he heard himself say.

"Gloria told us. How would she know if you hadn't told her?" Payaso cried. "Eh, *cabron?* How would she know?"

Suddenly Stepanovich was punching and kicking Payaso uncontrollably. He was pulled off by Black and Arredondo.

Payaso wobbled to his feet. "Her name is all you're gonna get from me, pig."

"What's this cocksucker talking about?"

"It's a lie. She wouldn't—she didn't."

Black and Arredondo stood there looking at each other for a moment, and Stepanovich could tell they didn't believe him. Pulling his gun, he aimed it at Payaso's face. "Who were the shooters?"

Payaso's eyes widened. He raised his hands defensively and backed away. Stepanovich advanced on him.

"Go ahead and kill me," he cried. "But I'll never roll over on my homeboys. I'm not afraid to die."

Stepanovich caught his breath. Both hands were holding his revolver and he was ready to shoot.

Arredondo moved backward from the potential line of fire.

Eerily, Black covered his ears in anticipation of gunfire.

Stepanovich aimed the revolver to Payaso's right and down. He snapped the trigger. There was a sharp fire blast and the sound of a bullet ricocheting along the cement riverbed.

Payaso shrieked and dropped to his knees.

"Kill him," Black said. "If we let him go, he'll turn us in to internal affairs."

"I ain't no stool pigeon."

"It's his word against the three of us," Stepanovich said, shoving his gun back into his holster. He walked to the sedan and climbed in. Black and Arredondo looked at each other for a moment and joined him in the car. Black started the engine and they drove away, leaving Payaso standing alone in the middle of the moonlit river.

Stepanovich, sitting in the back seat, could feel his pulse pounding rapidly at his temples as Black sped up the incline and out.

"Did you tell her about the surveillance?" Arredondo said.

"Drop me off at my car," Stepanovich said.

Black lit a cigarette. "We have a right to know—"

"I said, drop me off at my car," Stepanovich said, cutting off the conversation. "I'll meet you later at the Rumor Control."

EIGHTEEN

"I don't know what you're talking about," Gloria said, turning her head slightly to avoid eye contact.

Seething, Stepanovich stepped inside the door of her apartment and closed it behind him.

She retreated to a floor lamp in the darkened living room and turned the switch. "You look tired," she said, a quaver in her voice betraying her.

She couldn't look him in the eye. Instead she clutched her robe and tugged it together with both hands. She was lying, he could tell, and he felt like choking her.

"Are you OK?" she said. He could see the fear in her eyes.

"We were talking in bed and I mentioned a stakeout at Hazard Park."

"I don't remember—"

"You figured out what we were up to and dropped a dime to White Fence."

"No, I never—"

"That's why you acted funny at the hospital when we brought Fordyce in," Stepanovich interrupted. "He was killed because of you. And at Catalina, I could tell something was bothering you. Now I know what you meant by saying you didn't want anything to come between us."

Her chin quivered. "I would never do anything to hurt you. I love you."

"You rotten, treacherous bitch."

Both of them just stood there for a while and the room seemed to become smaller. Her eyes glazed with tears. "I tried to stop the killing," she said. "I tried to stop people from being hurt."

"What is that supposed to mean?"

"I passed the word to White Fence to stay away from Hazard Park," she cried.

"Who did you tell?"

"A nurse's aide in my ward, Dora Lemos. She's a White Fence *chola*. Her nickname is Sleepy."

"You fingered us."

"It wasn't like that!"

"Fordyce is dead because of you."

She sobbed and covered her face. "I was trying to stop people from being shot."

"Exactly what did you tell her?"

"Just that the police were expecting Eighteenth to ride on the park," she said, taking her hands away from her face. "I thought this would keep them away from the park. I just wanted to keep people from getting hurt."

Gloria slumped onto the sofa and reached in the pocket of her robe for a handkerchief. "When I heard about what happened, I wanted to die," she said, her voice cracking.

"I should have kept my mouth shut," Stepanovich said regretfully.

"I wanted to tell you about this at the hospital and at Catalina, but I was afraid you wouldn't want to ever see me again," she cried. "As God is my witness, I never meant to hurt anyone."

"Fordyce is dead and it's my fault."

Gloria wiped her eyes with the handkerchief and looked at it. "This is what happens when people are living in fear," she said resentfully. "Everything turns to hatred and violence."

Stepanovich, feeling naked and vulnerable, crossed the room to the window. On the street below, a pair of headlights came slowly down the grade on City Terrace Avenue and passed briefly under the illumination of a streetlight. It was a black-and-white police cruiser, but Stepanovich was unable to see the faces of the officers inside. It could be anyone, he thought.

He turned away and headed toward the door.

"Where are you going?" she said fearfully as he reached for the door handle. "You and I are the same," she said. "We're tied to the neighborhood, to the past. It's killing us." As he pulled the door open, she ran to him. "We can leave all this. There's nothing stopping us. We can walk away from it all."

"Walk away to where?"

"There are other places to live and work. You could be a policeman in a small town somewhere. And I can always get a job as a nurse. We're not locked up in East L.A."

"I'm not going to run away. I'm a cop."

"What does it mean—'I'm a cop'? Being a cop has nothing to do with you and me. Can't we just be two people who love each other?"

"I have a responsibility to the others . . . to the police department."

"You are more important than the police department or the neighborhood or those you work with. You are a person. Can't you see what's happening?"

He stepped outside.

"You're not seeing things clearly," she shouted as he made his way down the steps.

Feeling confused and alone, he sped to the Rumor Control Bar. Inside, he made his way through the crowd of cops now huddled at the bar and at tables, drinking fast and generously buying rounds because it was pay day.

Arredondo and Black were sitting at a corner table with bottles of beer. Stepanovich, his stomach in a knot, sat down with them.

Neither acknowledged his presence in any way.

"I want you both to understand something," he said in a tone low enough so that those at the bar wouldn't hear. "I mentioned to Gloria that we were going to be working Hazard Park. Because White Fence are her people, she tipped them off—told them to stay away from the park to avoid getting busted. She didn't mean to hurt us." He cleared his throat. "What happened is my fault."

"Women can't keep their mouths shut," Arrendondo said after a while.

"She's a good woman and she didn't mean any harm," Stepanovich said.

"White Fence could have just as easily spotted the motor home on their own," Black said. "The same thing could have happened whether she said anything or not. So fuck it. It happened and that's that. No one's to blame."

"I appreciate that, C.R.," Stepanovich said. "But from now on this beef is between White Fence and me. I carry the weight on this."

Nothing was said at the table for a minute or more.

"I say we're all carrying the weight," Black said finally, cocking his head toward Arredondo.

"That's the way I look at it too," Arredondo agreed. "We're homeboys."

Black shoved his beer bottle to Stepanovich. Stepanovich picked it up slowly and drank, then set the bottle down on the table. "The problem is, if Payaso won't talk, how are we gonna learn the identity of the shooters?"

"The White Fence *veteranos* would have been on the ride—Gordo, Lyncho—and since Smokey ended up with nothing more than a couple of pellets when we blasted him at Greenie's place, he's probably healthy enough to ride. I'll bet he was right there calling the shots. It's a damn shame we didn't kill him."

"But there's no way for us to prove that," Stepanovich said.

Arredondo nodded and gave a nervous laugh. "You're right. We know White Fence did it, but like every other drive-by, we're never gonna know for sure which of the gangbangers actually pulled the trigger. Hell, if it wasn't for the fingerprint, we'd have never known about Payaso."

Black lit a cigarette. "They didn't know who was in the motor home when they opened fire. They just wanted a get-back. And that's exacty what they got."

"We'll make one of them talk," Stepanovich said. "Gordo is on parole. And Lyncho—"

"They're not gonna talk," Black interrupted. "These cocksuckers have been arrested their whole lives and they've never talked. That's how they gained respect from the other rotten motherfuckers in their gang. That's why they are *veteranos*. We can arrest 'em and flap our jaws, offer 'em deals, kick their asses until we're sore, but they're not gonna talk. They're not afraid of jail. They're not afraid of us. And they'd rather die than be a rat."

Stepanovich's face felt flushed as he stood up and headed to the bar. He pointed to a bottle of Early Times. Sullivan stopped reading the newspaper and poured him a shot. He picked up the shot glass with two fingers and threw it back. The whiskey burned his lips, tongue, and throat, and then he felt a mist of perspiration forming on his forehead and upper lip. He picked up a cocktail napkin and dabbed his face.

Black and Arredondo followed him to the bar and Sullivan poured more whiskey. Stepanovich reached into his pocket and set money on the bar for the drinks.

"What's the difference which of the gangbangers were in the car?" Black said. "We know they were White Fence gang members."

Stepanovich thought he saw Sullivan shake his head disapprovingly, but didn't care. He was not only a confirmed alcoholic but a has-been.

"You're right," Stepanovich said disconsolately. "We're never gonna find out."

There was a faint pop as Black took a drag on his cigarette. He sucked the smoke from his mouth up into his nose. "Now, I guess, we either sit back like bunch of fairies and accept the fact that White Fence has gotten away with murder," he said, "or we retaliate."

Arredondo said, sipping his drink, "White Fence is probably celebrating right now. They killed a cop and got away with it."

"We can roll out the troops and arrest every member of the White Fence gang in the city," Stepanovich said reluctantly. "One of 'em might talk."

"That still wouldn't give us enough evidence to prosecute anyone," Black said glumly.

There was a long silence as the men stood at the bar, rattling the ice in their drinks.

"We need to catch White Fence right in the act," Arredondo said. "Catch 'em with guns in their hands. Then we could let 'em have it, those *chingasos.*"

"They've hit and now they're sitting back waiting for us to come around with search warrants, make a few bum pinches. But they're not worried. They know we don't have any evidence," Black said.

"I can hear them laughing about it right now," Arredondo said.

"I say we get White Fence to forget about us. Make them worry about somebody else. Get them to drop their guard," Stepanovich offered.

"If you have an idea," Black said, "stop beating around the bush and let's hear it."

"When we were staked out on Eighteenth Street and White Fence came gunning, it was a crime in progress," Stepanovich said. "It was open season. We were gang cops using reasonable force to stop a gang shoot-out."

"After killing Fordyce, White Fence isn't going to move against anyone else."

"You're right. But they would defend themselves if attacked by another gang."

"This is getting interesting," Arredondo said.

"If the White Fence *veteranos* were inside a pad and they had word they were going to be hit, they would be ready. Any shooters would get a warm reception. Now, if we were watching and we catch White Fence *veteranos* with guns in their hands, they're ours. We can give 'em what they deserve."

Black leaned back against the bar. "I see what you mean," he said. "It's complicated, but it could work."

NINETEEN

When Stepanovich walked through the gate at Sparky's
tow yard the garage door was open and a light was on
inside. Sparky had his feet up on his desk as he ate a
thick hamburger. Because there didn't appear to be
anyone else around, Stepanovich stepped past the fence
and sauntered in. Sparky noticed him and turned.
"Did prints come up with anything?" he said.

Stepanovich nodded, moving past Sparky to the black
Chevrolet. "We came up with one latent belonging to
a White Fencer. But he won't talk."

Sparky shook his head. "That's too bad," he said
sincerely. "Damn. Where do you go from here?"

Stepanovich touched the tarp covering the Chevrolet.
"Only so much we can do," he said somberly. "Without help."

Sparky stopped eating. Slowly he came to his feet
and tossed what was left of the hamburger into a
brimming wastebasket. He yanked a shirttail from his
trousers and wiped his hands. "I'm an ex-marine," he
said. "You don't have to beat around the bush with
me."

"Is anyone else working tonight?"

"I'm the only one here all weekend," Sparky answered warily.

Stepanovich set his hand on the fender of the Chevrolet. "I need this car."

Sparky pointed to a greasy clipboard hanging on a hook. "The evidence log is right there. Sign and it's yours."

"I don't want to sign for it."

Sparky stared at him for a moment, suddenly realizing it was odd that Stepanovich had arrived on foot. He turned and looked toward the street. "I could lose my tow contract with the city by letting somebody tamper with evidence."

"I'll bring it back in an hour."

Sparky wiped something shiny from his chin and examined it. "But technically the car never left here, right?"

Stepanovich nodded.

Sparky ran his sooty hands through his hair. "If you have an accident, I'm still responsible for the car."

"If I'm not back here in an hour, you can report it stolen. You can say you left the tow yard for a few minutes and when you returned, the car was gone."

Sparky licked his rough lips nervously. "Actually report it stolen?"

"That way you'd be covered."

"What about the mileage reading on the impound form?"

"I'll handle that."

"I'm still sticking my neck out."

"If there is any fall to take, I'll take it," Stepanovich said, looking Sparky in the eye. "You have my word."

Sparky rubbed his hands together for a moment. He tugged the sleeve of his grease-stained shirt and checked his wristwatch. Then he extended a set of keys from the shiny retractable key chain attached to his belt. Using both hands, he freed a key and tossed it to Stepanovich.

"That's the key to the front gate. I'll be back in an hour and a half."

As Stepanovich stood there holding the key in his

hand, Sparky stepped to his desk and flicked a switch on his answering machine. He headed out of the garage and climbed into his tow truck. After it turned over a few times, the engine started and the truck rattled out the driveway and turned onto Mission Road.

Stepanovich located the ignition key to the Chevrolet on the keyboard behind Sparky's desk. He looked about and spotted a flashlight among a pile of other tools on a greasy workbench. He picked it up and, approaching the Chevrolet, grasped the tarp and pulled it off. Using the key, he unlocked the driver's door.

Bending down to look under the dashboard, he used the flashlight to find the odometer cable, then unscrewed it. Without turning on the headlights, he drove slowly out of the garage and past the gate.

Once on the street, he stopped the car and pulled the heavy sliding gate closed behind him. Using a thick chain and padlock hanging over the top rail, he locked the gate securely. He checked his watch and climbed back behind the wheel, then sped down Mission Road to the parking lot.

Standing by the police sedan, Black and Arredondo looked extremely nervous as he pulled up beside them. Black opened the trunk of the police sedan and took out a pump shotgun. He climbed in the rear seat of the Chevrolet, and Arredondo climbed in front.

Stepanovich turned the steering wheel sharply and stepped on the gas. As the caper car made a U-turn, there was the sound of the front tires rubbing the wheel wells.

"Any trouble getting Sparky to go along with the program?" Black asked as Stepanovich sped past a railroad utility yard.

"He's solid," Stepanovich said, turning on Soto Street and heading south past Wabash Avenue.

At Seventeenth Street, Stepanovich slowed down and pulled to the curb. Black cranked the beavertail of the shotgun and chambered a round. Arredondo reached inside his windbreaker and pulled out his six-inch revolver. He snapped open the chamber and checked rounds. With a flick of his wrist he snapped the chamber shut again.

Stepanovich's palms felt damp on the steering wheel. "Eighteenth knows this car," he said, driving on. "That means we get one pass only. So wait until I get us into position."

"Let's go for it," Arredondo said, climbing into the backseat.

As they neared Eighteenth Street, Stepanovich was scanning left and right. The area was quiet and no one was on the sidewalks. He made the right turn onto Eighteenth carefully, eyes still roving to either side of the street. Then, his decision made, he accelerated steadily to the middle of the block. Reaching Greenie's apartment house, he slowed and veered to his left. The sedan lurched as the front wheels, then rear wheels bumped over the curb and across the sidewalk onto the lawn in front of the apartment house. In the middle of the lawn he swerved and braked; the car came to a stop with the driver's side facing to the front of the dwelling. Black and Arredondo readied their weapons.

Stepanovich pressed the horn three times. It seemed louder than any sound he'd ever heard. There was no movement at the window of Greenie's apartment. He leaned on the horn again.

"We can't sit here all night," Black said nervously.

Finally someone pulled the curtain back from Greenie's window.

Stepanovich pulled his revolver. "Now," he commanded. He and Black rolled the windows down. Stepanovich aimed his revolver up at the apartment and pulled the trigger in rapid fire.

Black fired his shotgun and the car rocked with a deafening blast. Glass crashed as the apartment window shattered. Firing rapidly, Arredondo emptied his revolver out the same window.

"Barrio White Fence!" Stepanovich shouted. "Barrio White Fence!"

"Viva White Fence!" Arredondo shouted.

Stepanovich dropped his revolver onto the front seat and slammed the accelerator to the floor. He steered the Chevrolet across the lawn, sidewalk, and, with the sound of metal bumper scraping cement, over the curb into the street. Swerving to the right, Stepanovich headed to the corner at full speed. Turning left, he slowed down a little to avoid drawing attention from passing cars. As he weaved through side roads in the direction of Soto Street, his eyes burned from the acrid odor of gunsmoke inside the car.

"I hope we got some of 'em," Black said.

Arredondo laughed nervously. "They'll never figure out what happened."

Having made a series of rights and lefts through residential areas, Stepanovich was relieved to finally turn onto Soto Street. He glanced at the speedometer, making sure he was traveling under the speed limit.

As he neared the freeway, flashing red lights suddenly appeared in the rearview mirror. Stepanovich's stomach muscles snapped taut and terror gripped him.

"Oh no. Oh shit," Arredondo uttered without turning his head.

Suddenly the red lights swung to the left of the Chevrolet and sped past. It was a fire department sedan with a flashing red light.

Black laughed nervously. "What are you worried about, homes?"

Arredondo let out his breath.

Stepanovich felt wetness under his arms. His hands were shaking.

Arredondo broke into laughter and, hidden from the eyes of East L.A. by the smoked windows, Stepanovich and Black joined in. They laughed hysterically and Stepanovich felt tears of relief at the corners of his eyes.

Minutes later, Stepanovich pulled into the parking

lot where they'd left the police sedan. After Black and Arredondo climbed out of the car, he sped out of the lot and down the street to Sparky's impound yard.

The gate was still locked.

Stepanovich checked his wristwatch. He'd been gone exactly twenty-nine minutes. He climbed out of the car, unlocked the gate, and shoved it open. Quickly he slid back behind the wheel and steered the car into the garage. After he parked it in the same spot, he hurried to close the garage door to insure that anyone passing by on Mission Road couldn't see what was taking place. Shielded from the street, he used rags to wipe down any possible fingerprints from the car's interior. Then he reattached the odometer cable. With this task completed, he hurried to the gate, rolled it closed, and locked it with the chain and padlock.

Being careful to remain in the shadows of the billboards and buildings lining the street, he ran back to the parking lot and climbed into the police sedan.

There was static coming from the police radio.

"A shots-fired call just went out," Black said. "But no requests for an ambulance, so I guess we didn't hit anyone."

At the Rumor Control Bar they slipped in the back door one at a time, Stepanovich last. The bar was now three deep with cops wearing the LAPD off-duty drinker's uniform of T-shirts and Levis. The crowd was divided into the usual huddles by rank, job classification, or cabal, and the jukebox was blaring a country and western tune. Even though it was Friday night, the noise level was subdued and there was no ass grabbing or drinking contests, which Stepanovich attributed to the recent funeral.

Brenda, serving drinks behind the bar, was wearing her seashell halter top, tennis shorts, and had her hair drawn to the top of her head and tied with a flourescent orange ponytail holder. Stepanovich slid between a couple of leather-faced motor cops at the bar and got

Brenda's attention. Even as he ordered a scotch and water, she spun the cap off a bottle of Teacher's.

"Where's Sullivan?" he asked.

"He got sick and went home," she said, filling a glass with ice. "He used to go fishing with Fordyce and he's just taking it real hard."

As Stepanovich picked up the cocktail, he realized his hand was shaking. "Any calls for me?"

Brenda shook her head, reaching into a cooler for a frosty beer mug, and lifted it to a tap spigot. Stepanovich stepped away from the bar.

"You guys gonna be around later?" she said, drawing beer.

Stepanovich pretended he hadn't heard and made his way to the corner booth where Black and Arredondo were seated. He slid across the red leather seat and took a sip of scotch.

"We did it," Arredondo said, sniggering mischievously. Black joined the laughter and Stepanovich found himself laughing too.

When the phone rang, though, they all stopped laughing. Brenda picked up the receiver. She looked about, spotted Stepanovich, and waved. He made his way back to the bar.

"It's Harger," she said, handing him the receiver.

"Stepanovich."

"Just got off the phone with the Hollenbeck watch commander," Harger said. "Somebody just shot up Greenie's apartment in a drive-by. You'd better get over there and see what you can find out."

"That's a roger."

Stepanovich set the receiver down and returned to the table. "There's been a drive-by at Greenie's," he said, smirking.

"Hijo la," Arredondo said in mock surprise.

There were a lot of gawkers standing around in front of the apartment building: ghetto zombies shuffling about on the sidewalk in the glare of flashing red lights. As at most crime scenes, no matter what the hour, at least half of the crowd was made up of children.

Stepanovich parked the police sedan in a space at the curb between two black-and-whites. A short female officer was standing in the middle of the front lawn making notes on a metal clipboard as she interviewed a tall, obese Mexican woman in a pink chenille robe and hair rollers. The young officer's uniform had been tailored to complement her striking hourglass figure. Her police utility belt and holster were shiny patent leather, which meant that she had purchased it herself rather than wear the standard department-issued equipment. It occurred to Stepanovich that when he'd joined up, there had been height requirements for police officers, and uniforms as small as the officer was wearing were sold only to police explorer scouts.

Stepanovich waited until she had completed her interview before he approached.

"What do you got?" Stepanovich said.

"Who are you?"

"Sergeant Stepanovich. O.C.B. CRASH. Special Detail."

"A gang detective?"

Stepanovich nodded, irritated by her obvious inability to recognize another cop when she saw one. On the other hand, he thought, without the uniform he wouldn't have guessed she was a police officer in a million years.

"You got an ID card?"

Feeling irritation turn to angry goose bumps on the back of his neck, Stepanovich took out his police identification card and showed it to her. As she examined it, he noted her name tag: Forest, C. Now he remembered. Candi Forest.

She nodded diffidently. "I was the first car to arrive," she said. "It's a drive-by—a black Chevy. But no one got a look at the occupants because the car had smoked windows." She pointed to the place in the lawn a few feet away. "They drove up onto the lawn

210

about here and fired into that apartment. Two witnesses heard them yell, 'White Fence.' They sped off the lawn back into the street and headed south. Because of the grass, there are no tire prints."

"Any hits?"

"Nope. The people in the apartment said they were sleeping on the floor. There are no clues, if that's what you came here to find out. This is just another gang drive-by shooting."

"Who do you think is responsible?"

"For the shooting?" Candi Forest said.

"For the shooting."

"Probably some gang just shouting White Fence to throw off the investigators: a false clue," Candi Forest said, arranging notes on her clipboard. "Look, I'm busy now. Why don't you just pick up a copy of my report tomorrow?"

"Sorry to bother you," Stepanovich said, gritting his teeth.

Officer Forest lifted her well-painted eyebrows again and folded her arms defensively across her flat, bullet-proofed chest.

Stepanovich made his way up the stairs to Greenie's apartment. The door was open and, inside, the glass from the shattered window littered the living room floor. Greenie, wearing only khaki trousers, was standing in the middle of the room angrily whispering in Spanish with Loco and Gato, a couple of dissipated, similarly dressed Mexicans whom he recognized immediately as Eighteenth Street gang members. They stopped talking as he entered.

"Who was it?" Stepanovich said.

Greenie looked at the others. "We ain't got no idea, man. It was a drive-by."

"You wouldn't tell me even if you'd gotten a look at them, right?"

"We ain't no fucking stool pigeons."

"Try to stay cool," Stepanovich said, thinking it sounded like something he might say if in fact there really had been a gang-related shooting. "This neighborhood has enough problems without another drive-by shooting." The gang members just stared at him with dumb looks on their faces, and for a moment Stepanovich wished the rounds he and the others had fired through the window had killed them all.

He sauntered back down the stairs and followed a cement path along the side of the apartment building to the alley. He looked about to be sure no one was watching, then took out a pen and pad, and noted the license numbers of those vehicles parked nearby he thought might belong to the gangbangers he'd seen inside Greenie's apartment. He knew any gang member's car might be used in a drive-by shooting at some time or another.

As he was returning to his car, Harger pulled up to the curb in a full-sized Mercury sedan with a whip antenna and a cellular phone. He climbed out. "What's up?"

"No hits."

"Does it look like White Fence?"

Stepanovich smiled. "It *looks* like 'em, all right. The shooters were driving a black Chevy with smoked windows."

"But Payaso's car is at Sparky's impound yard."

"I said, it *looks* like them."

Harger furrowed his brow. "I don't get it."

"It looks like White Fence, but it may have been . . . another gang."

Harger stood there for a moment, watching the apartment house. A look of understanding crossed his face. "I see."

"But there's no doubt that Eighteenth thinks it was White Fence. Therefore, they'll ride, probably to Payaso's house. There'll be trouble."

"And you'll be staked out there."

"It's the only way to gain the element of surprise," Stepanovich said.

Harger licked his lips. "Then I'm all for it."

"I want you to know that if we're there and shooting starts, some White Fence people are gonna get killed."

Harger's hand clamped Stepanovich's shoulder. "The Chief wants them finished off. I want them finished off."

"We may need to rent a room nearby for an observation post."

"The Department will pay for it."

"We need your support on this," Stepanovich said.

"You have it. Go for it. Go."

TWENTY

Back at the Rumor Control Bar, Stepanovich found Black and Arredondo sitting at the same booth. As he sat down, they watched him anxiously.

"Don't just sit there," Arredondo said.

Stepanovich smiled. "It worked. Greenie and his homeboys saw Payaso's car. They'll ride."

Both Black and Arredondo laughed as they slapped Stepanovich on the shoulder. Arredondo signaled Brenda for another round of drinks. She pursed her lips into kisses to acknowledge the order.

"My guess is they'll hit Payaso's house," Stepanovich said.

Black leaned close. "What makes you so sure they'll hit there rather than shoot up Hazard Park or do a drive-by somewhere else in White Fence turf?" he said in a conspiratorial tone.

"They saw Payaso's car so Payaso's definitely in the bull's-eye."

"He's right, C.R.," Arredondo said.

Black laughed. "And since the White Fence homies aren't responsible for the drive-by they won't be expecting anything."

"It's what Eighteenth thinks White Fence thinks that's important," Arredondo said.

"Actually, it's what we think that's important," Stepanovich said. "Because when they make their move, we're going to be there to finish all of 'em."

"Did we hit anyone on the drive-by?" Black said, tearing open a fresh pack of Camels.

"No hits."

"Too bad."

"Setting up on Ortega Street isn't going to be easy," Arredondo said.

"There's an apartment complex across the street from Payaso's house," Stepanovich said. "I saw a vacancy sign when I drove by."

Brenda came from the bar carrying a tray of drinks. "You guys are so quiet this evening," she said. "But I guess it's not the same without—"

"Sit down for a minute, Brenda," Stepanovich said.

Looking pleased at the request, she slid in next to Black, her abalone-shell halter top knocking against the edge of the table.

"Brenda, would you be willing to help us on something?"

She looked at the three of them suspiciously. "I'm not going to go down on another woman so you guys can watch. I just don't get anything out of it."

"It's nothing like that. We want you to help us on a case."

"Which case?"

'We can't tell you, but it's an important case and it has something to do with catching the people that killed Fordyce."

"This is for real?"

Stepanovich nodded. Glancing at everyone at the table, Brenda could see they were serious. "I don't want to get in trouble."

"What we want you to do is perfectly legal. The only thing we ask is that you never tell anyone about it. Ever."

"If it's not illegal, I'll help."

"As long as you keep your mouth shut, you'll have nothing to worry about."

She giggled. "I always wanted to be a cop."

Early the next morning, Stepanovich waited at Manuel's taco stand while Black and Arredondo made intermittent passes by Greenie's apartment in an unmarked sedan. They were supposed to notify him immediately if there was any movement from the location.

Brenda arrived shortly after ten and pulled her twelve-year-old Mazda into a parking space in back. She walked to the patrol car and climbed in the passenger side. She was wearing a faded flower-print dress. He was thankful she proved to have enough sense to wear something other than her seashell halter for her undercover assignment.

She handed him a rental application and a key attached with a piece of string to a tag that read: "APARTMENT 13." "The landlady barely spoke English. She looked at me real funny at first when I asked her about renting the apartment, but things eased up when I signed a Mexican name on the application. I think she figured I was married to a Mexican. But everything was OK the moment I showed the cash you gave me for the down payment."

"Good work, Brenda."

"You're so serious today," she said mockingly. "She thought it was great when I told her my brother and some of his friends were going to be over to paint the place before I moved in."

"You did fine."

"I should have been a cop. In fact, I signed up to take the civil service test once, but I forgot and went the wrong day. Do you want me to do anything else?"

"That's about it, thanks again."

Brenda placed her hand firmly on his thigh. "I've always liked you better than the others," she said. "You're shy. It's cute when a guy is shy."

"I have to be on my way."

"If you want it right now, you don't have to be shy," she said without looking him in the eye.

"Thanks anyway, Brenda, but I've gotta run."

"You have a girlfriend, don't you?"

Stepanovich nodded.

Brenda smiled wryly. "I can always tell when a guy has a girlfriend."

He shrugged. At that moment, perhaps because it was morning and he was used to seeing her in the dim light of the Rumor Control Bar, Brenda suddenly seemed much older. Her crow's-feet, the few wiry gray hairs interwoven through her ponytail, and the light spray of aging freckles across her nose and cheekbones seemed to stand out. In the daytime she seemed dumpy, lonely.

Like the other women who hung out at the Rumor Control Bar, she viewed her own life as a series of uncontrollable events hammering her mercilessly. In her case, it was a couple of completely wrong men. Her first husband, a compulsive gambler, lost their house and all their furniture. Her second husband abused her and kidnapped her daughter when they split up. A few months later, the child was killed in an automobile accident and the husband was sent to jail.

Stepanovich felt sorry for her and even before he'd met Gloria, had avoided her offer of sexual favors, except when he was particularly horny.

"Just forget you rented the apartment," he said.

She pinched him on the cheek. "If you guys can't trust good ol' Brenda, who can you trust?" She climbed out of the car and headed toward the Mazda.

Stepanovich lifted the radio microphone from the hook on the dashboard and pressed the transmit button. "CRASH three-four to five and nine. I'm ten-seven at the greenhouse." The word "greenhouse" was a code he'd arranged earlier with Black and Arredondo meaning they should meet at Manuel's.

* * *

An hour later, Black and Arredondo were downing a box of Manuel's tacos while Stepanovich sipped Coke from a paper cup.

"Brenda handled getting the apartment real well," he said.

"She probably ate the landlord," Arredondo said with his mouth full.

"If we come and go from the place, the neighbors are going to get suspicious," Stepanovich said.

"I have painter's overalls and buckets," Black said. "We go in like we're to put on a coupla coats of latex."

"Good idea."

Arredondo pulled napkins from a metal dispenser on the table and roughly wiped his mouth. "And since there's no telling how long we're gonna be in there, we'll need some chow."

"Johnson's market," Black said. "The night manager, Javier, likes cops. He's good for all the lunch meat and bread we can carry out."

Arredondo finished his Coke. "Get a jar of mayonnaise. I can't eat a dry sandwich—"

"We need some heavy iron for this caper," Stepanovich said.

Black's eyes lit up. Smiling proudly, he led the others to his police sedan and unlocked the trunk. Inside, laid out neatly on an olive drab blanket in military-inspection style, were two well-oiled Uzi submachine guns, an Ithaca pump shotgun, and a case of ammunition. "I signed out the tommy guns from the metro division armory."

"What did you put on the equipment roster?" Stepanovich asked.

"Possible warrant service. There's always an arrest warrant we could say we were thinking about serving."

The next few hours were spent returning cars to the motor pool, buying groceries, and procuring the rest of the necessary equipment, including bullet-proof vests, binoculars, and radios.

At his apartment, Stepanovich searched through his carport storage box and found his Army duffel bag, figuring it as the perfect camouflage for the weapons when entering the apartment. He tossed the bag in the trunk of the police sedan, then checked his watch. It was almost four, an hour before Gloria would go on duty at the hospital. He climbed in his car and drove straight to her apartment.

As he drove up, he spotted her in the parking lot walking toward her car. He pulled up next to her and climbed out. They embraced.

"You look worried," Gloria said.

"I have a lot on my mind right now, but I wanted to catch you before you went to work."

"What is it?"

"I want you to pass some information to White Fence," he said, forcing himself to maintain eye contact.

"I don't understand," she said fearfully.

"Eighteenth is planning to ride on White Fence. Soon."

A look of confusion came over her. "After what happened, I don't understand why you would—"

"I love you," he interrupted. "Do you love me?"

"You know I do."

"I'm asking you to simply pass on some information," Stepanovich said. "Will you do this for me?"

"I don't want anyone else to get hurt."

"Eighteenth is planning to hit a White Fence *vato* named Payaso."

"Dora has mentioned his name."

"Eighteenth is planning to kill him. They're going to hit his house on Ortega Street, and they're probably going to do it soon. Just relay that information. Please." He leaned down and kissed her on the lips. Aware he was late, he headed back toward the sedan.

"When will all this be over?"

"Soon," he said, climbing back behind the wheel. "I promise."

* * *

After dark, Stepanovich and the others returned to Manuel's taco stand, and made a final check of equipment. Everything seemed to be in order. To avoid the danger of parking even an unmarked police sedan anywhere in White Fence territory during the surveillance, Stepanovich phoned Brenda and asked her to drive them in. She readily agreed. Arriving a few minutes later, she remarked that she thought they looked cute dressed as painters.

With all the surveillance equipment, the three of them barely fit into the Mazda.

On Ortega Street, Brenda drove slowly down the darkened street and came to a stop in front of the apartment house across the street from Payaso's house. Stepanovich surveyed the street carefully. There was no one in sight.

"OK," he said. "Let's go for it."

"Be careful, dudes," Brenda whispered as they climbed out of the car, dragging the equipment with them.

Brenda drove off. The three hurried along a cement walkway and entered the open chain-link gate at the entrance to the apartment house. Without speaking, they moved quickly to the door of Apartment 13.

The place was vacant. A threadbare shag carpet was spotted and worn, and the walls were covered with nail holes. The air was warm, stale, and held the faint reek of Lysol. Stepanovich closed the door behind him and set the equipment he was carrying on the bare living room floor. The living room window facing Payaso's house was covered with tattered drapery. In the kitchen and bedroom, the windows were cloaked with a combination of cheap curtains and sheets he figured would shield them adequately.

In the living room, Black had removed the shoulder weapons from the duffel bag and laid them out carefully in front of the bay window. He was leaning close to the window, peering out through a break in the curtain, when Stepanovich joined him. There was a clear view of the front of Payaso's house. "This is perfect," Black whispered.

Arredondo handed out bullet-proof vests and the three men helped one another don the gear, fastening the velcro ties tightly around their torsos to keep the vests from hindering arm movement if they had to shoot.

At the sound of footsteps and voices outside, Stepanovich hurried to the window. Three men were approaching Payaso's house.

Black reached behind him for the Uzi submachine gun. There was a ratcheting sound as he cocked it. Arredondo grabbed a shotgun and ran to the kitchen window.

The door at Payaso's house was opened. Payaso allowed the men to enter and they stood in the doorway conversing. After a while he looked both ways in the street and closed the door.

"They're White Fencers," Stepanovich said. "Gordo and Lyncho . . . and here comes Smokey. They must have parked the car down the street."

Smokey, carrying a long, thin piece of what looked like rolled carpet, hurried onto the porch and went inside with the others.

Arredondo returned from the kitchen. "It's working," he said, unable to hide his zeal. "They're here. They're waiting for Eighteenth to hit."

Black had a sardonic, toothy smile. "Pray for Eighteenth to show."

"They'll show," Stepanovich said confidently. Leading the others away, he took out a pen and pad, and drew two lines to represent the street, squares for Payaso's house and the apartment, and X's for windows and doors. "And when they do, they won't know White Fence is waiting inside."

Black lit a cigarette. "If White Fence sees a car pull up, they're not going to just sit inside and wait to get shot up. They gonna let loose."

Arredondo coughed. "They'll probably come flying out the door shooting."

Stepanovich drew two lines to form a triangle emanating from the front door of Payaso's house. "When they do, we let go. C.R., you'll have the Uzi. Arredondo and I will take the blow guns." He pointed: "This is the direction of fire."

"Ready on the right," Black said, cigarette dangling from his lip. "Ready on the left. And ready on the firing line."

"They start it and we finish it," Arredondo chimed in, staring at the diagram. "The element of surprise."

Stepanovich cleared his throat. "Does everyone agree with this plan?"

"They wasted Fordyce so we're gonna waste them," Arredondo said bitterly.

"After it's over, no matter what happens, we all see things alike?"

Black formed a cruel smile. "The party line until the end of time."

Stepanovich put out his hands and, standing together in the musty room, the others clasped them forcefully. The next half hour was spent loading weapons and ammunition clips, double-checking bullet-proof vests, and quietly opening the windows to better hear any movement on the street.

The evening passed slowly and, taking turns being posted at the window or resting on the musty carpet, they said very little to one another.

About nine o'clock Stepanovich suggested to Arredondo that they affix flashlights to the barrels of the shotguns with wide strips of black electrician's tape. To ensure the tape didn't affect the action of the gun, Stepanovich tried flicking on the flashlight, aiming at the wall, and dry-firing the piece a few times. Arredondo did the same.

With the weapon readied for night action, Stepanovich set it on the sink within easy reach and stood at the kitchen window, because he thought it provided the best nighttime view of both the street and Payaso's house.

Because the windows were open and traffic was infrequent, every car turning the corner was cause for alarm, and as the evening passed, the tension mounted. He tried counting cars for a while to kill time. At twenty-eight he tired of the pastime and stopped.

"This is the way I like it," Black said.

"You like smelly apartments?" Arredondo said.

"Midnight to eight is where it's at. The night watch. Being the invisible man. I hate working during the day."

"You're nuts."

"In the middle of the night it's us against the crooks and no one else gets in the way. If a dude is cruising with a piece at four A.M. and gets stopped, he expects to get his ass kicked. Don't fuck with the night watch. That's the word on the street. The ten years I spent on nights was the happiest time in my life. It cost me a couple of wives, but it was worth it."

"So why did you transfer to detectives?"

"A new captain took over the division. He hated me, said I was nuts."

"We should have brought Brenda with us tonight," Arredondo said awhile later. "I can use some trim."

"Brenda would make a good wife," Black said.

"The captain was right. You really are completely fucking nuts."

"Think about it," Black said. "She never nags or complains and doesn't ask for money. She's clean and knows how to give a world-class blow job. What more could a man ask?"

"She's done half the department."

"She's no virgin, all right. But neither were my first two wives."

A few hours later, Stepanovich, feeling hunger pangs, dug bread and lunch meat from the store of groceries. He slapped together a sandwich and ate quietly, staring out the kitchen window.

Black took his time lighting a cigarette. "I have the feeling it's not gonna happen. We're gonna be here all night for nothing."

"Maybe they know we're here," Arredondo said.

Stepanovich held his wristwatch up to a shaft of moonlight coming through the window. It was 2:13. Unlike hundreds of other surveillances he'd been part of, he felt no fatigue whatsoever. Occasionally his feet, back, or knees would feel stiff, and he would pace back and forth a few feet, balancing on the balls of his feet to increase circulation. Uncle Nick had taught him this beat policeman's trick when he was a child, while they were waiting in long lines at the Griffith Park pony rides. He could picture Nick, wearing his hat and looking like Dick Tracy, standing with his hands behind his back and demonstrating the position.

The night passed and nothing happened.

TWENTY-ONE

As the sun came up, Stepanovich and the others began to alternate taking one-hour catnaps. The food they'd brought with them was their only comfort in the bare apartment, and Stepanovich and the others found themselves munching frequently. Perhaps because he didn't feel Eighteenth would hit during the daytime the day passed slowly. Finally darkness fell and Stepanovich found himself stalking from room to room to get some exercise.

His mind wandering, he moved to the kitchen sink and fumbled in the darkness for the faucet. Leaning over, he splashed cold water on his face. Wet and dripping, he closed the tap, took a clean handkerchief from his back pocket, and dried himself.

"Funny," Arredondo said. "Across the street the White Fence homeboys are waiting for the same thing we are."

Black lit a cigarette, one of perhaps a hundred since they'd initiated the surveillance. "What are we gonna do if White Fence gets tired of waiting and decides to leave?"

Stepanovich coughed and cleared his throat. "We'll worry about that when the time comes."

There was the sound of a car engine.

Stepanovich stepped to the window. A pickup truck rounded the corner. It was going slow—too slow, he decided. "Heads up," he said, picking up his shotgun. As the automobile continued down the street, it passed under a streetlight. It was red, the color of the caper car used at the church shooting.

At Payaso's house there was no movement.

Keeping the barrel of the shotgun pointed toward the floor, Stepanovich flicked on the flashlight attached to the barrel. When he looked, Black and Arredondo had already grabbed their weapons.

The pickup truck swerved close to the curb and cruised slowly closer to Payaso's house. The windows were down and there were at least three men in the bed of the truck. Stepanovich felt his pulse quicken. His mouth suddenly felt dry.

"Shooters," he said, and the sound of his voice echoed through the darkened apartment.

Black and Arredondo ran to the door and quickly cocked their weapons. Stepanovich pulled the curtain open to get a better look. Just as the pickup truck came to a full stop across the street, there was movement in the bushes on the west side of Payaso's house.

Suddenly the sharp crack of gunfire roared from those bushes. White Fencers firing revolvers rushed from the side of Payaso's house toward the pickup truck. The men in the truck fired back and the front of the residence and the street was lit with fire flashes.

Stepanovich dashed out of the apartment with the others.

As the barrage of gunfire, including automatic-weapons fire, continued, he and the others dove for cover behind a Chrysler parked in front of the apartment. There were screams, glass breaking, and slugs slamming powerfully into the doors and fenders of the pickup truck.

Black lifted his Uzi over the fender of the Chrysler to fire, but Stepanovich pulled him back. "Wait."

The engine of the pickup truck revved and the car

lurched forward, slamming into the curb. After another barrage of gun fire and shouts, the shooting stopped.

Figuring White Fence was out of bullets, Stepanovich came to his feet, pulling the butt of the shotgun gun into his shoulder. The powerful flashlight beam picked out Smokey Salazar. "Now!" he shouted.

At the same moment he squeezed the trigger and the powerful blast hurtled Salazar backward onto the lawn.

Gordo, running for cover toward the house with a revolver in each hand, was suddenly caught in a storm of tracer rounds from Black's Uzi, and his body spun and rolled and flopped onto the lawn as it was torn apart.

Stepanovich, aiming his death light quickly and without hesitation, was running across the street, firing, cranking the action to chamber a round, and firing again. Black and Arredondo were at his side firing rapidly, and in the din he could feel the hot empty cartridges sting his neck and cheek as they ejected from Black's raging Uzi.

Payaso, standing at the side of the house, turned to run. Arredondo fired, but Payaso had disappeared into the bushes.

Lyncho, lying wounded, was desperately fumbling with his Uzi trying to reload. Stepanovich fired and Lyncho's efforts ceased to matter.

In the bed of the damaged pickup truck two of the wounded were trying to climb out and escape.

Black, screaming shrilly in the heat of battle, ran madly into the street and raked them with fire. Then, commando-style, he poked the barrel of the submachine gun into the cab. Holding the weapon in one hand, he emptied a clip at full automatic and the bodies inside tossed wildly and then lay still.

Suddenly the shooting stopped and there was a momentary lull.

Stepanovich, using the shotgun shells in his shirt

pocket, reloaded quickly. With eyes darting and every muscle in his body taut, he roved about the lawn, checking to see if anyone was moving. The shotgun felt like it was welded to his hands.

Black, wild-eyed, hyperventilating, yanked open the passenger door of the pickup truck and reached in. He pulled out the lifeless body of a young man wearing a watch cap and allowed him to fall. His head thumped to the pavement.

Arredondo knelt on the lawn and handcuffed Gordo's lifeless hands behind his back.

Black backed away from the pickup truck holding his Uzi in one hand. He threw his arms around Stepanovich. "We did it! We got 'em!"

"Viva CRASH!" Arredondo shouted.

Standing on the tiny lawn among the bodies, the three detectives, perspiring and out of breath, slapped one another on the back and exchanged hearty embraces.

One by one the lights in the windows on the street were coming on. "I'll handle the questions about renting the apartment," Stepanovich commanded anxiously. "On the shooting itself, we keep it vague. You were in fear of your life."

The others nodded and the heavy night air was filled with the sound of approaching sirens.

Stepanovich heard something and turned toward the house. A middle-aged woman with long black hair came out the front door. Obviously terrified and walking cautiously, with clenched fists under her chin, she walked from the threshold to the steps.

"Where is my boy?"

Stepanovich, figuring she was probably Payaso's mother, ran up the steps and past her into the house. In the living room, beer cans were strewn about and there was the distinct odor of marijuana. He found the telephone on a lamp table next to the sofa and picked up the receiver. He dialed the emergency number, identified himself, gave the address, and requested an ambulance. He went back outside.

The woman moved from body to body on the front lawn. "Where is my Primitivo?" she cried.

A minute later, a police car with siren blaring sped around the corner and slammed to a stop in front of the house. The driver's door swung open and Officer Candi Forest stepped out. Her hand on the butt of her holstered revolver, she sauntered in front of the car and onto the lawn. She shone a flashlight in Stepanovich's face.

"Get that flashlight out of my face."

She complied. "What the hell?"

"We've had an officer-involved shooting," Stepanovich interrupted. "Notify the responding units that one of the suspects escaped on foot eastbound. Request the captain, the shooting team, and the coroner to respond to this location, then start sealing off the street."

"You're with narco, right?"

"Gang detail."

"OK, I'll block off the street," she said, retreating with her flashlight.

Ambulances and paramedics were the next to arrive, then some television news crews, and finally two well-groomed young investigators from the district attorney's office. Stepanovich knew them. They were sent to the scene of officer-involved shootings to determine if the force used by police officers exceeded the limits of the law.

Harger arrived a few minutes later with siren screaming. He climbed out of his radio car wearing a button-down shirt and tie and his zebra-skin holsters. It occurred to Stepanovich that though it was the middle of the night, Harger had taken the time to shower, shave, and dress neatly before leaving home.

Harger moved briskly about the lawn examining the bodies, then took Stepanovich aside, out of the glare of the news crew lights.

"Jesus, we have seven dead bodies here. What the fuck happened?"

"We spotted some White Fence suspects at Payaso's

house and staked out. Eighteenth showed up and started shooting. We tried to make arrests and were fired on. We fired back."

"I'm gonna need more than that to keep the press off our backs. Houlihan is going to dig into this one. And those pricks from the DA's office—"

"I thought the Chief was behind us."

"He is," Harger said, staring at the bodies on the lawn. "He is."

"Tell him we paid White Fence back for Fordyce."

Harger turned to look at the camera crews setting up across the street. With some difficulty he cleared his throat. "The heat is going to come down on this. Jesus H. Christ."

"What the hell is that supposed to mean?"

"I didn't tell you to kill seven people."

Though the night was warm and muggy, Stepanovich felt a sudden chill.

Payaso's mother was standing at the side of the house, staring down at one of the wounded. "Where is my baaaaaby?" she wailed. "Primitivo!" Officer Forest tried to pull her away, but the woman would not budge. Forest threw her arms around the woman's shoulders to restrain her. The woman pulled away and Forest slipped and fell on the lawn, her police gear rattling.

"That's interfering, bitch!" Forest screamed, coming to her feet. She grabbed a handful of the woman's robe. "You're under arrest!"

As Payaso's mother struggled with Forest, two uniformed officers standing nearby rushed to help. Payaso's mother continued to wail.

Harger stood there watching the melee as if it was on TV.

"They're all shooters," Stepanovich said. "Every one of them is good for a murder."

"Seven bodies. The police commission is going to shit."

"It'll go a lot easier if you say we were authorized to

stake out gang shooters if we saw them. That isn't enough to put you or the Chief on the spot, but it would give us something to lean on."

"It's probably better not to say too much to anyone other than the shooting team at this point," Harger said.

Stepanovich felt anger welling inside him. "Hey, remember me? The sergeant who works for you and the Chief?"

Harger grasped his arm firmly. "Everything will work out," he whispered. "The Chief has the right to review the decision of any trial board. He's on your side."

"Trial board?" Stepanovich said, pulling his arm away.

"Seven bodies. The police commission will demand it. When you're interviewed by Houlihan, keep in mind he'll be trying to tar me for Captain Ratliff. He'll be trying to lay this entire thing on me, to ruin my career and make himself deputy chief." Harger straightened his necktie, then marched across the street into a blaze of camera lights.

Standing there in the artificial light with his heart beating double-time, Stepanovich suddenly felt a peculiar sense of relief and excitement because he hadn't been shot. There was nothing like this feeling, nothing he could ever admit to anyone. The seven dead men were killers. They had taken the lives of Fordyce and little Guadalupe Zuniga and countless others shot in drive-by murders, and now they had sucked their last wind.

His hands were shaking, his ears were ringing, and his mind was clouded with the rush of emotion, but he felt no guilt. As far as he was concerned, a wrong had been set right.

Stepanovich, seated in a basement interview room in Hollenbeck Station, heard the creaking of footsteps above, which meant the captain had come in from home in the middle of the night—a sure sign of a major police flap.

Jack Houlihan, wearing a blue sports coat and a white shirt with a soiled collar, sat across the small table from him. "What made you stake out Payaso's house?" he said. It was the third time he'd asked the question, having phrased it differently each time.

"We were on routine patrol and I observed White Fence gang members enter the location," Stepanovich said, repeating his word-for-word answer with a sleepless, headachy feeling that somehow he was no more than a bystander in the night's events.

"So you decided to stake out the house?"

Stepanovich nodded rather than spoke.

"Pardon me?" Houlihan said, giving away the fact that he was secretly recording the interview.

"Yes. I found an apartment with a view of the house and asked the renter if we could use it for a police surveillance. She agreed."

"What was her name?"

"I don't remember."

"You used someone's apartment for an observation post without knowing their name?"

"That's correct," Stepanovich said because there was no regulation against doing so.

"And she just said OK and left all of you in the apartment with all of her property?"

"There was nothing in the place. Bare floors."

"Convenient," Houlihan said, referring to his notes. "Getting back to the shooting itself. Once you saw the pickup truck pulling up to the residence, how long did it take you and your men to deploy outside?"

"I don't recall."

"Surely you can give me an estimate."

"We saw the vehicle and moved outside to get closer. I don't know how long it took."

Houlihan tweaked his nose and looked at his fingers. "Then the shooting started."

"Yes."

232

"And you, Black, and Arredondo identified your-selves as police officers and tried to make arrests."

"Then they started shooting at us," Stepanovich said.

"What happened exactly? Moment by moment?"

"We were in fear of our lives and fired back to keep from being killed."

"Who did you shoot? Like specifically?"

To piss off Houlihan, Stepanovich shrugged rather than give a verbal answer.

"Answer verbally," Houlihan said impatiently. "You're clever enough to have figured out this inter-view is being recorded."

Though he didn't feel like smiling, Stepanovich smiled. "I don't recall."

For the next hour Houlihan asked the same ques-tions over and over in every possible way. Stepanovich noticed that rather than getting irritated, Houlihan seemed to be holding his temper rather well, a sign that he was waiting to reveal some unsettling piece of information at the end of the interview.

Finally Houlihan closed his notebook and folded his hands. "I guess that's about it."

Stepanovich nodded and rose from the chair. At the door, like an actor anticipating his cue, he hesitated to allow for Houlihan to drop his bomb.

"Uh, one more thing," Houlihan said in the manner of a snappy television detective.

Stepanovich turned.

Houlihan held up a Polaroid photograph of the black Chevrolet parked in the garage at Sparky's tow yard.

Stepanovich consciously avoided making an expres-sion of any kind.

"Well?"

"Well what?"

"Have you ever seen this car?"

"It looks like the White Fence caper car we found up in Happy Valley," Stepanovich said.

"Sit down."

Stepanovich stepped back to the table. "I'm tired of sitting down."

Houlihan, looking up, bit his lip nervously. "There was a drive-by at Greenie's apartment, and a car just like this one was used."

"So what?"

"I'd appreciate it if you'd sit down."

"I've been in this room with you for two and a half hours and I'm tired of sitting down," Stepanovich said coldly. "If you have more questions, ask them and let's get it over with."

Houlihan came to his feet. "Did you remove this car from Sparky's tow yard after it was impounded for evidence?"

Stepanovich avoided the urge to clear his throat. "No," he said.

"Do you have any knowledge of any person using this car after it was impounded?"

"No."

"Is there any reason the fingerprints of either you, Black, or Arredondo might be found anywhere on this car?"

"Yes," Stepanovich said. "We might have touched the car when we impounded it. Mistakes happen."

"But neither you nor anyone removed the car from Sparky's impound yard and shot up Greenie's apartment?"

Stepanovich stopped breathing for a moment. "Of course not," he said. Even if Sparky cops out, he told himself, Houlihan will still have trouble proving they did the shooting without a confession. Relieved, he allowed himself to breathe again.

Houlihan nodded, forming his lips into a priestly, condescending smile.

At the Rumor Control Bar, Stepanovich found Black and Arredondo sitting at what had become their favorite corner table. The few customers in the place, some between-shift drinkers and a couple of Valley homicide detectives, noticed him as he entered and a few nodded to acknowledge his presence. But, as it was whenever someone was riding a heavy beef, there was more whispering than expressing support.

"Did Houlihan hit you with the black Chevy?" Black said as he sat down.

Stepanovich nodded. "He saved it for the end."

"Same here," Arredondo said, slurring his words because he was already drunk.

"They don't have shit," Stepanovich said. "Nothing. A zero."

"They have our prints on the car."

Stepanovich motioned to Sullivan for a drink. The barkeep nodded and picked up a glass. "So we touched some evidence."

"Sparky can hand us up," Black said.

"Sparky can hand only me up. I'm the one who asked him for the car."

Arredondo sipped his drink. "Houlihan must know something or he wouldn't have brought it up."

"It doesn't matter what he knows. It's what he can prove. As long as we keep our mouths shut, there is nothing he can do."

"What about Brenda?" Black said.

"Neither of you had anything to do with getting the apartment. I handled that."

Black wiped a streak of moisture from his cocktail glass. "Even a shithead like Houlihan will be able to find out it was Brenda who rented the place."

"Maybe, but Brenda has serviced a lot of Department brass. He'll press her, but I don't think he'll want to press too far."

Sullivan brought drinks to the table. "Everyone will be avoiding you while you're under investigation," he said, setting the drinks on the table. "The moment you're cleared of charges, they'll all want to buy you drinks. That's the way cops are these days."

"Tell us how it was in the old days," Black said.

"You making fun of me?"

Black shook his head. "Of course not," he said wryly.

Sullivan sat down and slid the cocktail glasses to their proper places at the table. "Houlihan phoned me this morning. He wanted to know if the three of you were in here at about eleven night before last."

Nothing was said at the table. Black fumbled for a cigarette.

"Ain't you cowboys gonna ask me what I told him?"

"What'd you say?" Stepanovich replied.

"I told him I'd have to think on it. That way I knew I'd have time to talk to you boys and find out what I should say."

"Thanks, Sully—" Stepanovich said.

"No need to get all sloppy. Just give me the word and I go. That's the wonderful thing about being retired. I can lie like a motherfucker and there's not a thing Houlihan or anybody else can do about it. Lying is part of the Bill of Rights—as long as you aren't in front of a grand jury."

"We were sitting right at this table. All night."

Sullivan snapped his fingers. "Now I remember. You were sitting right at this table all night."

"We never left," Arredondo said.

Sullivan winked. "The three of you closed the bar. That's what I'll tell him. By the way, in case you don't know, Houlihan is Ratliff's right-hand man, and Ratliff and Harger are both gunning for the deputy chief slot." He turned and shuffled back to the bar.

Stepanovich sipped his drink. By the hushed tones around the bar, it became obvious to him everyone was talking about the shooting.

It was after midnight when Stepanovich left the bar. Though his senses were dulled by alcohol and he was exhausted, the shooting, a vivid technicolor nightmare, was still at the forefront of his consciousness. On the way to Gloria's apartment, he relived it a few times in what he estimated was real time: a minute perhaps for the entire shootout. As he well knew, violence always happened quickly. It was something to get over with as soon as possible. It had an objective.

TWENTY-TWO

The sound of helicopters clacked overhead.

Payaso, exhausted and unable to run full speed because he still hadn't fully recovered from his wounds suffered at the Queen of Angels Church, jogged rather than ran along Third Street.

A police car with red lights flashing turned the corner.

Payaso ducked and scooted behind some bushes, and the police car sped past. At the end of the block the car skidded to a halt and two officers, a man and a woman, climbed out. They activated flares and dropped to either side of the car in order to block the street. Because he knew from experience that when someone escaped from the scene of a crime, the police always tried to trap him by blocking the streets, he knew he was safely out of the perimeter. With his T-shirt soaked with perspiration from running, he lay there in the bushes trying to catch his breath.

Finally he came to his feet and, staying in the shadows so the policemen at the end of the block wouldn't notice him, resumed jogging. Though the street was illuminated intermittently by the powerful searchlight from one of the police helicopters flying overhead, he made his way another two blocks to Evergreen Cemetery. He climbed a six-foot chainlink fence and dropped onto the cemetery grounds.

Keeping an eye out for the powerful helicopter searchlight, he dodged sprinklers and made his way past crypts and tombstones all the way to the guard booth at the front gate. Through the gate he could see that Fourth Street was deserted. Still hyperventilating, he looked about on the ground. There was a loose brick lying near a sprinkler that was waving a powerful stream of water into the darkness. Picking up the brick and stepping to the guard booth, he smashed out the window glass just above the door handle and reached inside to open the door.

Inside, there was a telephone on the small desk. He picked up the receiver and, leaning close to read the dial, he touched numbers. The phone rang three times. Sleepy answered.

"It's me, baby."

"Parrot just called. She said Smokey and—"

"Listen to me," he interrupted. "I'm running and I need to do something."

"Are you hurt?"

"No, I ain't hurt, but everyone else is dead. The pigs were waiting."

She broke into tears.

"I'm at Evergreen Cemetery. Get my car at Smokey's and pick me up at the front gate. If there's *la chota* on the street, just drive past and come back in an hour. If you get pulled over, tell them you are on your way to work. Do what I tell you, homegirl."

Payaso set the receiver down and stepped out of the booth. Lifting his T-shirt, he pulled his .38 revolver from his belt holster. He reloaded with the six rounds in his right pocket and dropped the empty rounds on the grass.

From the left pocket he took a tiny paper packet and unwrapped it. There were four white pills. Though his mouth was dry and he knew it was going to be difficult to swallow, he tilted his head back and dropped the pills back in his throat. He swallowed three times, but the pills wouldn't go down. He knelt at the sprinkler and, cupping his hands, took water into his mouth. He swallowed until the whites went down, then stood and moved near the fence so he could keep an eye on the street.

He felt renewed energy almost immediately. The first sign was the warmth of surging blood starting at his temples and spreading across this face and into his extremities, including his cock and balls. Closing his eyes for a moment, he saw himself, gun in hand, shooting it out with the cops in front of his house and the cops falling.

By the time Sleepy arrived, he was supercharged.

He climbed over the fence, hurried to the driver's side of the car, and climbed in. Sleepy was wearing a tight sweater and skirt. She threw her arms around him.

He shoved the car into gear and accelerated.

Frightened, she pulled away from him. "How did they know you were—"

"It had to be the one who told you. She set us up for the cops."

"Gloria? She would never—"

"Gloria este la rata."

"No. She would never do anything to hurt anyone. It's not her way."

"Her boyfriend is a pig."

Sleepy cried quietly. "She's in love, but she wouldn't . . ."

Sensing the full effect of the whites, Payaso leaned back in the seat. If he wanted, it seemed, he could bend the steering wheel into a knot or shove his hands through the windshield or even fly through it without suffering injury. His gun felt warm and alive as if it were part of his body.

He turned left into a dead-end street and pulled to the curb directly under a streetlight. Killing the engine, he cupped Sleepy's chin. There were tears streaming down her face.

He lifted her skirt.

"People can see," she whispered.

He pulled down her panties and massaged her fuzzy softness.

"Not now, Payaso," she whispered. "Payaso. Payaso."

Leaving his trousers and revolver in place, he slid his zipper down and exposed his erect cock. He pushed her down on the seat. Arching into her, he grasped her breasts tightly. She held his shoulders and moaned deeply as he pounded into her.

"Please, not so hard, baby," she said, her voice shaking.

At that moment he came powerfully into her, then sat up immediately. He arranged himself quickly and secured his zipper.

Sleepy sat up. Staring at him, she pulled down her dress. "Are you high?"

Payaso grabbed the steering wheel and started the engine.

She slid next to him. "Payaso?"

He made a U-turn, and headed south on Fourth Street.

"That's a red light!" she screamed as he drove through a four-way intersection. "Please be careful."

"Everybody is dead," he said.

"Where are we going?"

"White Fence *rifamos*."

Stepanovich drove down City Terrace Avenue to the Tahitian Arms apartments. As he pulled into the parking lot, he mulled over what he was going to say to Gloria. Hell, he regretted not having come directly to the apartment from the station rather than stopping at the Rumor Control Bar.

As he climbed out of his car, he noticed a blue customized Chevrolet parked at the curb across the street—the kind of car Payaso owned.

Stepanovich's breath caught in his throat and his muscles tightened. He looked up at Gloria's apartment. The lights were on.

*   *   *

Payaso, with his hand on the butt of his revolver, stood back from the doorway. Sleepy, standing in front of the door, was shaking with fear. "Do it," he whispered.

"Please. Don't make me—"

"Do it, homegirl."

Sleepy wiped her eyes and, with her hand shaking, knocked on the door lightly. After a moment the door opened. "Gloria."

"Dora. What's wrong?" Gloria said.

Payaso stepped in front of Sleepy and shoved Gloria to the floor. He pulled Sleepy inside. He grabbed Gloria by the hair and put his gun in her face.

"You set us up, bitch."

"Dora. What is this?"

Sleepy broke into an uncontrollable bout of tears. "I told him what you said about Eighteenth coming to his house."

"The cops were waiting," Payaso said. "They killed the homeboys—"

"I'm sorry," Gloria cried, coming to her feet. "I didn't want anyone to get hurt."

Payaso slapped Gloria with an open hand. Her head snapped back and she cried out. He aimed his revolver at her.

"No! Please don't hurt her!" Dora cried.

Payaso's face was tingling with heat. He felt light on his feet, potent, and invincible as he cocked his revolver. Out of the corner of his eye he spotted movement at the open door and whirled about.

Stepanovich grabbed Dora from behind and held his gun to her head. "Let Gloria go, Payaso." Payaso considered firing at Stepanovich, but hesitated because Dora would certainly be shot. Payaso kept his gun aimed at Gloria. "Your bitch is dead, pig," he said.

"She has nothing to do with what happened. Drop your gun."

"Fuck you, pig."

"Payaso, you pull the trigger and your woman is dead."

Suddenly Payaso realized with a start that although Stepanovich was using Dora for a shield, he himself was exposed. He tried to pull Gloria in front of him, but she resisted.

There was the sharp crack of gunfire.

Payaso felt himself being ripped backward and down as Stepanovich came at him firing. Though he knew he was getting killed, he restrained the urge to fire back because he might hit Sleepy, his *ruka*. With the sound of Sleepy shrieking and the gunshots and the cop screaming, "Drop the gun!" he was exploded over and over again. Lying there breathless, he watched Stepanovich kick him in the ribs to roll him over. His arms were pulled behind him, and handcuffs clamped his wrists for the hundredth time in his life. As blackness took him, Payaso's last thought before lapsing into unconsciousness was that he was thankful for dope. Because of the pills he'd taken, there was little pain.

And to die without pain was good.

Stepanovich picked up Payaso's gun from the carpet and came to his feet.

"You killed him!" the woman screamed. She seemed stunned as Stepanovich frisked her. Sobbing loudly, she dropped to her knees next to Payaso.

Gloria, her hands doubled under her chin and eyes wide with fear, was standing with her back to the wall, staring at Payaso. Stepanovich walked over to her and reached to take her in his arms. She pulled away.

"Everything's OK now," he said, feeling his pulse in his mouth.

"Deeeeeeaaaaaaadddd!" Dora wailed.

From outside came the sound of sirens and rushing footsteps on the stairs. He pulled his badge from his belt and held it up as two young Hispanic officers burst through the doorway with revolvers held in the two-handed combat stance.

"Everything's code four," Stepanovich said.

The officers lowered their weapons.

"Call an ambulance and notify the watch commander by land line. Tell him there's been an officer-involved shooting."

"What do we have?" the taller officer said.

Stepanovich turned. Payaso's eyes were open and white foam was bubbling from his mouth. "Gang retaliation. He had a piece and I did him." Stepanovich nodded at the woman. "Take her in for murder."

The other officer hurried to the woman and snapped handcuffs on her wrists. "Payasooooooo!" she screeched hysterically. "My Payaso is deeeeeaaaaad!"

The officer pointed at Gloria. "What about her?"

"She's a witness. I'll take her to the station myself."

The sound of footsteps was followed by the arrival of more uniformed officers. Stepanovich briefed them quickly. Two uniformed city paramedics arrived. A younger man carrying a medical case knelt down next to Payaso and held a stethoscope to Payaso's chest.

"No vital signs," he said brusquely. "Looks like we're not needed."

His partner, a balding man, glanced at his wristwatch, then reached to his back pocket and took out a blue-printed pad the size of a traffic citation book. He filled out the top page quickly, tore out the carbon copy, and handed it to Stepanovich.

Stepanovich looked up suddenly and found Gloria staring at him.

As officers began stretching yellow evidence tape across the doorway, Stepanovich took her by the arm and led her outside to his car. He opened the door for her and she climbed in.

"Do you feel OK?"

Gloria stared straight ahead.

"Try not to think about what happened."

TWENTY-THREE

Stepanovich drove Gloria around the corner to the two-story house where her sister lived.

He helped her out of the car. "I'm going to the station. When the shooting team investigators arrive, I'll send them over here to interview you," he said, leading her up the short walkway. He could hear a vacuum cleaner going inside.

Without looking at him, she knocked on the door.

"Are you OK?" he said, realizing his hands were still shaking.

The vacuum stopped. The door opened and Gloria's sister, Armida, a handsome woman resembling her, frowned in concern. "Gloria. What's wrong?"

Gloria broke into tears and Armida threw her arms around her.

Stepanovich returned to Hollenbeck Station to brief the shooting team investigators. He spent the next seven hours answering questions and writing reports about the two shootings. With these duties finally taken care of, he hurried back to Armida's house. Armida came to the door and told him Gloria was lying down and would be with her for the night. He told her he would be back in the morning.

At his apartment, Stepanovich fished a key from his

pocket and unlocked the door. He had a horrible, nauseating headache.

In the kitchen he opened a drawer and fished among kitchen utensils, supermarket coupons, and some plastic corn-cob holders Nancy had left behind until he found the bottle of aspirin. He spun the cap and tipped three of the white pills into his cupped hand. Filling a glass from the dish drainer, he tossed the pills back and washed them down.

In the living room the red light on his answering machine was blinking. He touched the PLAY button: a message from the landlord reminding him to pay the rent. He turned the machine off. In the bathroom he stripped and took a long shower, soaping up and rinsing himself three times.

In bed, though the aspirin had made the headache disappear, every time he closed his eyes he pictured Gloria and heard gunshots.

Unable to sleep, he turned on the radio and flipped through channels for a while, finally stopping on a talk show featuring a panel of motorcycle gang members. Then he turned off the radio and lay there in the dark, intermittently reliving the shootings and seeing Gloria and Payaso holding the gun to her head. After an hour or so of tossing and turning, he concentrated on the persistent hum of the freeway floating through the open window and managed to drop into fitful sleep.

In the morning, a loud knocking woke Stepanovich from a frightening dream in which he was naked, precariously riding a motorcycle on a wire extended between skyscrapers.

He opened his eyes. It was light. Still half asleep, he staggered to his feet and pulled on his trousers. The pounding on the door continued as he shuffled through the living room to the front door. Stepanovich used the peephole. It was Houlihan and two other grim internal affairs detectives.

Stepanovich rushed to the telephone and picked up the receiver. He began to dial Arredondo's number, then stopped when he realized the phone might be bugged.

"Internal affairs!" Houlihan shouted. "Open up!"

Stepanovich set the receiver down on the cradle, took a deep breath, and walked back to the door. He unfastened the chain lock and pulled the door open quickly.

Houlihan stepped back as if startled. "Internal affairs investigation," he said nervously. The other detectives, athletic-looking men with closely cropped hair, Stepanovich recognized by face but not name. They were dressed in neat but obviously cheap suits and ties and were carrying briefcases. Both avoided looking him in the eye.

Stepanovich, carefully avoiding making any expression whatsoever, just nodded at Houlihan.

"I guess you know why we're here," Houlihan said nervously.

Stepanovich forced a smile. "Looking for your wife?"

Houlihan's face turned a purplish red. "You are the subject of a personnel investigation. Captain Ratliff, Commander of Internal Affairs Division, has ordered us to search your apartment."

"I hope you have that in writing."

Houlihan reached inside his coat, proudly displayed a folded sheet of paper, and handed it to Stepanovich. Because he figured Houlihan wouldn't have the guts to do anything without official backing, he handed the paper back without reading it.

Like a magician doing a silk scarf trick, Houlihan hid the paper inside his coat and came out with a small plastic-laminated card. He read: "You have the right to refuse consent for this search, but if you do, the Department may choose to legally close and secure this dwelling and seek the issuance of a legal search warrant from a duly authorized judge—"

"I know my rights. What's the allegation?"

"CUBO," Houlihan said. "Conduct unbecoming an officer."

"Go ahead," Stepanovich said, believing there was nothing in the apartment of evidentiary value, and stepped back from the door.

Houlihan moved past him into the living room and the others followed. As Houlihan pointed the detectives toward rooms, Stepanovich stepped into the kitchen, picked up a coffee mug, and filled it with water. He opened the cupboard and took out a small glass jar of instant coffee.

"I'd appreciate it if you would stay in one place and not move around while we search," Houlihan said.

Stepanovich glanced into the living room to make sure they were alone and there were no witnesses. "Fuck you," he said in a tone low enough so that if Houlihan wrote him up and accused him of refusing to cooperate with an internal affairs investigation the others wouldn't be unable to corroborate the allegation.

Houlihan knew what Jose was doing. He just stood there glaring, red-faced. Stepanovich twisted the cap from the coffee jar, picked up a spoon, and measured a heaping teaspoon into a cup. As Houlihan watched, he opened the microwave door, set the cup inside, and fixed the digital timer for two minutes. He closed the door and touched the ON switch. The microwave hummed.

Cautiously, keeping his eyes on Stepanovich, Houlihan began to casually sort through the stack of mail on the kitchen table.

With the coffee heated, Stepanovich carried it to the table and sat down. He slurped the coffee loudly and looked Houlihan directly in the eye.

"I'm just doing a job," Houlihan said.

Stepanovich stared at the mail in Houlihan's hand. Guiltily Houlihan set the mail down and left the table to explore the living room, checking thoroughly under sofa cushions and thumbing through some *Serb World* and *American Legion* magazines piled in the corner.

When the detectives returned to the living room, the taller one, standing with his back to Stepanovich, handed something to Houlihan. "This was on the dresser."

Stepanovich picked up his coffee cup and sauntered across the room.

Houlihan, staring at the carbon of the weapons receipt Black got for the shoulder weapons, was smiling broadly. He looked up. "Looks like you were planning a heavy operation without the knowledge of your superiors."

Though Stepanovich felt like grabbing the receipt out of Houlihan's hand, he just sipped his coffee.

Houlihan shoved the receipt in his suit jacket pocket. "Did you hear what I said?"

"Yes."

"It's your name and your handwriting, isn't it?"

"Probably," Stepanovich said, knowing that he would be violating a Department regulation by not answering. Besides, a police handwriting expert would be able to identify his handwriting.

"You might as well tell us the truth and save yourself a lot of trouble."

"Is your search completed?" Stepanovich said.

"You could say that."

"Do you have any further questions?"

"Not right now—"

"Then get the hell out of my apartment."

"Do you want a receipt for the evidence?"

"No," Stepanovich said, opening the door. "I want to go back to sleep."

Houlihan and the others had barely stepped across the threshold when Stepanovich slammed the door. He walked to the window and pulled the curtain back a few inches. The detectives walked down the stairs and stopped by the car to converse animatedly. Houlihan looked pleased. Finally they climbed into their police sedan and drove out the driveway and around the corner.

Stepanovich ran into the bedroom and threw on a T-shirt and shoes. He shoved some change into his pocket, and jogged back through the living room and out the door.

At the pay telephone across the street from the apartment, Stepanovich dialed Arredondo's number. The phone was answered on the first ring. Stepanovich, articulating clearly, read off the phone number of the pay telephone.

"Got it," Arredondo said in a tone indicating he recognized Stepanovich's voice.

Stepanovich hung the receiver back on the switch hook.

Less than five minutes later, the phone rang.

"Are you at a pay phone?" Stepanovich said.

"If you're going to warn me about IA, they've already been to my place and gone. Black just called. They hit him too."

"Did they get anything?"

"They didn't get anything at Black's, but they took my address book."

"Is Brenda's number in there?"

"I think so."

"Shit."

"They're going to try to hang us," Arredondo said.

"We're OK as long as we keep our mouths shut."

"When they were leaving I heard 'em talking about the grand jury. It sounded like they're taking it to the district attorney. They want to get us indicted."

"Harger won't let that happen."

"You'd better talk to him," Arredondo said. "Things are moving fast."

"Meet me tonight at the Rumor Control."

At Hollenbeck Station, a group of Hispanic men, women, and children were parading in front of the entrance carrying picket signs saying: "COPS GET AWAY WITH MURDER" and "PROSECUTE POLICE MURDERERS." Stepanovich drove around the corner and pulled into the parking lot in the rear. He made his way down the stairs to the CRASH office. The squad room was empty.

The door to Harger's office was cracked a few inches, and Stepanovich peeked inside. Harger, his necktie askew, was seated at his desk busily writing on a thick legal pad. Stepanovich rapped on the door to gain his attention. Harger looked startled as he said, "Joe." He quickly turned over the tablet. "I thought you had the day off—"

"Internal affairs searched my apartment."

"I only have a few minutes before I have to be at the Chief's office," Harger said apologetically.

"They searched Arredondo's and Black's places too. They're trying to put a case together on us."

Harger picked up a pencil and drummed on the tablet. "This thing is taking on a life of its own. The DA, the politicians are getting involved."

"Why hasn't the Chief held a press conference?"

Harger stopped drumming. "A press conference?"

"If the chief expresses support for us, it'll take off some of the heat. Internal affairs will back off."

"Sure. I'll bring that up with him."

"Captain, I'm as solid as anyone on this department, but you and I both know that once the ball starts rolling on something like this, every bureaucrat, every political hack, every reporter in this town will get in on the act. They'll make punching bags out of us."

"That's not going to happen," Harger said. "Things just look like they're getting out of control at this point. I want you and the others to just hang in until we see what we're up against. The chief doesn't want to play his cards too soon."

"I've been around long enough to know that's not how it works. Somebody has to take a stand on our behalf or we'll never make it."

"Hey, you guys blew up seven people. I can't just wave a magic wand and make it go away. There's going to be a lot of televised funerals and coroners' inquests and rehashing in the press before this incident is washed. You have to be patient."

"Unless we have somebody out there on our side, the system will eat us alive."

"I understand," Harger said, coming to his feet. "The chips are down and nothing is lonelier than riding a beef. I've been there and I know. My advice to you and the others is to try to keep your mind on something else for the time being. If you sit around watching the Monday morning quarterbacks and the bleeding-heart Mexicans crying on the news, you'll go crazy."

The phone rang at that moment, and Harger snatched up the receiver. "Harger," he said, turning away from Stepanovich. "Yes sir. He's with me right now, sir." Stretching the telephone cord, he returned to his seat, grabbed a pen, and made notes on the reverse of the legal tablet. ". . . Got it. Yes sir," he said somberly.

He set the receiver down slowly.

"That was the Commander. You, Black, and Arredondo have been relieved of duty pending a trial board."

"Does the Chief know about this?"

"The Commander gave me a direct order not to talk to either you or the others until the investigation is completed."

"There's no one else in this room except you and me. I want to know what the fuck is going on."

Harger stepped to the door and shoved it closed. "This whole investigation is pro forma because there were so many people shot. The police commission is demanding a shake-out to look good for the Hispanic rights groups. It's a game, a scenario."

"The police commission was the one asking for more gang enforcement."

"They were. But that was then. Look, I know you're upset. You have a right to be. But I want you and the other guys to stay cool until this blows over. Just hang in there. Hang tough."

"Are the internal affairs investigators going to present evidence to the district attorney?"

"I've been ordered not to talk to you or the others named in the allegation."

"But at this point there is no formal allegation," Stepanovich said.

"Nevertheless, I've been ordered not to talk to you."

"All along I've been assuring Arredondo and Black the Chief is behind them."

Harger picked up a leather folder from the corner of the desk. He unzipped it and shoved the legal tablet inside without turning it right-side-up. He zipped it closed. Moving past Stepanovich, he grabbed his suit jacket from a coat rack. "I want you guys to hang in," he said, shrugging on his coat. "It'll work out."

"You're not leveling with me."

"There's something else," Harger said, ignoring the remark. "I'll have to ask you for your badge and gun." Stepanovich's lips felt slightly numb. "The Commander sent someone out to collect Black's and Arredondo's equipment too. This is just until the trial board comes back with a finding."

Stepanovich unclipped his silver police shield from his belt and handed it over. He reached inside his jacket, unholstered his revolver, and handed it, butt first, to Harger.

"Consider it a free vacation," Harger said, slipping the gun and badge into his leather case. He slapped Stepanovich on the shoulder and left the room.

TWENTY-FOUR

Stepanovich drove from Hollenbeck Station to the downtown Criminal Courts Building. At the entrance to the building's underground parking lot he pulled up to a guard booth. A young, sleepy-eyed county building guard looked up from a copy of the *National Enquirer* and nodded.

Stepanovich drove inside and cruised along the long rows of automobiles until he found Howard Goldberg's car, a ten-year-old, primer-spotted Oldsmobile with a hand-control accelerator device on the steering wheel. He tried the door and found it unlocked. Looking around to make sure no one was watching, he climbed in. Sitting behind the wheel, he took out his wallet and removed one of his personalized LAPD business cards. Using a pen in his shirt pocket, he printed the following on the reverse of the card:

"Relieved of duty. Meet at Evergreen."

He affixed the corner of the card under the steering wheel accelerator knob where Howard wouldn't miss it and climbed out.

Because he hadn't eaten all day and knew it would be at least an hour before Howard left his office, Stepanovich drove down Alameda Street to Philippe's sandwich shop and parked in the crowded parking lot.

~~The outside of the ancient delicatessen had recently~~
been repainted in its original beige with new green
canvas awnings to make it look like it had in the
twenties.

Inside, the restaurant's long, narrow tables were
filled with customers eating off trays. Making his way
across the sawdust-covered floor to a crowded counter,
he ordered two lamb sandwiches, a side order of po-
tato salad and set them on a brown plastic tray with a
cup of coffee. At a corner table he ate slowly, finishing every morsel, returning to the counter for a coffee
refill, because he had time to kill before meeting Howard. On the way back to his table, he stopped at the
sundries counter near the front door and purchased a
copy of the *Los Angeles Times*.

On the front page was a large photograph of the
sheet-covered bodies lying on the front lawn in front
of Payaso's house. The headline read: "POLICE PROBE
IN TEEN SHOOTINGS." Unfolding the newspaper, he read
the article:

Reliable law enforcement sources report that a major
internal investigation is under way in the deaths of
seven alleged gang members on Ortega Street last night
at the hands of an elite unit of the police gang detail.
Undercover officers allegedly exchanged fire with the
gang members in an attempt to defend themselves
during a street gang battle they allegedly happened
onto. Efriam Verdugo, president of the local chapter
of the Coalition Against Cop Abuse said it was obvious the officers had used excessive force. "Isn't
seven bodies enough to convince anyone that Los
Angeles Police Department treats Hispanics as second-
class citizens? Can you imagine what would have
happened if they had killed seven white teenagers?"

Mr. Verdugo alleged that police abuse has been
covered up by LAPD higher-ups for years and that
investigations of police shootings are invariably biased
in favor of the police officers involved.

Police Public Affairs Spokesman Merle Gates said

that the victims of the shooting were not teenagers and in fact were adults with extensive criminal histories. When questioned as to the nature and background of the special gang unit involved in the shooting, he declined further comment.

Feeling frustration, anger, and guilt welling within him, Stepanovich stopped reading and shoved the paper through the door of a nearby plastic trash can.

Outside, he walked along Alameda past the Terminal Annex Post Office to Olvera Street, a sloping cobblestone throughway between a few buildings someone had designated as historical landmarks. He moved briskly past the small stalls selling plaster *toros,* serapes, and crude, Mexican puppets with stick torsos, wood and wrought-iron personalized nameplates, and other tourist gimcracks.

At the end of the street a circle of vagrants relaxing on cement benches surrounded a pigeon-stained plaza. A single-file line of school children awaiting the daily Olvera Street historical tour cuffed, teased and wrestled as youthful school teachers shouted and blew whistles to restore discipline.

Standing there without either gun or badge, Stepanovich's mind wandered. There had been other moments like this. Gloomily he recalled his mother informing him of Uncle Nick's death by heart attack. And Nancy, in her businesslike way, informing him that she was leaving to live with Bruce the interior decorator.

Stepanovich parked his car in an alley off Third Street where it couldn't be seen from the street and walked the few blocks to Evergreen Cemetery. Behind the high hedge near the entrance, where he and Howard had once waited for the ice cream truck, he sat on the grass. Through the high, spiked fence surrounding the graveyard he could see the area where Uncle Nick was buried.

A few minutes later, Howard's Olds cruised into the

driveway and pulled up. Howard waved and Stepanovich climbed in the passenger seat. The glum expression on Howard's face told him Howard knew something.

"Are we going to ambush an ice cream truck?" Howard said.

"We're just lucky we never got caught."

"We'd have survived."

Stepanovich forced a smile. "You've heard?"

"Everybody in town has heard."

"I'm worried, Howard."

"You should be."

"The White Fence punks we wasted were the ones who killed Fordyce. The others were killers too—"

"Oh, I understand," Howard interrupted. "I grew up here, remember?"

"I've been suspended from duty pending a trial board."

"And you'd like to know if the internal affairs people have been over at my office?"

"If you'd rather not tell me, I'll understand."

Howard leaned forward, his arms embracing the steering wheel. "You really did it this time. Houlihan had a one-hour meeting with the district attorney himself. Weber and I sat in. Houlihan pushed for us to file conspiracy to murder on you and the others. Weber readily agreed, of course, because he thought that's what the DA wanted to hear."

Stepanovich felt his throat turn dry.

"I pointed out the weaknesses in the case—told them there really is no case—but Houlihan was really gilding the lily for excessive use of force. He and Weber were on the bandwagon like a couple of vigilantes. Weber kept making statements like 'We have no way out. It looks to me like we have to file charges.' But you lucked out. The district attorney agreed with me that the case was weak and could not be prosecuted in a criminal court."

Stepanovich let out his breath and ran his fingers through his hair. "Thank God."

"The reason the DA won't prosecute is that he's going to run for state attorney general as a Republican in the next election, and it would be bad politics for him to file on cops at this time. He told me that three weeks ago, but failed to tell Weber because he's a pipeline to the Democrats. Therefore, you lucked out. In the last election, when filing on cops was the thing to do, he was digging through old cases trying to find a cop to put in jail." Howard turned and stared at the cemetery. "Timing is everything." He pointed: "That's where we used to hide and eat the ice cream, isn't it?"

Stepanovich nodded.

"Hitting the trucks is the most exciting memory of my childhood," Howard said. "Almost sexually exciting —right up until I fell off. I remember the sound of the ambulance and lying in the street unable to move. You were looking down at me and crying."

"Now that we aren't going to be prosecuted criminally, internal affairs will probably make it extra rough on us at the department trial board."

Howard cleared his throat. "Do you have any brass on your side at the Department?"

"Yes."

"Like who?"

"The Chief."

"You've talked with him personally?"

"He sent the word down through Captain Harger. He's been behind us from the outset."

"If you have the Chief in your pocket, you'll be in good shape in front of a trial board. Kangaroo courts don't go against the wishes of the chief Kangaroo."

At a rustle in the nearby bushes, Stepanovich turned. A pack of sniffing, snapping wild dogs wandered through a break in a hedge and trotted briskly along the length of the cemetery's fence line. Remaining in pack formation, the skinny mongrels stayed close together all the way to Third Street.

"I'm sure we have the Chief's backing," Stepanovich said.

"If you had his complete backing, I doubt if a brown nose like Houlihan would have been sitting in the DA's office begging to get criminal charges filed on you."

"That's just the way Houlihan is. He likes it."

"Is it true he's the guy who used to collect the urine samples from the police recruits to see if they'd been using dope?"

"None other."

Howard just shook his head. "Let me put it to you gently: if the Chief isn't willing to stick his neck out a little for you guys and get the internal affairs people to back off, then you'd better stand by for the ram."

It was standing room only at the Rumor Control Bar. A vice detective had just been promoted to sergeant.

Stepanovich found Black and Arredondo at the bar talking to Sullivan. The three looked grim.

"We're home free on criminal charges," Stepanovich said. "This comes straight from the DA's office."

Neither Black nor Arredondo changed expression.

Sullivan picked up a folded letter lying on the bar in front of them and handed it to Stepanovich. As he tried to read in the dim light, Sullivan picked up a flashlight from behind the bar and shone it on the paper.

FROM: Chief of Police Levester C. Burrel
TO: Stepanovich, Jose L. Det., Sgt. Ser.#613845
     Arredondo, Raul A. Dept., Ser.#257491
     Black, Cyrus R., Det., Ser.#992318
     A personnel investigation is being conducted, and it has been alleged that all of you violated the following penal code sections and department regulations:

1. Conspiracy to commit murder
2. Conduct unbecoming an officer

3. Failure to notify a supervisor of an ongoing investigation
4. Excessive use of force
5. Use of unauthorized weapons
6. Making false and misleading statements to a supervisor
7. Acquiescing in the failure to report a felony crime and violation of department regulations per the above
8. Conspiracy to commit all the above

All of you are here by relieved of duty without pay pending a Los Angeles Police Department Board of Rights hearing concerning these allegations.

"They can't prove any of this," Stepanovich said weakly. He knew, however, that the rules of evidence at a trial board were rigged so that charges were adjudicated by the "preponderance of evidence" rule rather strict courtroom rules, enabling the board to convict anyone for anything and to issue findings that would be laughed out of a legitimate court of law.

Sullivan poured some scotch into a cocktail glass and slid it to Stepanovich. "When they throw in this many charges, it means they are trying to fire you," Sullivan said.

"He's right," Black said, lighting a cigarette. "The conspiracy to murder charge is just for show, but they'll end up proving CUBO, acquiescing, and excessive use of force."

"If the Chief was behind us, they wouldn't have listed so many allegations," Arredondo said.

"They have to make it look good for the police commission," Stepanovich said.

"Maybe it'll look really good if they fire the three of us," Black said.

"Which is exactly what they can do with a shit list like this one."

"Did you talk to Harger?" Black asked.

"He said the trial board is just pro forma and the Chief is behind us."

"And the check is in the mail," Arredondo said.

"Harger was sticking his neck out even talking to me."

"He was sticking his neck out?" Black said. "What about us?"

Sullivan grabbed a bottle of Early Times from the well rack and filled a shot glass. Forming his mouth into an alcoholic grimace, he tossed back the drink. Shaking his head, he turned and moved down the bar cleaning ashtrays.

"Harger will come through for us," Stepanovich said.

Black jammed out his cigarette and picked another from an open pack on the bar. "I'm beginning to have my doubts."

"We knew some heat was going to come down," Stepanovich said.

"But this is starting to look like the real thing," Arredondo said. "They actually want to fire us."

"It's too soon to say that."

"With these kind of allegations we'll be lucky to end up with a penalty of six months without pay," Black said. "I have a house payment, a boat payment, and child support."

"Just hang in," Stepanovich said. "I'm sure we'll get some word from Harger very soon on how this is going to be fixed."

Black lit another cigarette and blew out the match. He smiled broadly. Arredondo turned to him. "What the hell are you smiling about?"

Black positioned his hands to hold an imaginary shotgun. "I was just thinking about wasting all those homeboys. Boom! Boom! Boom!" He laughed.

"You're nuts," Arredondo said. "One hundred percent certifiably insane Okie."

Black laughed even louder and, perhaps out of nervous tension, Stepanovich found himself laughing too.

Soon the three of them were in a frenzy of laughter and Stepanovich found himself wiping away tears.

Brenda, dressed only in bra and panties because the air conditioner was on the blink, finished washing the dishes in the kitchen and set them in the drainer on the cracked Formica sink counter. She wished she had enough money to have the sink fixed. As a matter of fact, the kitchen linoleum, most of the major appliances, and the tile in the bathroom of the two-bedroom tract home needed repair. Hell, for all intents and purposes, the entire house, like the rest of the cheapie tract homes in the neighborhood, was falling apart. Wiping her chapped hands on a dishtowel, she resolved that the first thing she would do when she got her next paycheck from the Arroyo Grande Cardboard Box and Container Company, where she worked as a box inspector, was to have whining ex-husband's junked car towed off the front lawn. She told herself she would have taken care of this earlier, but it was more fun to hang out at the Rumor Control Bar rather than to try fixing up a house that was, God knows, completely shot.

There was a knock on the door. She hurried into the bedroom and threw on a robe.

At the front door, she opened the peephole.

"Yes?"

"Lieutenant Houlihan, Los Angeles Police Department," said a man fitting the description given her by Stepanovich. He held up a police identification card. "I'd like to ask you some questions."

"I'm not properly dressed."

"I can wait for you to change."

"What's this about?"

"Would you mind opening the door?"

She complied.

"May I come in?"

"I'd rather talk right here."

Houlihan bit his lip. "OK, then. I'm here about the apartment you rented on Ortega Street."

"I heard the TV news about the shooting. Awful."

"How is it that the officers came to use your apartment?"

"They asked me and I said yes. I believe in supporting my local police. You know, you shouldn't bite your lip like that."

Houlihan took out a note pad and pen. "Which officer spoke with you?"

"He had a Russian-sounding name."

"Stepanovich?"

"That's it."

"Had you ever met him before?"

"I'd seen him at the Rumor Control Bar."

"What do you mean you've *seen* him?"

"We're both customers of the place. I've seen him sitting at the bar. Haven't you ever just seen somebody somewhere?"

Houlihan bit his lip. "Did he ask you to rent that apartment?"

"No."

"Why did you want to live on Ortega Street?"

"I just decided to sell my house and move into an apartment. I was driving by and saw a "FOR RENT" sign."

"Is this house for sale?"

"No. I was going to list the house with a realtor, but after I saw the TV about what happened—the shooting and all—I decided to stay right here."

"Are you aware you could be prosecuted for lying to a police officer when he is in the performance of his official duties?"

"Are you calling me a liar?"

"I didn't say that."

"I'm kinda busy today. Is there anything else?"

"May I step inside for a moment? I need to get down what you told me in writing and have you sign it."

"I think you better stay where you are," Brenda said.

"I'm sure you have no objection to signing a statement, right?"

"Can you arrest me if I don't sign the statement?"

"No."

"Then I'm not signing it."

"You can be subpoenaed into court."

"You got a subpoena?"

He shook his head.

"Then, if you don't mind, I'm busy," she said, closing the door in his face. Having set the chain lock, she hurried to the front window. With her heart pounding, she watched Houlihan walk past Gary's junk, climb in his police car, and drive off.

In the bedroom she struggled into a pair of tennis shorts and her abalone-shell halter and fixed her hair into a ponytail on top of her head that C.R. Black called "his love handle."

In the bedroom, she used an atomizer to spray some Obsession perfume on her neck and wrists, then headed out the door.

Stepanovich was sitting on a bar stool working on his third drink when Brenda walked in the front door. She looked ill at ease.

"That guy Houlihan came over to my house," she said, crawling onto the stool between him and Black. She placed her cheap leather purse on the bar and took out a plastic cigarette case. "He wanted to know why I rented the apartment on Ortega Street." She picked a cigarette from the case and Black lit it for her. She puffed, waved a hand through smoke. "I told him I rented the place on my own and you guys asked me to use it. But I don't think he believed a word I said."

"You did good, woman," Black said, putting his arm around her. She smiled demurely.

"Brenda always does good," Arredondo said.

Black glared at him and Brenda looked pleased.

"He'll be back to talk to you again," Stepanovich said "He'll have more questions."

"What should I say?"

"Stick by your story. If he presses, just cut him off. Tell him you don't want to get involved."

There was an uneasy silence as Sullivan brought Brenda her usual and retreated to the other end of the bar.

"He won't accept that," Brenda said.

Stepanovich sipped his drink. It tasted bitter. "Just tell him you don't want to get involved and if he wants more information he'll have to get a subpoena."

"I can I get in trouble for lying to him, can't I?"

"If you're subpoenaed to the trial board, you repeat your story and that's that."

"But I can get in trouble, can't I?"

"Only if you change your story."

As the evening wore on, the conversation dwindled, as if somehow everything, for once and for all, had been said. Stepanovich, matching the others drink for drink, grew numb from the alcohol and long before closing time he had the feeling that he was trapped inside the bar; the doors were locked and he would be staying here in the darkness and the smell of booze-soaked floors and red leather and stale cigarette ashes.

The next morning, Stepanovich awoke on the floor of his living room. There were beer cans strewn about and Arredondo was asleep on the sofa with his mouth hanging open.

He staggered to his feet and walked into the bedroom. Brenda and Black were lying on the mattress naked with arms around each other.

In the bathroom, he stared at himself in the mirror, trying to remember what had happened the night before. He recalled purchasing six-packs of Coors from Sullivan and then climbing into Black's car outside in the parking lot. The rest was a blank. He opened the bathroom door and stared at Brenda and Black as they slept. What was Gloria doing? he wondered. He picked up the phone and dialed her number. She answered on the first ring.

"Are you feeling better?" he asked.

"A little."

"May I come over?"

"Joe, I've got to get away for a while. I'm flying down to Albuquerque to stay with my older sister for a week or so."

"We need to talk."

"My head is spinning."

"I love you," he said.

"I love you too."

"Can we get together before you leave?"

"I'd rather wait until I get back . . . until I've thought things out. I'll see you when I get back."

"Sure."

TWENTY-FIVE

Two weeks later, the board of rights hearing for Stepanovich, Black, and Arredondo was scheduled to convene in the eighth-floor hearing room at Parker Center. Because of the extraordinary interest shown by the Los Angeles press corps, a number of folding chairs had been set up in the corner of the room as a makeshift press pen. In addition, the police public affairs representative had set up an elaborate display board with framed photographs of the department's current chain of command officer. The color eight-by-tens of the neat, trim commanders, all in uniform and wearing gold braided police hats, were arranged around a larger photograph of Chief of Police Levester C. Burrel. A distinguished, soft-spoken black, he was popular not only with the officers and detectives who'd worked for him as he climbed the ladder from the Wilshire vice squad to the eighth floor at police headquarters, but also with the real estate developers, powerful lawyers, and their city council pawns who secretly controlled the city.

A nervous Stepanovich, dressed in a suit and sporting a fresh haircut, sat at the defense table with Black and Arredondo, who were similarly dressed. Howard Goldberg had obtained special permission from the district attorney to act as volunteer defense counsel for the three accused while on unpaid leave from his regular duties. He was leaning over the table, thumbing quickly through a thick stack of notes.

Seated in the twelve rows of padded seats in the room were detectives assigned to internal affairs division, deputy city attorneys concerned with potential civil litigation arising from the Ortega Street shooting, note takers from the chief's and mayor's offices, the police commission, the American Civil Liberties Union, Hispanics rights groups, and potential witnesses, including Sparky, Brenda, Sullivan, Officer Forest, Harger, and a coroner's investigator.

The stage where the board would sit was usually used for prisoner line-ups. The steel-reinforced door at the rear of the stage opened and a hush came over the room. The members of the Board of Rights, Captain Homer L. Ratliff, Captain Dexter C. Kefauver, and Captain Chauncey K. Lively—all wearing full uniform and sporting fresh haircuts—moved to their table and sat down.

The manual said that the senior captain would chair any board of rights. That meant that Ratliff, Harger's nemesis, would be in charge. "Board of rights," Stepanovich said to himself. "It should be called the board of No rights."

"This disciplinary trial board is called to order," said Ratliff, a tall, lanky man with deep-set eyes. Known throughout the Department not only for his uncanny ability to ace promotional examinations but his unbridled ambition and lack of common sense, he had a grayish pallor that made him look much older than his forty-nine years. In fact, other command officers called him "The Mummy" because it was said he'd wait an eternity for the Chief to retire so he could finally get his promotion to top cop.

Enunciating carefully, Ratliff introduced the other board members, then read the allegations out loud. This completed, he read a long paragraph from the manual advising Stepanovich and the others of their rights. In so many words, a policeman had a right to hire an attorney, but, as Howard had pointed out, only if he paid for one himself. Also, there was no right against self-incrimination. "Having completed those preliminaries," Ratliff said, "I'd like to read a letter sent to this hearing by Chief Burrell."

Howard cleared his throat. "The defendants object to any such reading on the grounds that it is prejudicial."

Ratliff smiled condescendingly. "The objection is overruled." He thumbed a page and read: "As the head of this department, I want all parties to know that the sole purpose of any board of rights hearing is to ascertain the truth and once that is done, to return a finding and penalty commensurate with the evidence developed. In my book, *Administrative Law and Police Justice,* I warned that in dispensing justice, a board of rights must always be aware of the desirability of sworn officers being allowed to function without fear of reprisal, but also the danger to the citizenry if officers of the law acted under a clear cloak of administrative protection from misconduct. I wish all parties well."

Howard leaned close to Stepanovich. "Who wrote the book for him?" he whispered.

"His brother teaches administrative law at USC."

Howard nodded.

"This board wishes to thank the Chief for his thoughts," Ratliff said. He turned to Houlihan. "The Department may call its first witness."

Houlihan, the department advocate, rose from his table and introduced himself. "The department calls Sergeant Jose Stepanovich."

"Mr. Chairman," Howard said loudly, "the defense moves that you be replaced as chairman of this board of rights on the grounds that you are clearly prejudiced in this matter. You are a close personal friend of the investigating officer, Lieutenant Houlihan, and are, in fact, the godfather to his son. You attend the same church and have taken family vacations together."

Ratliff blushed. "Police departments are very close-knit organizations, Mr. Goldbloom—"

"Goldberg."

"Yes, Goldberg," he said to the press area. "As I was saying, the fact that officers are acquainted with one another socially is not in and of itself reason to disqualify someone from sitting on a police trial board. If that was the case, we'd never be able to discipline ourselves, and the public interest wouldn't be served. Your objection is therefore overruled. The department may call its first witness."

Houlihan stood up. "The department calls Sergeant Jose Stepanovich."

"The clerk will swear in the witness," Ratliff said, making a note.

Stepanovich, his stomach fluttering, rose and approached the witness stand. He raised his hand. Rose Fujimoto, a busty young Oriental woman with a bouffant hairdo who everyone in the Department knew was the Chief's current girlfriend, administered the oath in a heavy Japanese accent.

Stepanovich said, "I do," and took a seat on the witness stand. His throat felt dry and he felt the underarms of his suit jacket must already be stained with perspiration.

Houlihan, wearing what looked like a new suit, looked composed. "Please state your name and assignment."

Stepanovich complied.

"For the record, the defense objects to the fact that the accused is forced to testify against himself in this hearing."

Ratliff thumbed through some paperwork and took out a typed page that Stepanovich guessed had been prepared for him by Houlihan or some other flunky. He read: "The proceedings of a board of rights hearing involves administrative rather than criminal law and is initiated as a fact-finding body to reach a decision without undue interference from restrictive limitations. Our job here is not to become entangled in a web of technicalities. This would defeat the purpose of this tribunal. Our aim is to keep things informal and to avoid quibbling over witnesses and the admissibility of evidence."

"May I be heard?" Howard said.

"Certainly, Mr. Goldbloom."

"Thank you, sir," Howard said, glaring. "In the context of this informal atmosphere, I'd like to point out that the defendants are on trial for their careers without the benefit of the guarantees provided in the Constitution of the United States, and that this 'tribunal' as you call it, is nothing more than a tribute to injustice, bureaucratic intrigue, and the whim and caprice of the police chain of command. In short, it's an institutionalized kangaroo court and you are the head kangaroo."

Ratliff maintained a poker face as cameras whirred from the press area. "Lieutenant Houlihan, you may continue."

"Sergeant Stepanovich," Houlihan said confidently, "during the course of your duties while assigned to the Central Bureau CRASH gang detail, did you have occasion to seize any vehicles as evidence?"

"Yes."

Houlihan stepped forward and handed him a Polaroid photograph of the black Chevy belonging to the White Fence gang. "Does this appear to be a Chevrolet you caused to be towed to the police impound yard?"

Stepanovich said yes. As his knees began shaking, he was thankful that the witness stand hid them from view.

"Our investigation has shown that you and the other defendants stole this vehicle from the impound yard and used it to fire rounds into a dwelling on Eighteenth Street—"

"Objection! Who said that?" Howard shouted. "There is no factual basis in the evidence for such a question!"

"The objection is overruled," Ratliff said diffidently. "Per Section 140.75 of the board of rights manual, this board is empowered to develop any and all pertinent facts. The witness is directed to answer the question."

Houlihan smiled. "Sergeant Stepanovich, did you and the others violate the penal code of the state of California by firing into an inhabited dwelling in order to incite gang warfare?"

Stepanovich cleared his throat. "No," he said, surmising that Houlihan was bluffing because if Sparky had talked, he'd have been the first witness called to the stand.

"Where were you and the members of your unit the night after you impounded the Chevrolet?"

"We were at the Rumor Control Bar."

"Do you realize you are testifying under oath?" Houlihan said.

"I'm directing my client not to answer that non-question!" Howard interrupted. "Even though this is a star chamber proceeding and he obviously has no legal rights, he is still a human being and has the right not to be badgered and humiliated. The question has been asked and answered."

Ratliff and the others captains conferred in whispers, and there was the sound of cameras whirring. Finally Ratliff sat back. "Objection sustained," he said.

Undaunted, Houlihan turned a page of his legal tablet. "Sergeant Stepanovich," he said, "on the date listed in the allegation, did you take part in a surveillance on Ortega Street in the city of Los Angeles?"

"Yes."

"And you were the ranking officer at this surveillance?"

"Yes."

"What led you to initiate the surveillance?"

"During routine patrol we observed known White Fence gang members coming and going from the residence."

"You staked out simply to monitor gang members you observed entering the location?"

"That's correct," Stepanovich lied.

"Isn't it true that you and your unit were fired on by White Fence gang members on August nineteenth and a member of your unit, Officer Timothy Fordyce, was killed."

"Yes."

"Isn't it true that you requested one Brenda Marie Teagarten to rent an apartment on Ortega Street to enable you and members of your unit to observe Estrada's residence?"

Stepanovich swallowed dryly. "No."

"You're saying you just went to the door of this apartment and asked her permission to use the place for a police surveillance."

"That's right."

"Had you ever seen her before?"

"I've seen her at the Rumor Control Bar."

"And she is a friend of yours, is she not?"

"I only know her as a customer in the bar."

Houlihan smiled wryly, and Stepanovich had an urge to rush from the witness stand and smash his teeth down his throat.

"During the surveillance and the shooting that occurred on Ortega Street, would it be safe to say that you were in charge?"

"Yes."

"And that, as ranking officer, you accept responsibility for all that occurred?"

Stepanovich swallowed. "Yes."

"And is it safe to say that you kept Captain Harger apprised of what you were doing by regular briefings as prescribed in Section 8926.71 of the Los Angeles Police Manual?"

"Yes," Stepanovich said because he knew there was no other answer to the question.

Later, Howard was allowed to cross-examine Stepanovich. A portion of the transcript read as follows:

Howard: Sergeant Stepanovich, isn't it true that your supervisors were aware of the activities of the CRASH special unit?

Stepanovich: Yes. I kept Captain Harger briefed on our activities.

Howard: But you hadn't informed Captain Harger specifically of the stakeout at the Estrada residence?

Stepanovich: Yes.

Howard: Such stakeouts are routine, for your unit, isn't that correct?

Stepanovich: Yes.

Howard: And isn't it fair to say that such a stakeout to monitor the activities of East Los Angeles street gangs was specifically what your unit was designed to do?

Stepanovich: Yes sir.

As the questions continued, Stepanovich noticed the captains wore the familiar police mask: I could give a shit, but it's my job to listen. The same expression he himself had worn when listening to burglary or car theft or purse-snatch victims telling their musty tale of unresolvable woe. This smug veil and the fact that the three board members had avoided eye contact with him since he'd taken the stand told him without any doubt that the verdict as well as the punishment had been decided before the trial board had even convened.

Stepanovich's testimony was concluded by three o'clock, and Ratliff announced a ten-minute break in the proceedings. The crowd of spectators, reporters, and cameramen stood and stretched, lit cigarettes, and filed into the hallway to line up at vending machines.

Stepanovich huddled with Arredondo, Black, and Goldberg at the defense table.

"He's making you the fall guy," Howard said, tapping his pencil nervously.

"The captains aren't asking any questions," Arredondo whispered. "They've been told what finding to come back with."

"They're going to hang it on our asses," Black said, lighting a cigarette.

"We'll know by who they call for the next witness," Howard said.

"The Department calls Captain Robert Harger," Houlihan said in a loud, clear voice.

The door was opened by one of Houlihan's assistants, and Harger marched in wearing a dark suit, pastel blue shirt, and tie. After being sworn in by the Chief's girl friend, he took the stand and stated his name.

"Captain Harger," Houlihan said, "are you in command of the CRASH special unit that includes the four defendants sitting at the defense table?"

Harger said he was.

"Did you authorize this unit to engage in a surveillance on Ortega Street for the purpose of observing White Fence gang members?"

"No, I did not."

"So in other words, the members of this unit acted without your authority?"

"That's correct."

Stepanovich suddenly had a clammy, cold feeling, as when his mother informed him of Uncle Nick's death.

"*Hijo la,*" Arredondo muttered.

"If Sergeant Stepanovich had asked your advice on such a surveillance, what would you have told him?"

Howard slammed his fist down on the table. "Supposition! A hypothetical question! I move this entire line of questioning be stricken from the record. How does anyone know what they might have done in a given situation at some date in the past?"

Ratliff coughed dryly a couple of times. "This board of rights isn't going to get bogged down in a lot of technicalities. The question stands."

Harger, the picture of a movie detective, rubbed his palms together. "I would never have approved the surveillance," he said.

"So, in violation of the LAPD police manual, Sergeant Stepanovich failed to notify you of his plans?"

"It certainly seems so."

Stepanovich turned to Howard. "Delay this thing. Get a continuance," he whispered.

"They'll never go for it."

"I need some time, Howard. Before this thing goes any further, I need some time. Just a day will do it."

"Mr. Chairman, I'd like to ask the indulgence of the board to permit us to break early."

Ratliff let out his breath. "On what grounds? We're right in the middle of important testimony."

"I'm under a doctor's care and on time medication that I inadvertently left at my residence."

Ratliff turned to the others on the board.

"I'm feeling very nauseous at the moment. I'd very much appreciate your indulgence."

"Very well," Ratliff said through gritted teeth. He rapped a gavel. "This hearing is adjourned until tomorrow morning at nine."

Harger hurried off the stand and out the door. The spectators began to clear.

Neither Stepanovich, Black, nor Arredondo moved from the defense table. Howard was staring at Stepanovich.

"What the hell is this all about?"

"I'll talk to you tonight," Stepanovich said.

Howard nodded and began gathering his paperwork.

Stepanovich motioned to the others and they followed him out of the room. "They're gunning for you, homes," Black said, stepping into an empty elevator.

Stepanovich nodded as the elevator descended. "Sullivan was right about Harger."

Arredondo unwrapped a stick of chewing gum. "I guess you had no way of knowing." He slipped the gum into his mouth and stared at the floor.

"I took the man at his word. I—I'm sorry."

"At least they don't have anything on the caper car," Arredondo whispered as they stepped out of the elevator into the underground parking lot.

"They don't have enough to prove it was us," Stepanovich whispered. "And since they can't prove it, they'd rather keep it from the press."

"They don't need that to fire us," Black said with a sardonic smile. "They're pinning the allegations on you, and then at the end they'll get us for acquiescing. That with CUBO is enough for termination. As I see it, the three of us are finished."

Stepanovich just stood there as Black and Arredondo shuffled across the parking lot to their cars. Rather than heading for his car, he started walking. He followed First Street and trudged up the grade to the bridge. As rush hour traffic whipped past him, he hiked to the center of the span and stopped. Below, the white cement riverbed extended north toward Boyle Heights. Across the river in East L.A., the spire of Our Lady Queen of Angels Church glinted in the sun, forcing him to blink. Looking below for a moment, he imagined jumping, falling rapidly, then slamming to the burning cement below.

Finally he made his decision. With the bridge traffic whizzing at his back, he headed back to the police building to get his car.

TWENTY-SIX

Because it was Thursday, one of Harger's regularly scheduled racquetball days, Stepanovich drove from the police building along North Broadway through Chinatown. At Solano Avenue he turned left and wound through the Elysian Hills to the Los Angeles Police Academy, a cramped training complex comprised of a two-story brick building, a shooting range, and an athletic field hidden in a canyon near Dodger Stadium. He steered slowly into the parking lot.

Harger's car was parked in a space near the stairs leading to the building housing the racquetball courts. Stepanovich pulled into the space next to it and turned off the engine. He rolled the windows down for air and leaned back in the seat.

About two hours later, Harger came down the stairs and headed for his car. Stepanovich opened the door and climbed out. Harger stopped dead in his tracks.

"Have a nice game?"

Harger nodded without speaking and continued toward his car. Stepanovich stepped in front of him. "I came here to talk."

Harger glared. "I'm not allowed to talk to you during the trial board and you know it."

"What is the board going to do to us?"

"I have no idea."

"You and the Chief sat down and figured the best way to get the heat off."

Harger started to move toward his car, but Stepanovich didn't budge.

"Get the hell out of my way."

"You're going to fire all three of us, aren't you?"

Harger shoved Stepanovich aside and took out his keys. As he unlocked the door, Stepanovich said, "I'm gonna take you down with us."

Harger turned toward him. "What did you say?"

"I said, I'm gonna hand you up to internal affairs."

Harger forced a smile. "For what?"

"At first I considered telling them about how you gave us the green light from the beginning—all that bullshit about the Chief being behind us all the way."

"Go ahead and tell the board anything you want. It's your word against mine. You have no corroboration and I outrank you. Who the fuck do you think they are going to believe?"

"You're right. They're going to hand down the party line because they're a bunch of suckasses like you."

Harger stepped closer to him and aimed an index finger in Stepanovich's face. "You're about to add insubordination to your list of charges," he said angrily.

"That's why I have a better idea. Remember those Polaroid shots you took at Brenda's house?" Harger's face became flushed. "I'm going to send them to the police commission. Sure, I know because you're a Captain, it's not enough to warrant a trial board. But it'll end your chances of ever getting another promotion. You'll never make deputy chief."

Harger's face was visibly flushed. "You son of a bitch."

"I thought that would get your attention."

Harger stepped closer. "I want those photos."

"I want to know what's going to happen to my people."

Harger grabbed him by the shirt. Stepanovich thought

about it for a second, then punched Harger squarely in the jaw. The blow knocked Harger backward and off his feet. Stunned, he touched his lip and looked at the blood.

Then he came to his feet swinging.

Stepanovich backpedaled and countered Harger's blows. Catlike, calling his punches, he administered powerful rights and lefts. Harger lunged at him. Stepanovich dodged and kicked him fully in the stomach. Harger doubled over and his head thudded loudly against the fender of his car.

Harger reached to his waistband.

On fire with anger, Stepanovich kicked him in the ribs. As Harger doubled over in pain, he pulled the gun from Harger's inside-the-belt holster and snapped the chamber open. He thumbed the extractor rod and bullets fell into his hand. He threw them in Harger's face. Then he took the gun and threw it out of the parking lot into the street.

"You better go home and tell the wife she's married to a permanent Captain." Stepanovich turned and headed toward his car. At the sound of footsteps behind him, he whirled. Harger stood there, rubbing his head. A trail of blood extended from the right corner of his lip to the bottom of his chin. Stepanovich thought, he's shrunk somehow in the last few seconds.

"I don't know what the trial board is going to do. You have this all wrong."

"What's the verdict, motherfucker?"

"Termination," Harger said finally in a barely audible voice.

"Termination for who?"

"You, Black, and Arredondo. I'm sorry. But it was the Chief's idea."

"You're going to change his idea," Stepanovich said.

"I don't think I can."

"Then you take a fall with us. One big happy family."

"The police commission wants someone's head—the publicity."

"You can talk the Chief into figuring a way out."

"There's no way. Someone has to get fired."

"Bullshit."

"As God is my witness, I see no other way to resolve this thing. I'm telling you what can and cannot be done. The atmospherics."

Stepanovich swallowed twice. "Then I'll resign. That'll satisfy the police commission."

Harger licked his lips. "The others can't just walk away. The press will know it's a fix—"

"You can transfer them out of the division."

"That means nothing and everyone will know it."

"It'll satisfy the press. That's all the Chief is concerned about anyway."

Harger wiped blood from his lip and looked at it. "I'm not sure I can pull it off."

"A professional bullshitter like you should be able to handle it. If not, the photos get full distribution."

As Harger stared at the ground, Stepanovich turned on his heel and marched to his car. Watching Harger from the corner of his eye, he opened the driver's door and climbed in.

Harger was still staring after him as Stepanovich drove out of the parking lot. He drove across town to Howard's modest tract home just off the freeway in Encino. The street was crowded with cars, and he had to drive around the block to find a place to park. Walking back to Howard's house, he noticed that three syles of stucco homes on the block varied only slightly from one basic design. Just as at his apartment in Glendale, there was the endless whiz-hum of the freeway.

Though most of the other houses had family name plaques: "THE YEES," "THE KRAUTHAMMERS," "THE SINGER FAMILY," Howard's plaque was bare because he was a prosecutor and had received numerous threats on his life.

Stepanovich walked up the wheelchair ramp and knocked on the front door. Howard's sister Miriam opened the door. She was a well-groomed woman in her forties who wore her dark hair in a ponytail. The conservative green business suit and designer eyeglasses made her look like what she was: a lawyer. She worked for a private firm in Century City specializing in civil cases. She threw her arms around him and hugged him tightly.

"Joe, you never come over anymore."

"I've been busy."

"Baloney. You'd better get over here and eat a decent meal once in a while. You're probably living on greasy hamburgers. You don't have to call, just come over. You know when we eat," she said, ushering him in.

"OK, I will."

Howard was at a desk in the corner. He closed the book he was reading. "Leave him alone, Miriam," Howard said. "He has a girlfriend."

She gave Stepanovich a pinch on the cheek. "True love never dies," she said on her way to the kitchen.

Howard wheeled to Stepanovich. "You look awful," he said. "Sit down."

Stepanovich sat on the sofa. Though he'd been in the house many times, he noticed for the first time the furniture in the place looked packing-crate new because Howard never used it.

Later, Howard sat slumped in his wheelchair sipping wine, listening attentively as Stepanovich finished explaining what had taken place at the police academy. "You're crazy," he said darkly.

"I got everybody in trouble and I'm going to get them out."

"You call beating the shit out of a superior officer getting *out* of trouble?"

"There's no other way to save Arredondo and Black from getting fired."

"I could have appealed the trial board finding in Superior Court."

"It would have taken years and in the end we would have still gotten fired."

"Thanks for the confidence."

"You know that's not what I mean."

"What you did was stupid. Harger is probably at the DA's office right now swearing out charges against you."

"Let him take his best shot. Then I'll take mine."

Howard, who seldom drank because he said it gave him headaches, poured his fourth glass of wine, drank it down, and made a sour expression. "Out of touch with reality," he said to the glass.

"Huh?"

"Sometimes I wish you and me could go back and start over. Just start over again as kids."

Miriam came into the room and ushered them into the kitchen for a meal of halibut, potatoes, broccoli, and squash. For dessert there was fresh fruit and cheese.

After dinner, Stepanovich tried to help with the dishes, but Miriam forced him out of the kitchen. He told Howard he'd see him in court in the morning and headed to the door.

"Don't go to your apartment, Joe. If they're going too arrest you, I'd rather have them do it in the hearing room tomorrow morning so I can post immediate bail rather than have them book you tonight. You're welcome to stay here, but if a complaint has been filed, they might even come here looking for you."

Taking Howard's suggestion, Stepanovich decided to sleep at his mother's house rather than return to his apartment. He drove past Vega Street, turned, and parked his car in the backyard of a family friend where the car couldn't be seen from the street. Using a route he used to take when he was a kid, he made his way through an alley and a couple of backyards and entered his mother's house through the rear entrance. Waking her, he told her that if police officers came to the door not to allow them inside.

In his room, Stepanovich turned on the color television. Robert Mitchum, dressed in an army uniform, was inside a wide storm-drain tunnel running full speed toward the camera. Stepanovich stripped to his T-shirt and shorts and climbed into bed.

He awoke to the "Today" show and turned off the television. While shaving, he noticed the puffiness under his eyes caused by a night of tossing and turning and dreaming about Gloria.

At the kitchen table Mrs. Stepanovich served him a plate covered with bacon, fried eggs, and pancakes.

"I'm not very hungry, Mom."

"Eat what you can," she said, sitting across from him, the way she had when he was a child.

He shrugged and took a few bites.

"Do you want to talk about it?"

"What's that?"

"The trouble you're in. You're my son and I have a right to know."

"We were in a shooting and the Department is taking us to a trial board over it." Because of the way he felt, the food seemed tasteless.

"When you were growing up, I knew you'd turn out to be a policeman. Every time Nick would stop by, you'd be swaggering around like him for days after." Her tone was muted, serious, unlike other times she'd made similar comments to him.

"It'll all blow over," he said to his plate.

"You're in real trouble, aren't you, Jose?"

"You're gonna be late for work, Mom. I'll give you a ride."

"I don't need no goddamn ride," she said angrily. "I need my son to talk to me!"

"Everything's OK, Mom."

" 'Everything's OK,' " she said sarcastically. "Everything's *not* OK. You're talking to me like a cop talks to someone he meets on the street. Your Uncle Nick was a cop twenty-four hours a day. Your Uncle Nick was your big hero—"

"You're talking about the past—"

"Nick never gave of himself. He was a cop and he was above that. And now you're just like him. You've grown cold. I can see it in your eyes. Nothing is hidden from a mother." She wiped away a tear, stood up, and moved to the end of the sink. She grabbed a paper towel and blew her nose.

"I'm sorry if I upset you coming here—"

"I want you to quit the department. To hell with them. You can find another job. Or go to college and be a lawyer like Howard."

Stepanovich stood and took his plate to the sink. Turning on the faucet, he washed the contents of the plate into the garbage disposal and set the plate on the sink. He checked his wristwatch. "I have to go."

Mrs. Stepanovich, her jaw set, just shook her head.

Neither said a word as he drove her to work. When they arrived, she kissed him lightly on the cheek. "Please think about what I said, Jose."

He stepped off the elevator at the police building. The hallway, usually crowded with gawkers, police gossipers, and informants for various high-ranking officers, was empty.

Stepanovich took in a breath, grasped the door handle, and sauntered into the hearing room. Though the crowd was as large as the day before, Harger wasn't there. Houlihan was standing in the corner of the room, speaking furtively with a couple of sharply dressed detectives. He was sure they were staring at him as he walked to the defense table and joined Arredondo and Black.

"Something's going on," Arredondo said. "The Chief's adjutant has been running in and out of the room."

Black sipped coffee from a styrofoam cup. "My guess is they've come up with a zinger. Maybe Brenda copped out . . . or that fuckin' Sparky."

"I think I'm about to get arrested," Stepanovich

said under his breath. Black and Arredondo looked at him in astonishment.

The swinging doors from the hallway opened and Howard, with a pile of books on his lap, maneuvered his wheelchair down the short aisle and joined them. His eyes were puffy from drinking and his hair was matted on one side.

As if on cue, Ratliff and the other members of the board entered and took their respective seats. Unlike yesterday, they were carrying neither notebooks nor briefcases. Stepanovich wondered whether Houlihan would handcuff him right in the hearing room or wait until he was out in the hallway.

"This board is called to order," Ratliff said, pulling his swivel chair close to the table. He picked up a plastic pitcher, poured water into a paper cup, and took a sip. From his uniform breast pocket he removed a folded white envelope. He blew into the flap and took out a piece of paper. "Let the record note that the accused are present with counsel."

"This doesn't look good," Howard whispered.

"Per Section 288 of the board of rights manual, in the event an officer submits a resignation subsequent to filing of a complaint but prior to the completion of the board of rights hearing on the charges," Ratliff said as cameras and lights clicked on in the press area, "the chief of police may instruct the board to close the file and adjourn. Due to the resignation of Officer Stepanovich, the Chief has done so."

"The other accused would ask clarification of their status," Howard said loudly and distinctly.

Ratliff nodded. "By special order from the Chief and in no way connected with the allegations, Officers Black and Arredondo are transferred to new assignments as of the next deployment period. This file is now permanently closed and the board is adjourned."

Reporters rushed out the door to the bank of phones in the hallway.

Black leaned close. "You didn't have to—"

"Yes, I did," Stepanovich said.

Houlihan came to the table with two transfer forms and set them in front of Black and Arredondo. As Howard gloomily examined the paperwork, Stepanovich stood up, took a deep breath, and walked out.

TWENTY-SEVEN

Standing at the door of Gloria's apartment, Stepanovich heard the television inside: a news report concerning the board of rights hearing.

When Gloria opened the door, her face was devoid of makeup, and from the darkness under her eyes, he could tell she'd been crying. She was wearing a fluffy white sweater, tight black pants, and her hair was pulled back sternly. He threw his arms around her.

She pulled away from him and pushed the door closed.

Standing there in what should have been comfortable surroundings, Stepanovich suddenly felt horribly uncomfortable.

"Did you have a nice trip?" he said.

"I feel a lot better now—have you eaten?"

"I'm starving."

She moved past him into the kitchen, opened the refrigerator, and took out a package of corn tortillas, hamburger meat, and a bowl of something that looked like refried beans. Without saying a word, she poured oil into a pan and began frying the meat.

Stepanovich moved to the kitchen table and sat down. "I'm sorry about everything."

Gloria opened the refrigerator again and took out a

can of beer. Popping the cap, she set it on the table in front of him and returned to the stove. "I heard about you on the news. I'm sorry you had to resign."

"I'm leaving L.A. and I want you to go with me, Gloria. My cousin Jack Mornarich is the mayor of Glide, Oregon, and he can get me on the sheriff's department there. And he said they have a nursing shortage at the hospital in town."

She avoided looking at him.

"Gloria, I love you and I always will. I want you to be my wife."

The meat was done. Without a word she heated a couple of tortillas, scooped on the fried meat, and sprinkled a handful of grated cheese, tomato, and shredded lettuce. She turned off the burners and brought the plate to the table.

"Did you hear what I said?"

"That night you waited for me outside the hospital," she said, setting the plate down in front of him. "After I came home, I thought about you all night. I was infatuated."

"I felt the same way—"

"That isn't something I'm used to," she said, sitting across from him. "I've been working in hospitals since I was eighteen years old. I've seen so much I've forgotten how to feel some things, I guess." She folded her hands in front of her. "Go ahead and eat."

Though he still felt uneasy, Stepanovich bit into the taco.

"We could have been born somewhere else," she said. "Have you ever thought about that? That we could have been born anyone, anywhere in the world except East L.A.?"

"But we weren't," he said, picking up the beer.

"You used me to help you trap the White Fence homeboys."

"That's over now." He took a big gulp and set the can down. He wanted to put his arms around her, to feel the softness of her sweater, of her arms holding him.

"You had to get even for what happened to Fordyce," Gloria said. There was a tear in the corner of her left eye.

"None of that has anything to do with you and me." He reached out to take her hand. She left the table and moved to the sink.

"Gloria, you and I didn't make it like this. It's just the way it is."

"You're right. East L.A. was divided into gang territories generations ago, and maybe it will always be divided: groups fighting one another. But I thought you and I were more important than the gangs, than the neighborhood—than the police department. I was wrong."

Stepanovich's mouth suddenly felt dry. "I'm truly sorry for what happened."

"There's nothing to apologize for. We can't help the way we are."

"I love you, Gloria."

"And I love you. But that doesn't change the fact that we're living in different worlds. I want to stop people from killing one another. Jesus, why should there be a hundred beds at the hospital just for people with bullet wounds?"

"Ask the gangbangers. They're the ones who are killing people."

"What do you mean, *'they'*?"

"You don't understand."

"Oh yes I do, Joe. I'm the one who watches kids die. I'm still living and working in the barrio, but I'm not part of it like you are. Your life is dedicated to more pay-backs, more turf battles, more death."

"I understand you being upset—"

Gloria used a knuckle to wipe away her tears. "Joe, I'm not going to go away with you."

Stepanovich shoved his plate slowly away and came to his feet. His temples were throbbing. "You sit me down and feed me and then tell me to get lost. I don't get it."

"When you shot that man, there was a look in your eye I'll never forget—"

"But he would have killed you!" he shouted.

She turned away and he grabbed her arm. "I can't help who I am, Gloria. But I love you."

"You love revenge. You love your surrogate family at the Rumor Control Bar," she cried. "You've become a gangbanger."

"I need you."

"Not more than you need your homeboys," she said coldly.

Stepanovich reached out to take her in his arms, but she pulled away.

"I'm as tough as you are, *vato*," Gloria said. Covering her face with her hands, she hurried to the bedroom. Without turning around, she slammed the door behind her.

Stepanovich, feeling tears in his throat, followed her, but stopped himself at the bedroom door. "If you change your mind, you know where to find me," he said loudly. Overcoming an urge to punch walls and tear apart her furniture, he walked to the door, looked back one more time and left.

Downstairs, as he unlocked the door of his car, he looked up. Though he couldn't see anything through the sheer drapes covering the window of Gloria's bedroom, he imagined her watching him.

TWENTY-EIGHT

Assisted by Arredondo and Black, who looked as hungover as he'd ever seen them, Stepanovich fit what he owned into two suitcases and three cardboard boxes and carried them to a U-haul truck he'd rented at a police discount from the equipment rental service down the street from Sparky's tow yard.

With his mattress and box springs and the remainder of his kitchen supplies shoved into the bed of the truck, he wrote a note informing the apartment manager he was leaving and that if she was able to rent the apartment to someone else by the time his rent was up at the end of the month, she could send the refund to him care of Jack Mornarich in Glide.

With the truck loaded, Stepanovich walked across the street and bought two six-packs of Coors. Back at the truck, he, Black and Arredondo moved into the shade furnished by the truck and popped open beer cans.

Arredondo tipped a can back and drank fully half of it. "They transferred me to the Drug Abuse Resistance Program," he said, restraining a belch. "I'll be assigned in a high school to teach the kiddies not to shoot dope. The school I'm going to has twenty single teachers and eleven of them are supposed to fuck like bunnies."

Black leaned against the truck. "As of midnight tonight, I'm assigned back to Wilshire morning watch. If I'm lucky, I won't have to see daylight until I retire."

"You guys'll have to come up to Glide. We can go fishing."

"Sounds real good," Black said.

"You say the word, homes."

As they were finishing their beers, Brenda pulled up to the curb up in her Mazda. A large sticker on the front bumper read: "SHIT HAPPENS." As she gave Stepanovich a hug, her seashell halter top poked him in the chest. "I wish you all the best, Joe."

"Thanks, Brenda."

"C'mon, honey," she said to Black.

Black shoved his empty beer can into a brown paper sack on the bed of the truck. He shook hands with Stepanovich. "You're as solid a cop as I've ever met," he said. "You take care, now."

Black and Brenda climbed in the Mazda. Black started the engine. As they drove off, they were sitting close together and her arm was around him.

Arredondo threw his arms around Stepanovich in an *abrazo.*

"Good luck with those teachers, Raul."

"I don't need any luck, homes."

"Of course not."

Arredondo swaggered across the street to his Chevrolet. He tooted the horn as he drove off.

On the way out of town, Stepanovich stopped by the Fordyce residence to say good-bye. The couple seemed to be adjusting to their loss as well as could be expected and at one point even discussed taking a train to Kansas City for a family reunion.

Stepanovich followed Interstate Highway 5 through Hollywood and the San Fernando Valley and finally out of Los Angeles and into the Tehachapi Mountains. The sun was setting as he steered the curving Tejon

Pass past the lonely truck stops of Castaic, Gorman, and Lebec.

Adjusting the radio volume to drown out thoughts of Gloria, he changed gears and steered down a long grade leading to Kern County. At the base of the mountains, the highway straightened to a band stretching due north all the way to San Francisco. With the ridge route behind him, Stepanovich stepped heavily on the gas pedal and accelerated into the darkness.

Late that night he was still on the road.

About the Author

GERALD PETIEVICH is a former U.S. Secret Service Agent. His father was a long-time Los Angeles Police homicide detective, and his brother was awarded a Los Angeles Police Department Star of Valor for his actions in a shootout with gang members. Mr. Petievich numbers among his novels *To Live and Die in L.A.*, *To Die in Beverly Hills*, and *Shakedown*.